"*Siân Griffith's emotionally resonant, crisply sentenced, beautifully built Scrapple is ultimately a meditation on how not-being-at-home feels like the fundamental human condition when it comes to youth, race, place, money, mystery, just getting by from one day to the next, and pretty much anything else. An impressive work.*"

—**Lance Olsen,** author of *My Red Heaven*

"*Scrapple starts with a bang and doesn't let up. Robert's quest to find his brother is gripping, but so is his quest to find his place in a new school, new neighborhood, and new city. In this suspenseful story, Griffiths still somehow makes space for moments of penetrating insight into what it's like to be a young person shouldering the weight of loss and unasked-for responsibilities.*"

—**Caitlin Horrocks,** author of *The Vexations*

"*Scrapple pulls off the impressive feat of writing about youthful friendships in a way that is realistic but still complex, smart, and challenging. The two boys at the center of this excellent novel are tormented by bullies as they face difficult questions about race, money, and sexuality, but they never lose their humanity or their youthful optimism. Siân Griffiths deftly ties all these threads together into a captivating story that will resonate with any reader who remembers being that age when you're too young to change your life, but just old enough to desperately wish you could.*"

—**Tom McAllister,** author of *How to Be Safe*

"Siân B. Griffiths is an enchanter, casting her spell with fresh, unusual words, with impeccable sentences and unerring details. I love the people in this wise and luminous book, a novel steeped in poverty, sexual harassment, and racial discord, a novel daring enough to begin with babies abandoned in an empty and derelict apartment. And then bad gets worse. I started reading slowly, hoping the book wouldn't end, hoping I wouldn't have to say goodbye to our hero Robert and the indomitable Jerome, young pals who face the constant threat of violence on the mean streets of Philadelphia as they try to solve the mystery of the babies' missing parents. Buy this book, friends, and you will thank me. You're not going to read many novels as powerful, as honest, and as compassionate as Scrapple."

—**John Dufresne,** author of *I Don't Like Where This Is Going*

SCRAPPLE

SCRAPPLE

Siân Griffiths

BRADDOCK
AVENUE
BOOKS
UNCOMMON BOOKS · UNCOMMON READERS

Printed in the United States of America
10 9 8 7 6 5 4 3 2 1

FIRST EDITION, June 2020
ISBN 13: 978-0-9989677-4-8

Book design & cover image by Karen Antonelli

Braddock Avenue Books
P.O. Box 502
Braddock, PA 15104

www.braddockavenuebooks.com

Distributed by Small Press Distribution

SCRAPPLE

Robert didn't know which was the greater crime, to fall in love in the middle of your father's funeral or to fall in love with your brother's wife, but he knew he was doubly doomed since he had done both on a single late October afternoon before he turned fifteen years old. 1997 was a year of good people dying—that's what Angela said. Mother Teresa had died and Princess Diana had died and now Robert's father because, she said, death comes in threes.

Angela and Sean had flown in from Philadelphia that morning. Seven weeks pregnant with twins, Angela hugged herself warm by the graveside, crying for a father-in-law she had never met. Her tears mixed with the Oregon drizzle. She did not wipe them away. She didn't pretend to have any words. She offered no sounds or murmurs. She only cupped Robert's chin in her cold, slender fingers, and brushed her thumb against his jaw. Before he could lean in, she turned away to focus her love on his little sister Bridget, wrapping her in a hug that outlasted any hug he'd ever witnessed.

Robert wanted to crawl into Angela's arms and lie there. No, more than that. He wanted to crawl inside her skin, to stay there like a bug. She would be his chrysalis, protecting and sheltering him until he developed a kind of shell. Everyone else tried to dodge the fact of his father's death, ducking away from Robert the way they ducked away from the constant rain. Only Angela had faced the facts with them, unflinching as the jack-o'-lanterns that looked out *from local porches.*

In her first trimester, Angela had looked more like a car model than a pregnant woman. She could have lain across the hood of a Lamborghini, her feet curved into those high, high heels, water beading on her chest and midriff. Her tanned thighs framed by the fringe of her cut-offs. Her breasts, soft as pillows, barely contained by a torn and translucent t-shirt.

That night, Angela was asleep in Robert's bed, and from his sleeping bag in the living room, Robert strained to make out his mother and brother's conversation. Sean cracked a fresh Coors from the fridge, drinking the last of their father's beer as if it didn't mean anything, as if there would be more beer, more days, more Dad.

Robert didn't hear his mother's low voice, only Sean's replies: "I know it's far." "There's nothing for me here." "But we like Philly." And later, "Angela's family is there." Now that Sean had dropped out of Hassler, his mother couldn't see a reason for Sean to stay gone. They spoke for hours; his mother's whispers were hushed but insistent. Robert couldn't imagine what she said. He couldn't picture his mother admitting that she needed help, let alone begging for it. Darkness spread on every side of the small white house, but they sat together, Sean's strong voice cutting through each of their mother's sh-shushing arguments.

None of it mattered. Days later, Sean and Angela got back on the plane and flew away, leaving Robert and his mother and sister to figure out what came next. Their mother scanned the paper each day, hoping to find someone, anyone, willing to hire a forty-year-old woman who hadn't held a job since high school. Herman was wrung dry, a town with nothing left. They finished out the school year and spent the summer packing up the only home he'd ever known. The U-Haul meant that they had given up, or it meant that they were starting new. But which?

A PRIVATE DARKNESS

August in Philadelphia was hot and thick. Hurrying Bridget through Penn Center, Robert tried not to stare at the buildings whose tops stacked like chevrons on a sergeant's sleeve. Staring would give them away as outsiders. Only tourists gawked at sky-scrapers, and tourists got mugged. But they weren't tourists anymore. For almost two weeks now, Philadelphia had been home, or something like it.

His mother's gaze was level, but Bridget, her hand hot in his, could not stop looking. Herman didn't have a single office over two stories. The ones that stretched around them now, all metal and glass, crowded out the sky. They were supposed to have been at Sean's ten minutes ago.

A shove laid Robert flat. He rolled to glimpse the hulking man who had barreled out of Brotherly Love Coffee. "The fuck?" the man bellowed as a slop of suds and dingy water splatted on the sidewalk inches from Robert's head. "How my customers supposed to get through this mess?"

The window washers responded with laughter and another splat of suds.

The coffee man growled and hocked. His loogie landed in the suds by Robert's hand. "They got no respect," he said to the air. "No respect for the working man."

Robert's mother stared as if her gaze could push the

man away and make him stay put. The fern she held dampened the effect, but it was intense nonetheless. Hazel and black-lashed, her eyes were the same as Sean's, but they cast an entirely different spell. Sean's said, *Love me*; hers said, *Back off*. Robert honestly had no idea how anyone ever braved their way past that look.

Bridget hopped back and forth over a crack running down the sidewalk, oblivious to the dangers. Robert smiled as he pulled himself up, letting his mother know that he was okay, that they would all be okay.

As they walked, the city grew smaller and older. Here, his mother's home-sewn cotton sack of a dress didn't look so strangely out of place. The buildings had little wooden doors that swung on iron hinges and gleamed with glossy layers of enamel. The bricks were weathered and rounded with time. Little brass plaques told of famous people and revolutionary conspiracies seeded in a city founded more than a century before Lewis and Clark trekked their way to Oregon. Buildings like this were where it had all started: America. The thought blew his mind. In the small rooms of these small houses, men had hidden together and dreamed up a country. He wondered what his friend Troy, the only guy he knew who could rattle off the names of all one hundred senators, would think of this place. If he ever saw him again, Robert might tell him about it.

Sunlight flashed off a passing car's hubcaps and burned stars in Robert's eyes. He checked the directions his mother had scrawled on an old envelope. They'd gotten off the bus too early, not close enough to the Schuylkill, though even here the air hung heavy with river smell. Sweat trickled in a little creek down Robert's spine. His mother shifted her grip on the fern, its plastic hook leaving an angry red mark on her fingers.

Three men leaned against the side of a building on the corner as if they were joists put there to hold it in place. Looking at his mother, they smiled in slow motion through mirrored sunglasses. "You need help, Mama?" one crooned. "We'll help you."

She shot him a look, but it had no effect. Their family passed into the cloud of the men's cologne, something heavy with leather and musk. The men looked as if they spent the whole summer this way, loitering in sleeveless shirts, flexing, commenting on passing women. "We'll show you everything you're looking for," the man said again, his yoyo eyes traveling up and down their mother's body.

Robert dropped his gaze to the fern, choking down the men's smell. His mother's dress was too thin; their eyes bored right through it. She needed wool, leather, chain mail. Every step was an assault. The maze of sidewalks stretched and hooked around them. His mother stopped at a gray stucco building. It wasn't old enough to be cool, just old enough to be old. Cracks ran up its walls as if it all weighed too much, as if the building had grown tired of holding itself up but couldn't make the final effort to fall down. The concrete stank of urine and its glass doors were smeared with something brownish green that Robert both did and did not want to identify. His mother glanced again at the scrawled directions. "This is the one."

Bridget crushed her body close to Robert as they walked. "This is where the green man lives."

The green man, her nightmare monster. She'd been talking about him more since the move. Robert rubbed her shoulder. "No green man here, Bridge."

The elevator with its old metal gate squealed and groaned as it pulled them up. Robert felt certain it would drop them, splattering them all like eggs in a box, but eventually it lurched to a halt and opened. He heard the twins crying through the thin walls even before his mother knocked.

The three of them stood, listening, first for footsteps and

then for any sound at all aside from crying babies—a television, voices, a sneeze—but all they heard was unbroken wailing. His mother shifted the fern from one hand to the other. In the damp hallway, Robert felt as limp and sodden as steeped tea. He hoped Sean had a window air conditioner like some of the people in their neighborhood. Robert had begged their mother to buy one, but she said they were loud and made the air taste weird.

His mother knocked again. Sean should have had the game on by now. The kickoff would be any minute. Strange, that they couldn't hear the TV when the twin's cries were so clear. Even though Sean had quit the team, he wouldn't miss a minute of Hassler's season opener. They had been planning this day for weeks. Sean had made them delay coming to see the apartment so that they would see it for the first time on game day. They'd made a thing of it. He'd called at seven that morning to make sure they were coming, repeating the bus numbers, asking his mother again when they would arrive.

Their mother knocked a third time, but the crying only sharpened. The apartment wasn't supposed to be that big—a converted hotel suite, Sean had said. Just a living room, bedroom, and galley kitchen. This was his third apartment in a year and the smallest yet, but, Sean said, it had a view of the Schuylkill through the gaps in the buildings.

"What's taking so long?" Bridget asked. She was five and impatient, and they ignored her.

Their mother handed Robert the housewarming fern, chosen because it reminded them of Oregon, all green and optimistic. Her face settled into a hard, stubborn worry. The tension built up in her; it pulsed from her skin in waves. She put the spare key in the lock, her mouth pressed in a line. She laid a hand on the knob.

Later, Robert would know that his world had folded

flat in that instant, though the moment was over before he was aware of it. He hardly saw a thing as his mother slipped inside. But he did see something. What, exactly? Already, he was trying to reconstruct the fragment of color and motion he'd glimpsed before his mother's hand caught him in the chest and pushed him back, before she said, "Wait here with Bridget," before she closed the door.

None of the things that should have been in the living room were there. No smell of popcorn hanging in the air, no ice-cold Cokes dripping on the table, no Sean smiling to welcome them. No couch, no coffee table, no big screen TV. The room was empty, except for a large, rectangular crib.

The crib wasn't right. It had a flowered bed sheet pulled over it, the corners tied down so that it looked like an oversized birdcage. And a little hand. Had he seen that at the sheet's edge? A small fist squeezing between the rails? Loud crying echoed in his ears, as if opening the door had increased the volume in the hallway even after the door had closed. He could feel the palm of his mother's hand on his chest where she'd pushed him.

"It smells out here," Bridget said.

She hadn't seen, he realized. She hadn't seen and he couldn't tell her. Robert stopped her as she reached for the door. "Mom said to wait."

"I don't want to wait."

"We're going to."

Bridget crossed her arms and stomped her pink shoe, but Robert didn't care so long as she was quiet. He strained his ears listening. "You want something to do?" he said. "You can hold the fern."

"I'm not holding that dumb thing."

Through the crying, Robert heard movement. Just one person. Maybe Sean had gone to look for them. But the game should have started by now. Hassler had a strong coach and a talented running back. Anything might happen, even against Notre Dame.

More minutes. More waiting. Finally, "Open up for me, Robert," their mother said, tapping the other side of the door with her foot. She had a baby in each arm and Sean's old duffel over her shoulder.

"Where's Sean?" Bridget asked.

And Angela? Robert didn't say.

"Press the down button, Bridget."

"But—"

"Press it."

He'd wanted to stay there a little longer. He'd wanted to wash the babies clean and call the police, but his mother had said there was no water in the apartment, no electricity, no phone, and no time if they wanted to catch the bus home.

They rushed blindly through unknown streets to the stop they hadn't found before. Robert and his mother each dragged their own set of anchors: Robert towed Bridget, the straining duffel bag, and the ridiculous fern; his mother cushioned the babies' heads, one in each palm, so that they weren't too badly jostled as she sped across the concrete. If Sean had gone looking for them, they should have passed him along the way. As they rounded the final corner, the bus was already rolling in. They didn't have a free arm to flag it down, but thankfully, the driver saw and waited.

The five of them plunked into the first open seats, panting in the stench of unchanged diapers. Around them, people frowned and covered their noses and mouths with their hands. His mother bounced the babies in her arms but made no sound. A strand of black hair had escaped her barrette and stuck to her hard lip, quivering as she exhaled, but she noticed only the twins.

"You know, they have this radical new technology called soap," some stranger said. "It's cheap and user-friendly. Even dummies can use it; you don't need a manual or nothing."

A few people chuckled, and the man smirked to himself, satisfied with his own cleverness. Their mother didn't so much as flinch.

Robert should have offered to carry one of the twins, but he knew he would barf. Already, his throat burned against the stink. He stared through the fern fronds and the street-grimed window, bracing against the stranger's remarks. Everything was everybody's business here. His mother juggled the babies in one arm, poop smearing the front her dress. Robert couldn't name the emotion on her face. Anger, yes, and concern, disgust—and something else, something like the look she'd worn at the funeral. Something forbidding.

Their mother nodded at Bridget as they got off the bus as if everything were okay, but even in their own neighborhood, people stared. Robert saw his family as the neighbors would see them: a small white girl whose red Hassler t-shirt stretched past her knees, a too-tall white boy with gawky elbows, a white woman carrying babies cradled like footballs. The neighbors paused, then went back to laughing and talking, only now they would be laughing and talking about them. Robert wondered if every Philadelphia neighborhood was as loud as theirs. Ever since they'd gotten here, someone always had a boom box in the window blasting hip hop or corridos, as though they were always having a block party and the Flannigans weren't invited.

His mother aimed her lion eyes forward, walking as if

she weren't shit-smeared and reeking. These kids looking at him would go to his school. In days, they would know him. They would remember.

Robert pulled their building door open, relieved to be at a place that didn't feel like home but was, at least, a private darkness. He tried to speak, but the babies' sourness, stronger even than the fungal smell of the stairway, moved like a cloud around his mother and choked him. *Not a word*, his mother's eyes said. *Not one little word.*

DEAD LINE

Robert dialed their old rotary phone, not knowing what he would say when Sean picked up. He hated this old thing, waiting endlessly, needlessly for the dial to whir back home before putting in the next number. Everyone else on the planet had switched to touch-tones a decade ago and now they were upgrading to cordless, but not the Flannigans. His parents had to be the last analog family of the digital age, tethered by coiled wire, stuck waiting for the *tick-tick-tick-tick* of each number. The babies' faces were purple and tear-stained. They kicked at the air, feet curled into fists. Only his brother's voice, deep and steady as a foghorn, could guide them through this storm.

What had they been looking for that day in the woods, years ago? Robert couldn't remember, but he remembered the chipmunk. He wouldn't have noticed it, a still, sodden brown thing in the still, sodden leaves. He only spotted it when Sean kneeled. The thing looked dead, but recently dead. It hadn't gone stiff or flat, it hadn't had its eyes eaten away, it hadn't begun to rot. Even so, Sean picked it up, so small in his strong hand, and rubbed it dry with his sweat-shirt. "It's breathing," he said. "I can feel its heart beating like crazy." And Robert could see it now too, the movement of the ribs. Its eye squinted open, and it startled awake, jumping to its feet. Sean leaned to return it to the ground, but before he could let it go, it bit his thumb. Robert watched as a bead of blood grew, but when he looked to see where the chipmunk had gone, it had vanished.

"You saved it," he had said. "It would have died right there if not for you. It was mostly dead already." Sean laughed and brushed the blood away. The sun speckling its way through the trees threw a dappled light on his brother's face. In Robert's eyes, he glowed like something holy, a guy with the power to give life to the dead.

The receiver warmed in his hand, ringing. Sean's answering machine should have picked up by now, but even the recording of his brother's voice had vanished. Robert returned the receiver to its cradle.

Their mother had that look about her that made him think of salt, of things crusted in sea spray. She barely paused to lay the babies on a towel before starting tub water, which was less rusty than when they'd first moved in.

"Electricity off, water off," his mother said. "Sean knew we were coming. He *knew*." She seemed to catch on that word and draw inside, her mouth sealing in a thin line.

The diapers stuck to the babies, the air-dried edges crusting to their tender skin. Their mother slid her fingers into the wetter mess, as gently as possible peeling the diapers away. Even so, rashes opened underneath. Spots of blood mixed with the diaper sludge on her hands and the sudsy water, tingeing the bubbles. The twins twisted and screamed. His mother's hard mouth quivered and an unattended tear clung to her lashes. She couldn't help the babies without first hurting them—he could see that—but knowing didn't make it easier to watch.

"Did he at least leave a note?"

His mother soaked a clean washcloth and soaped their bottoms. Her silence spoke: no note, then.

Robert picked up the receiver again and plopped himself on the living room couch. He had no idea whom to call. This didn't seem like a situation for 911. Nothing was on fire. No one was dying. Sean wasn't where he was supposed to be, that was all.

As their mother ran a fresh tub of clean water, Robert flipped through listings for the non-emergency police number, dialed one number, waited, dialed the next, waited. The lady who answered sounded either harassed or bored, he couldn't tell which. "I'd like to report a missing person," he said. "Two, I mean. My brother and his wife."

"Mm-hmm," the lady said. The station bustled behind her voice, someone crying, someone shouting. Robert described the morning quickly, unsure if she was even listening.

A pause. Maybe she was reaching for a pen, or pulling up a computer file? She asked for the full names of the missing, their home address. She asked if either Sean or Angela was of "diminished mental capacity," if either was medicated, was mentally ill, if they had an abusive relationship. She asked if Robert had any reason to believe they'd been threatened. She asked if either had a criminal record or if they had friends who participated in criminal behaviors. Robert answered no and no and no and no.

"We'll file a report," she said.

"Does that mean you'll send an officer over?"

"Have you told me all the pertinent information?"

Robert looked through the doorframe. His mother cupped water and poured it over the babies. If he mentioned them, would the police take the twins away? Put them in foster care or something? He didn't know. He wanted to put the conversation on hold and ask his mother.

"Sir," the lady repeated, "was there anything else?"

"No. No, I guess not."

"Listen, hun," her voice became deeper, more sincere, as she dropped the scripted lines. "I'm going to be honest with you. Our officers? They're busy. Your brother and his wife are grown. They could've gone down the shore, taken a break, you know?"

"Their apartment was empty. The furniture was gone."

"Like I said, we'll look into it, but they don't sound like a priority case."

Robert pictured a dusty room lined with shelves of files like the warehouse at the end of *Indiana Jones*. The woman would hang up on him and wheel Sean's file to a basket of files no one would ever open.

"But Sean's *missing*," he said again, as if he needed to clarify. He wanted to believe they were abducted, taken by force, but no one took adults and furniture and left children behind. "Angela is *missing*."

"Sometimes, that's how people do."

"They left their babies."

"Babies were left unattended?" The official tone was back, the boredom vanished. Maybe they would investigate now. Maybe he said the right thing after all.

But he needed to be careful. "The babies are safe. We have them."

"Ages?"

"Twins. Just a few months." Robert fought to remember the exact age, but the policewoman had already moved on.

"I'm adding a note that two infants were left unattended but are now in your care. Family and Children's Services will take that up with your brother if he turns up. Do you feel equipped to continue caring for them?"

They didn't have a single diaper. They didn't own a jar of baby food or a high chair or a stroller. He'd barely turned ten when Bridget was born; he'd never looked after a baby. His mother hadn't worked and his father had been there. His father, who looked like Paul Bunyan with a baby on his shoulder in place of an ax, who could change a diaper practically single-handed and then play a banjo lullaby.

His mother wrapped the twins in towels, dabbing their noses and smiling at them through teary eyes. One working mother. Four children.

"Yes," he said.

"Good. I'll file this then." She gave him his case number and the line clicked dead.

Robert fought the duffel's zipper to sort through onesies and washcloths, bottles and binkies. Everything was filthy. He soaked the bottles in the sink, wondering if he should add bleach to the dish soap, wondering what would wash the taste of sour milk from plastic.

The rage of one baby had settled into gasping sniffles. His mother silently stroked its head. Her love for the baby was in that motion, but the love was also an ache.

Robert turned and tripped over Bridget, who had slipped up behind him. "Which one's Sammy?" she asked.

Robert wanted to answer, but he didn't know how to tell the two apart. Sean would know. He always knew which baby was which, just like he knew how to kiss tears away and turn them into smiles. Sean had taken to fatherhood with the ease with which he did everything.

"When's Sean getting here?" Bridget's pigtails were loose, and reddish brown strands hung in her eyes. Her hair was getting darker every day, just as Sean's and their mother's had. By the time Bridget finished elementary school, it would be the same crow color as theirs. Robert unclipped her barrette and brushed her hair back. Just like Bridget herself, the hair never stayed put. He half-turned towards his mother. "Can I go in your purse for diaper money?"

"And formula," she said.

* * *

Robert kept a mental list of things that were gone. Dad was at the top of the list. When they moved, he added Oregon. Now, Sean and Angela.

Robert had always loved Oregon, but almost from birth, his brother wanted out. In second grade, he volunteered to do his American City report on New York. He papered his bedroom walls with tourism bureau posters of Boston and Chicago alongside posters for Rancid, Suicidal Tendencies, and the Dead Kennedys. Sean needed some place bigger and brighter than their small logging town. He needed only a vehicle: a bike, a car, college.

Robert held Bridget's hand as they walked to Wawa. The lady at the beauty shop had the mailman by the elbow, telling him a story that had them both laughing as if no one was watching. Across the street, a bunch of kids jumped and squealed around a leaking hose. Bridget looked at Robert, her eyes begging to join them, but he shook his head, so she darted ahead, flapping her arms to make the pigeons fly. The purple and green of their necks shone hot in the sun.

The final street was busy, and there wasn't a crosswalk. He ran to catch his sister's fingers as a Pontiac whooshed by. Her hand was sweat-slick, but he held it tight. They counted cars and looked for a gap through which they could run.

"When Sean comes," Bridget started.

"Hush." It was the word his mother used to quiet him when she told them their father wasn't coming home, that he wouldn't ever come home again. She hadn't said another word after that one, not for some time. Afterward, he understood. Words could open up more pain than a person could bear. Silence made walls for the box that contained the things that would consume you. Silence let you focus on what needed to be done: the sandwich to make, the dishes to wash, the diapers to buy.

* * *

The Wawa on the corner carried only one brand, squeezed on the shelf between emergency candles and toilet paper. He grabbed a package and a can of formula powder, glad not to have choices. He wouldn't have known what to get if there had been more than one kind. He added the total, figured the tax, and grabbed a tube of rash cream.

The cashier smacked her gum as she raked the pile toward her across the counter. He wondered how much of his life she could read through his purchases, how often she used her register to total the cost of someone's pain.

A man walked up behind them carrying Pringles, fuel injector cleaner, and a half gallon of milk. "Got a new baby, huh?" In Philadelphia, Robert noticed, strangers started conversations with strangers. Robert only nodded, hoping to keep the interaction short.

"Twins," Bridget said. "But they're not new. They're already over three months old."

"You sure you got the right diapers, then? You got newborns."

The cashier paused. "You want to swap them out?"

Every inch of Robert's skin burned. He looked at the package. Of course, they came in sizes. Any idiot but him might have guessed that. "I'm sorry," he said to the man. "You can go ahead of us."

"I'm in no rush."

Robert dashed the diapers back.

"Can I have a soft pretzel?" Bridget called.

Robert shook his head quickly as he laid the diapers on the counter, but again, the cashier hesitated.

"Sean would buy me one."

"We don't have enough." He whispered the words, hoping his voice was too low for the others to hear.

The cashier appraised him through dark eye makeup. She selected a pretzel from the case where they spun top-lit, as if they were jewels. She wrapped it in paper and slid it across the white countertop to Bridget. "Here you go, chica. Make sure your brother gets a bite."

Robert stopped Bridget's wrist as she reached. "I can't pay for that."

"It's cool. Probably time to change them out anyway. Put in some fresh."

"Thanks," Robert mumbled, too humiliated to meet her eye.

Outside, the heavy air hit him like a wet, hot fish slap to the face. *Jesus.* Bridget bounced next to him with her pretzel. God only knew how long it had hung in that case. She tore off hunks and popped them into her mouth. He couldn't decide which was more upsetting, the heat or her happiness. "You shouldn't have taken that."

"It's good. Want some?"

"You shouldn't eat stuff a stranger gives you."

"You'd eat it if we bought it."

"We couldn't buy it. That's the point." He should have just ignored her when she first asked. Then, he'd have nothing to be embarrassed about. He needed to watch his mouth. Be careless like that at school, and he'd be the same class-A reject he'd been in Herman. This was his one chance to reinvent himself.

The plastic bag hit his leg with every step. Already, its handle cut into his sweating hand. The summer seemed made of a kind of hot air pudding you had to slice your way through. Robert hadn't stopped sweating since the move. How Sean could prefer this to Oregon baffled him, but Sean convinced their mother easily enough. He'd be able to help them here, she said. He found them an apartment and lined her up with a job. He said they'd see the Liberty Bell and Independence Hall and Betsy Ross's house. He said they would eat cheesesteaks and scrapple and water ice. He said they'd go to D.C. one weekend and Ellis Island another. He said they would do all the things Robert had never yearned to do. What the hell was a scrapple anyway? It sounded like a board game played in church basements by little old ladies with beehive hairdos and diamond-studded glasses.

Bridget finished her pretzel and was at it again, prattling away as she always did. "Can we go to the park?"

"Mom's waiting."

"After we drop off the stuff?"

"We need to help with Sammy and Deacon."

"Babies cry too much," she said. "When's Sean coming?"

Robert hesitated, then shook his head. Bridget looked like she did when she counted on her fingers, adding things up. "Why won't anyone talk about Sean?"

Her shoelace was untied. He stooped to retie it, but she only waited for his answer. Finally, he said, "There's nothing to say."

Bridget's eyes filled. He'd caused that. Her hair had fallen loose again, and he smoothed it with his hand and re-clipped her barrette. "It'll be fine," he said.

"*What* will be fine?"

"The babies," he stammered. "The babies will be fine."

"Why are we buying diapers?"

"Babies need diapers, Bridget. You know that."

"Why didn't Sean have any? Why doesn't he bring some?"

"Come on."

"Why wasn't he there like he was supposed to be?" Hysteria sharpened her voice like it did after her green-man nightmares.

He couldn't breathe, so he shut his eyes and let all the words crowded in his throat escape. "Sean was gone, Bridget. He left us."

Robert pulled her to him, the swinging plastic bag thumping her back. "It's all right, though. We'll take care of things. Sammy and Deacon will be all clean and happy when we get home. Sean will come. Angela too. We just don't know when, okay? We'll be all right, but you've got to stop crying, Bridget. We've got to be strong."

By strong, what he meant was silent.

Bridget settled into snuffles as they walked. She wouldn't bother their mother with questions now. She wouldn't ask to play. When they got home, she would go to her room and cry enough for all of them while he and his mother tended the babies.

THE FIRST MORNING

Robert didn't look like he belonged to his family anymore. Not since his father died. His mother, Sean, and Bridget shared the same unmistakable gold-flecked eyes rimmed with black lashes. Sean had inherited the best from both parents, their father's Brawny Man build and their mother's striking looks. Sean had their father's strong shoulders and their mother's straight nose, their father's charisma and their mother's stamina.

Robert got only the leftovers, his mom's narrow frame and social awkwardness, his father's pale skin and lank red hair.

He should do something about it. Drink protein shakes, lift, run. Now and then, he could almost convince himself that his long, hooked nose made him appear sophisticated, like a kind of British aristocrat. Maybe he was the kind of guy who could dangle a pipe from his fingers and say "tut tut." Most days, though, he faced the truth: he could grow out his hair as long as he liked, let it flop over his boring blue eyes, but it still wouldn't hide his beak of a nose.

The night before, he'd helped his mother layer pillows and blankets in her bottom dresser drawer, making a cozy little bed, but even so the twins had hardly slept. Worse, Bridget had woken with another green-man nightmare. Now, their mother's skin hung on her face as she paced with the phone in one hand, its long cord shushing against the floor. The other hand gripped the receiver, pressing it against the side of her mouth so tightly that the skin went white. She sighed heavily and said "Leona" but was cut off before getting any further.

She had broken down and called Angela's mother. Robert couldn't quite process this. They didn't speak to Leona. Leona had wanted to kill the babies. "Abort," she'd said, like it was no big thing. That was what Angela told them. Her mother had it in her mind that Angela would be the first in their family to finish college. When Angela didn't listen, Leona told her she was a knocked-up slut like all the rest of the neighborhood whores. She said Angela had her whole future in front of her, that she was a fool to throw it away for some good-looking douchebag too stupid to wear a rubber. She said that Angela had better not run home when things went bad. Angela hadn't talked to her since.

Leona dumped all those pent-up lectures into his mother's ear, and she sat there, absorbing it. Slender as she was, his mother was hardly weak. She was built to endure over distance. She set her jaw now just as she did when she ran her long runs. She disappeared to clatter around in the dishes while keeping the phone shouldered to her ear. She emerged holding a full bottle towards Robert, but flinched as he took it, her body suddenly stiff. "Don't you dare tell me what she gave up. Sean gave up college and a pro career for that girl."

Their mother had been pregnant with Sean before she was seventeen. She told the story as a happy one. The best thing that ever happened to her. She skipped the part about having been the high school track star, though her records for the 800m, mile, and two-mile still hung in the Herman field house twenty years later. She missed state her senior year, too far along to run sprints. Lately, when she told the story, Robert wondered if pregnancy was the best thing that ever happened to her only because it cut her off from all the other possible best things.

Robert rubbed the bottle's nipple against the baby's lips. His mother shut herself in the bedroom, but her muffled voice filtered through the walls. The phone cord strained against the jack, making a line to the crack under the door. In his arms, the baby clamped down on the bottle. "I guess you were ready to eat," he said.

The twins were not identical. This baby's eyebrows were straight, like Sean's, but his eyes were darker brown. That's how he'd known this little guy, then. By Angela's dark eyes. The other's eyes were lightening towards Sean's hazel.

Their mother's door creaked open. From the way her shoulders hung, he guessed the phone call hadn't accomplished anything. She clicked on the radio and collapsed next to him on the couch. The local news talked of houses in Southwest Philadelphia sinking into the long forgotten swampland buried below. It was too awful to think of: someone, anyone, might be walking through their kitchen, not thinking a thing about it because the tile had been there for generations, when, with no more warning than a sharp crack, they fell through the floorboards into some murky, underground creek. A boy, perhaps, not unlike himself, hungry for a snack from the cupboard, suddenly immersed in the sludge. There would be no way to rescue him, not with three stories of house above and too much mud for screams. He would swallow the city with his last breath, just as it swallowed him.

He shook himself from these thoughts, which were too dark to be thinking around the babies. His mother smiled weakly at him, reaching to stroke the soft head of the dark-eyed baby. "Oh Deacon," she said. Robert filled in the unspoken question: *what are we going to do with you?*

JEROME

By the time the sun disappeared into the afternoon's haze, the last thing Robert could tolerate was a sweaty baby against his chest. The fan in the window blew dock smell from the Delaware: motor oil, fish, and cat piss. The twins cried and kicked at the quilts they lay on. They wore nothing but diapers, but they were hot and their tantrums made them hotter. There was just no reasoning with babies.

For the fifth time, his mother called the janitorial service where Sean worked weekends, but the answer was always the same; they hadn't seen him. Robert grabbed his father's old banjo, picking one string, then another, messing with order and sound.

The walls were thin, thrown up quickly when the row house was cut into apartments. He had heard the biker across the hall yelling at his girlfriend yesterday as clearly as if the man were standing in their living room. "Bitch," he'd yelled. "Who is he? Tell me who he is." Now, that guy would be the one hearing all their business. He was probably sitting in his front room now, fuming about the new family, the one that couldn't get their kids to shut up.

He was the only other white person in the neighborhood, as far as Robert could tell, but that didn't mean he was anything like them. His arms were bigger than Robert's thighs and covered with faded tattoos. Snakes, bare-breasted women, and decks of cards melded, rolling across his skin when his muscles moved. In Robert's mind, they did that now. The man, sitting in a greasy gold easy chair, a stack of weights in the corner and centerfolds taped to the walls, would throw himself up to storm around the room, ranting about their noise. He couldn't take much more. He'd bang on their door and bellow at their mother, the ends of his Yosemite Sam mustache jumping with each word. She would apologize, of course she would, but it wouldn't mollify him—he was past that, all fists and rage.

The banjo sounded nothing like it had in his father's hands. Robert tried to determine the key of baby crying, trying to harmonize. Perhaps he could soften its edge and make wailing bearable. His mother's back was to him, but he could see the tension in her shoulders pulling so hard she seemed likely to snap.

And then, just as he had imagined, a thumping fist rattled the door in its frame. Robert and his mother looked at one another. The person could have a gun, though if it were their neighbor, he wouldn't need one. A single jab powered by that bulging bicep would crumple any one of them.

Fear made him clumsy. Robert stumbled to the door, but though she never seemed to hurry, his mother beat him there. The spring in her step meant she thought it was Sean. Robert was inches from her shoulder, but their minds were miles apart. Sean, he knew, never would have knocked.

She swung the door wide to find a tall black kid, hair braided into rows, grinning at them through wire-framed glasses. "Man, those babies are *loud*." The kid addressed himself to Robert. He didn't seem to be complaining. "What's that?" He gestured to the banjo, which, to Robert, now seemed like some alien object growing from his arm. The kid didn't wait for Robert to answer. "I'm Jerome," he said, as if that explained everything. "You want to come out?"

Robert didn't know what to make of any of this. He looked at his mother. "Go on," she said.

"Don't you need help?"

"Go."

"All right," he said, half to her and half to the boy. His fingertips were raw; he hadn't played enough since the move. He'd have to toughen up. He shoved the banjo under his bed.

Robert had never known a black person. In Herman, the only people who weren't white were Native Americans or migrant farm workers. He supposed he should also include the Hongs, Fujiokas, Chins, and Yamadas, but their families had been working the railroads and mines in Oregon so long that he never thought of them as anything but white. Black had a different texture, a different history.

The sky, white with humidity and smog, lowered over the abandoned, boarded-up row homes down the block. Except for the graying plywood over the windows and doors, the condemned houses were identical to the one that had become his family's apartment, rectangular brick with bay windows bulging in the front. Jerome lived close if he'd seen them move in.

"You going to Garvey or East Catholic?" Jerome asked.

"Garvey."

"Me too! What grade you in?"

"Tenth."

This was a sore spot. Herman Junior High continued through ninth grade, but at Garvey, people started high school as freshmen. All the students in his grade already had a full year under their belts. When school started, he'd be the only sophomore still trying to figure out how things worked. He wondered if anyone would miss him if he hid in his bedroom until high school was over, slip in just in time for graduation and call it good.

In his oversized shorts and shirt, Jerome looked like a part of this place. He fit in. "Maybe we'll have some classes together."

"Maybe."

"I thought for sure you'd go to East Catholic. That's where most of the white kids go. You going out for sports?"

Where the white kids go? Philadelphia needed an instruction manual. "I don't know. You?"

"Football, maybe. But that might make the girls love me too much. Next thing you know, they be calling me all night, waking the house. Be on me like flies." He pantomimed flicking them off. His hands were almost feminine with their long, slender fingers. They reminded Robert of a piano player's hands, fine-boned and elegant. He couldn't picture those hands catching a football.

Girls on him like flies? "Sounds like a good problem to have."

"I'll let you know when I have it. You see *Slayers* last Tuesday?"

"We don't have a TV." Jesus. How much more fuel could he feed the inferno in which he was vaporizing his puny reputation? And it wasn't even true! They did have a TV, but it was only a 13" Emerson and, since his mother wouldn't get cable, they could hardly pull in any decent shows.

That was all too much to explain. To anyone looking, he was part of the baby-poop white family too backwards to even own a TV.

Jerome didn't seem to notice. "Next week, come watch at my house. My little brother talks over all the good parts, but I just throw sofa pillows at him until he shuts up."

He rattled on, talking about last week's episode,

about zombies and the tricks for killing them, tripping from one subject to another without thought or effort. Jerome talked like they were friends, like Robert was another kid from the neighborhood, like Robert being white didn't matter at all.

Friendship, like everything else, would be different in Philadelphia. In Oregon, friendship was a group of kids lying around on a Friday night playing D&D or Legends of Zelda until two in the morning. He wondered what Troy and Scott and Lara Lynn were doing now. They were three hours earlier, living in a whole different time of day. Maybe sleeping still. Maybe reading a book. Not thinking about him, that was for sure. Their friendship was like water. When Robert stepped out, it closed over his absence leaving no trace that he'd ever been there. Just like people were when his dad died, as if he hadn't been essential.

Jerome's legs stuck out from his baggy shorts like straight brown sticks growing out of basketball sneakers instead of pots. His calves had no muscle, not like a football player's. Maybe cross-country if he could run. He had that loose-limbed ropey-ness that sometimes came with speed or endurance, like his joints were held together with slack rubber bands so that he bounced just a little as he walked. Even when he wasn't smiling, his face looked ready to crack open again, like any excuse would do it. He was something solar-powered, collecting the sun so he could beam it back.

"What kind of music do you play?"

"I just mess around."

"You making your own kind of music, then. That's the best kind."

"I thought you didn't know what it was."

"The banjo? I ain't ignorant. I just never knew anybody who had one."

Robert smiled back at him. He couldn't quite find his feet

in this conversation, but maybe that wasn't so bad. "It was my dad's."

"Cool. Hey, you like Twizzlers? Want to go to Wawa?"

When Robert walked in, his mother smiled for the first time in days. He'd given her that, he realized, and he was glad. She put on Leonard Cohen and waltzed Sammy and Deacon slowly through the room. The dance lulled their crying and they lay open-eyed against her body. On the surface, it was an improvement. In spite of her smile, another unspoken worry haunted the corners of her mouth. He wished she'd take a long run—distance always lifted her—but the kitchen timer was beeping. Dinner was ready. She kissed each baby on the head and laid them on the quilts folded on the floor.

THE CHUM

Robert woke to find his mother on the end of his bed. She wore one of his father's undershirts—or it wore her. The seams of its shoulders falling midway down her arms. In it, she was small and tired and fragile. Her thick, unclipped hair curtained her eyes, and her skin, once tan from daily runs, was growing pale. The scent of Drakkar hung like a pleasant cloud, a memory that refused to budge. Everything about his father had been strong.

"Sean hasn't called."

Robert sat up. She started her new job today. "It's okay."

"I'll have to call in."

"I can handle it. We'll be okay."

His mother hadn't worked since her high school job at Dairy Queen. Now, she would start as receptionist at the vending company where Sean worked weekdays. She'd never had an office job, never even known anyone with an office job. "I don't own a suit," she had said. "You don't need one," Sean had told her, "even the boss wears jeans." She went to the Goodwill anyway and found a tan Chanel with a grease-stained lapel. She embroidered flowers over the spots, sewing each night before they left Oregon so that she would be ready. Robert hadn't realized how much the job meant to her until the moment she'd shown Sean the finished jacket, shy pride beaming through her sliver of a smile. Sean pulled her in for a hug and kissed the top of her head. "I told you, you don't need anything special," he'd said, but next time he came, he brought two silk shirts, one turquoise and one red, to match the flowers she'd sewn.

Last week. That had only been last week.

She stared out the door, the lines of her face settling into *the ways things are*. "I can't leave you with Bridget and the babies. It's too much."

"I can do this."

"It's not fair to ask."

"Then don't ask." Robert smoothed the old sheets, his fingers tracing the faded super heroes flying to the rescue of people whose problems were straightforward. Life wasn't fair. That's what adults always said. This last year, he'd come to know *isn't fair* personally. "They'll fire you."

"You start school next week. Who'll watch them then?"

"Sean will be back."

"Registration day is tomorrow, Robert. Tomorrow."

"I'll take them with me if I have to."

"That's not the start I want for you." Tired as she was, her eyes seemed almost colorless. He wished he could see her how she used to be, laughing as she ducked into the old kitchen with his father and baskets of blackberries, the juice staining the long-gone twin of the shirt she now wore, her cuffed jeans brown at the knees where she had kneeled to pick in low bramble.

Robert pushed back the sheets. "I'll fix the bottles. Let Bridget sleep."

Across the hall, a baby cried. His mother wavered.

"I got this," he said again. "Get dressed or you'll be late."

She looked so different in her suit. Her cheeks glowed against the silk of her shirt. He couldn't get over seeing his mother like this:

a glamorous person, a woman with an office job in the city. He imagined her punching at blinking buttons lining a beige office phone, putting people on hold, transferring them, helping the business run. She had always been important to him, but today, she would be important to other people. He wondered if that scared her.

"You worry too much," he called as she dashed out the door to catch the bus.

But once the door closed and his mother disappeared from the window's view, loneliness set in like nothing he had ever known. No one could help. He was in the middle of a city of over a million and a half people, but he might as well be on a raft in the ocean.

Bridget leaned over Deacon, asleep on the floor in his nest of blankets. She blew a long steady breath across his wispy hair like he was a set of birthday candles she wanted to put out. "Don't," Robert said, too late. They watched, still and breathless now as deer at the wood's edge, while Deacon drew pudgy fists to his eyes. The corners of his mouth pulled down, and the wailing poured forth. Light-eyed Sammy woke instantly. From then on, the morning would be a contest to see which brother could out-scream the other.

Bridget turned to Robert. "The babies don't do anything but cry."

"Deacon *was* sleeping until someone had to go and poke him."

"I didn't poke him. I didn't do anything."

"If you hadn't done anything, they'd be sleeping."

"I don't want the babies here anymore."

No one does.

He almost said it, and knowing that threatened to choke him. He couldn't allow no one to want Sean's babies. What he said instead was, "If we don't want these babies, no one will."

Bridget's eyes rounded. Kids were transparent when they were five and hadn't started school. The thought of an unwanted baby never crossed her mind. "I didn't mean it."

"I know."

Still, the babies cried and cried.

Three hours down, six to go. Each minute stretched. His skull was ringing. He needed to go to the bathroom, and he needed to be in there for a while, but he couldn't leave the twins with Bridget. Each time she lifted one, Robert was sure she would drop him. What if one found a marble or a cockroach or some other random object and put it in his mouth? What if one stopped breathing for no reason whatsoever? What if Robert failed?

Robert's gut cramped, his stomach twisting in knots. His skin was chilled with sweat, but his insides burned. Samson had settled a little, but Deacon kept wailing. Robert flipped through the old *What to Expect* book his mother had dug out. Crying could mean a million things, and each of those million things could be nothing or could be a sign of imminent death. The bottles should be washed, and he needed to fix them all lunch at some point. Bridget's sympathy gave out again after the first hour of crying. She begged him to go to the park, but he wasn't about to carry two babies on his own while she ran all over kingdom come. When begging didn't work, she stomped her foot and screamed, then sulked in her room, which, at this point, was fine with him. One less worry.

Robert put Sammy down and lifted Deacon, but this only made Sammy cry again while Deacon continued to scream at full pitch. They were too small to cry so hard for so long. Surely, they had to sleep at some point. His shoulders ached from carrying the babies. They just got heavier and heavier the longer you held them, two squirming bricks.

Bridget's door cracked open and her face peered through, tears still clinging to the fringe of her lashes. "Mom would let me go."

He shot her a look, and she slammed the door.

He was failing everyone. His mother's work number was written on the pad by the phone. One call and he could ruin their lives. Even if they didn't fire her for leaving early on her first day, no one else would watch the babies on the second. She wouldn't trust him. She'd call in and, just like that, the job would be gone. His stomach cramped again. His mouth filled with a wash of warm spit.

The door rattled on its hinges under another banging fist. "Knock" was too light a word. The person must have thought a deaf family lived here, or that the Flannigan's door had done some wrong and needed to be punished. Why did people in Philly always bang? Bridget ran to answer it, but Robert rose and stepped in front of her, mouthing "no." It could be a murderer for all they knew, some sadistic criminal with a butcher knife and a Jack the Ripper fixation.

"What if it's Sean?" she said.

Whoever it was thudded their fist again against the door. *Bang bang bang bang.* Gut knotted, head throbbing, hands full of screaming baby, Robert had no idea what to do. If everything would quiet for just a second, he could figure it out.

The knob turned. He had forgotten to lock the door! He threw his body in front of Bridget's. One little twist of the deadbolt could have saved them, but when his mother left, he'd forgotten even that.

The door creaked open, and Jerome's face appeared. "Why didn't you answer? I know you heard."

Robert was so relieved he thought his legs would give out. Jerome shook his head. "Damn, boy. You look rough. You were white yesterday, but you're *white* white today. Give that baby here."

"Make sure to support his head."

"I've got four little brothers and sisters *and* a baby niece. You don't need to tell me nothing. Sides, this guy's old enough to hold his own head. Go on, now. Take care of yourself."

Robert hesitated only for a moment before dashing to the bathroom.

They went to the park after lunch, Jerome showing Robert how to carry a baby draped over his arm to help with colic. The park was small and grassless, but a sprawling maple grew in the corner. The boys sat in its shade. Bridget did three quick cherry drops on the ancient jungle gym before running for the slide. Robert watched her lining up with the other kids. Already, she chattered away to a Latina girl in neat pigtails. Her hair looked like it had been parted with a laser and ironed flat to the base of her pink ribbons. Each curl looped in exact circles. Bridget had never been so neat.

Overhead, something buzzed in the branches, the noise rising and falling, giving a pulse to the summer heat.

"You know not to come here at night, right?"

Robert examined Jerome's face, trying to work out if he was just trying to scare him. That's what his dad would have done, telling him some goofy story about werewolves or flesh-eating zombies that came out by the light of the moon, grabbing Robert suddenly by the shoulders to make him jump. They'd laugh until every fear set below the horizon, distant as the sun.

But Jerome wasn't smiling. "I'm serious. Come dusk, clear out. It's all bangers, dealers, and pimps after that. You don't want to be anywhere near this place."

The girls ran a lap around the wood chips, then stood in the dust they had stirred. Bridget took the other girl by the hand and led her to the maple to show her how to make fairy houses in the tree roots, choosing out sticks and moss for tables, beds, couches, a crib. Perhaps "fairy houses" was an Oregon game. When he was her age, he built forts in the rhodies and once— only once—the blackberries. The brambles caught at his shirt like they were alive, little claws grasping to trap and devour him, vengeance, perhaps, for all the blackberries he'd eaten over the years. Some places, you didn't mess with.

"You been here at night?"

"Me? Hell no. The police roll by and think I'm packing? That's it."

"But you're not, are you? Packing?" The word felt weird in his mouth, large and furry. He'd only ever used it to fill moving boxes.

"Me?" Jerome snorted. "It's all perception. The whole world? Perception. Which is all well and good if you're fronting for the ladies, but it's nothing to mess with neither. Not with the po pos. Not here, not at night."

With the sun streaming through the trees and children laughing as they draped themselves along the jungle gym, the place looked harmless enough. In Oregon, it was the isolated cabins and trailers of the woods you had to watch, meth head country, but that danger seemed so distant. Yeah, in elementary school some kid got all burned up when her parents' lab exploded, but she was two years younger than Robert and not related to anyone he knew. He'd almost forgotten about her.

Robert glanced at his scuffed low-tops and realized that what he'd been nudging through the sand with the toe of his sneaker was a discarded vial. Sean said the neighborhood was okay, but he'd only seen the daylight version. Sammy, hot on Robert's arm, slept on, oblivious.

Jerome said, "Your dad split on you all?"

Robert didn't know how to answer. In a way, he had. Maybe it was best to say that. *Yeah. He split.* Easy. Better than how it had been when people knew. As soon as the story of the gunshot spread through Herman, his friends hadn't known how to talk to him. They edged away. When they finally gathered for their first game night after the funeral, the air around him seemed fragile as glass. They fixated on the battles, fighting, fighting, forgetting healing potions and regeneration, forgetting Cheetos and jokes, forgetting the way they controlled all the fate that the dice couldn't decide until death became inevitable and no one knew what to say. Robert didn't want to bring that weirdness here, not with Jerome, yet he heard himself saying the words: "He died."

"I'm sorry."

Robert shrugged, counting the seconds until Jerome found an excuse to take off. He stared at Sammy, counting his breaths. If Robert knew anything, he knew that you didn't bring up death with a person you just met. Any time now, Jerome would need to pick something up at the store, or check on his brothers, or—

"Let me guess. Drive by?"

Jerome was teasing, and Robert laughed. It felt strangely good to laugh about his father, like death was not so fierce. "Believe it or not, kind of."

"You playing."

"He worked for the city. Fixing potholes, striping the road, stuff like that." He paused, the familiar glue forming in his throat. He could see it all. It was a week before Halloween and there were pumpkins everywhere, waiting to have faces carved into them. Fake spider webs stretched on lampposts and shrubs. He cleared his throat and forced the words out: "Dad was patching asphalt when some guy got ticked off at his girlfriend. Said she'd been cheating. Guy came rolling up to her house with a gun. My dad went to cool him off, but the guy ended up shooting my dad and the girl both."

"They catch him, the guy who did it?"

"He didn't really run."

"That's the difference between a white guy drive by and a black guy drive by."

Robert didn't know if that mattered. Dead was dead. He didn't feel any better knowing that the guy was in prison. Afterward, everyone walked around all tragic, even people who hadn't really known his dad or liked him. Like Phil Tate. Dad always laughed about how lazy that guy was, a shovel leaner. Phil was always trying to blame his slowness on anyone else. Robert's dad approached every problem with jokes and patience. His mother only pursed her lips and said, "He'd throw you under the first available bus if it would save his job." And after all that? As soon as his dad was shot, who comes to their door but old Phil Tate, crying like they'd been best friends.

"That why you moved here? Your dad dying?"

"My brother and his wife are here. With the babies and all, my mom decided we might as well be closer to them."

"And your brother left the kids with you today?"

"Yeah." It was a half-truth, but the whole truth glided out after it like a tail following a kite. "Today and tomorrow and who knows how long. He left."

"Just what my dad did."

"Yeah?"

"Yeah." Jerome let that sit for a moment before saying, "These babies can't watch themselves when school starts."

"I don't know how to find him."

"Can't find a man who don't want to be found."

Bridget was trying to climb up the slide. Things had gone so far from the plan. Now that his mother was here to help, Sean was supposed to go back to school. When he finished, he'd get a good job and they'd all get a place together out in the suburbs. Narberth or Medford Lakes or Wynnewood, Sean said. They'd live in a place that sounded like an ocean fish or a fairy tale or both. The city itself was supposed to be temporary.

"The trees here are loud," Robert said. Sammy was hot in his arms.

"Cicadas. You don't have them in Oregon?"

"I don't think so."

"When your mom gets back, I'm taking you to meet Miss Martha. She watches all the kids in the Chum."

"What's the Chum?"

Jerome looked at him for a long moment before the grin slid over his face. "The Chum is where you're *at*, brother."

"We're in Philadelphia."

"Yeah, but there's white folks Philly and there's the Chum. There's Rittenhouse and Society Hill. There's Pennypack Park and East Passyunk and Penn's Port. Then there's us. A few blocks east, you're in Germantown. Head southwest a ways, you end up in Huntington Park. But here? This here's the Chum. And you, my man, are living right in the heart of it." The sun bounced off Jerome's glasses as he laughed, hiding his eyes behind light. His words slid out like liquid. "White boy doesn't even know where he lives."

Philadelphia was a warm, wet mouth, ready to swallow Robert whole. Angela had known how to live in the city. She said she was Italian, but she'd never been to Italy. She was Philadelphia-Italian, which was something all its own. She had that fight born into her. She thrust her chest out like it was armor. If even Angela couldn't make it here, if Sean too had cut and run, what chance did Robert have?

"You're all right, dawg." Jerome was still smiling. "You got no game whatsoever, no front, no face. That's cool. Not exactly typical, but cool. Unique. You want to find him?"

"Him?"

"Your brother."

"What happened to 'can't find a man who don't want to be found'?"

"Don't mean we can't try."

"Why? You want to look for your dad?"

"That asshole?"

"School's only a couple days away."

"So you don't want to look."

"No—I mean, I do. I just don't know where to start."

"Think about it."

"I will," Robert said, but his stomach was sliding into his shoes and he didn't know if the "it" he would think about was *where* to look or *whether*.

MISS MARTHA

Bouncing along on Jerome's shoulder, Deacon actually giggled. His face slid in a lopsided grin as his cheek tapped softly against Jerome's braids. Robert's mother carried Sammy, and for the first time that day, Robert's back started to unknot.

Each brick house was painted its own yellow, purple, or green. The bright color was all that made one different from the next. They were plain row houses, each with one long unadorned front window and a short set of steps leading to the door. Along the street, fast food wrappers and a pair of broken sunglasses mingled with the less obvious things that might or might not be there: vials, bullet casings, condoms filled with some John's cum.

Miss Martha was younger than Robert expected. He had imagined a gray-haired grandmother complete with knitting needles, half-moon glasses, and a quavering voice, but the woman who opened the door was only a little older than his mother, her hair black and her face unlined. Two children clung to the skirt of her bold-printed caftan. Behind her, another child cried for her mama. "Good evening," she said, in a precise, lilting voice so rich it made Robert think of velvet. If sound were a fabric, hers would be dark like that, picking up light along the folds.

"These folks need someone to watch their babies." Jerome jerked his thumb back towards Robert's family.

Miss Martha pursed her lips before speaking. "No

'Hello'? No 'How are you?' Jerome, I taught you better."

"Sorry, Miss Martha."

Robert's mother shifted Sammy to her shoulder and reached out a hand to shake. "I'm Beth Flannigan. We've just moved in, a couple blocks over. Jerome tells us you run a daycare."

Miss Martha waved them into her apartment and offered coffee and tea. She walked with a cane and a bad limp. Thick curtains made the room dark and the air hung heavy with incense. Bridget reached to pull a wooden elephant from the circle that marched in the lamplight of an end table. They were carved from some soft, easily broken wood, balsa perhaps, but stained dark as ebony with plastic tusks. "Don't touch," Robert hissed.

"Oh, she can touch them," Martha said. His mother followed her back into the room with a tray of mugs.

"They look fragile."

"I like to keep a little Africa here, but I don't own anything that can't be broken."

Bridget looked at Martha, her hand still hanging frozen in the air in front of her, then looked again at Robert and dropped it to her side.

"You said this wasn't official," their mother said. "Does that mean you're unlicensed?"

"I'm on disability, so technically, I don't work. Watching kids just helps folks out. Of course, a little money helps me do that, but you won't be able to claim me on your taxes, if that's what you're thinking."

His mother's face looked as tired as her wrinkled suit. He guessed that was not what she'd been thinking. Her eyes fell to Martha's cane. "It's just you? No help?"

"The older kids help with the younger."

One of the skirt children from the doorway came up to Bridget, staring at her. Bridget stared back.

"How many kids?" their mother asked.

"A handful." Martha waved her hand vaguely, as if the question were inconvenient smoke that could be cleared away. She didn't seem too bothered by his mother's cross-examination. Her cane was twisted, gnarled wood. Now that it rested against Martha's ample thigh, Robert could see that the knob was carved in the shape of a skull with bared teeth and hollow eye sockets.

Miss Martha's gaze rested on him, like his skin was so light that she could see every fear shining through, incandescent. She said, "These two are, what, maybe three, four months old?"

His mother nodded. "They're my son's boys. My oldest son's, that is."

Jerome slurped his tea, perfectly at home. Another child walked in, looked at them with wide eyes, and walked out again. Robert wondered how many children were here, hiding in the paneling or behind the furniture. Miss Martha was like some kind of Pied Piper, collecting them all. Her tea was like nothing he'd ever tasted, a potion, perhaps, to calm them into doing her will.

Miss Martha said, "Take your time and think about it. Talk to people. See what they say. I raised half the children on this block."

"I will." His mother folded the paper with Martha's number, putting it carefully in her purse. Her face had not softened, but she said, "I'm sure I'll call soon."

His mother was quiet that night as she chopped the green beans. Lately, she'd been serving half the meat and twice the veggies. Sometimes she said it was healthier and sometimes she said it was environmentally friendly and it was probably a bit of both though, personally, Robert would have voted for more protein. She paused now, the knife balanced in her hand, to switch the radio away from reports of the houses collapsing into the buried Schuylkill swampland and of the sentencing of the two junior high kids who'd shot up their school in Jonesboro, Arkansas. She opted for Nirvana instead, like she always did when she was missing his dad.

Robert turned Miss Martha's place over and over in his mind, the fake African ornaments, the dark rooms, the endless children. "Martha is definitely different," he said.

His mother froze, tense as a startled rabbit, but she soon started chopping again with new speed. He liked watching her chop, how quickly she could turn a stringy mess of whatever into a neat bowl of dinner. His childhood was infused with misting rain, sunlight made green as it filtered through leaves, and the quiet knowledge that his mother was always close. The twins wouldn't have any of that.

"Jerome seemed to do okay there."

His mother did not look up.

"I mean, all those kids seemed safe enough."

Chop, chop, chop.

"They'll be okay there, right? You don't think we need to keep looking?"

Tension pulled her shoulders tight under the thin blue silk.

"Can we afford it?"

His mother dropped the knife and gripped the sides of the counter so hard that the skin of each knuckle whitened against the bone. It took him a minute to realize that she was crying. He'd never seen her cry before. Not when Sean left for Hassler, not when she told him about his dad, not even at the funeral itself. Always, she set her face in stone and, as she put it, kept herself to herself. He'd wanted her to cry when his father died. He'd wanted her to show any emotion, to prove to the town how deeply she'd loved him. Now, her back to Robert, she cried so quietly that her sobs seemed closer to hiccups, and Robert was too terrified to move. Perhaps he should hug her or stroke her hair or say that they would be okay, but none of these seemed right. "I'm sorry," he said.

His mother straightened and quickly dashed her tears away. "It doesn't matter," she said. "I'll call Martha tomorrow." Her voice was unwavering, as if there had been no doubt or tears. She was decisive: the twins would start there Monday. Bridget would join them two days a week, Mondays and Wednesdays after kindergarten, so that Robert could get some undisturbed study time.

She went about dinner like nothing had changed. He watched her back. Did she want to move back to Oregon? He might as well ask if she wished Dad were alive again or if she would like to run a marathon on the moon.

The phone's aggressive ring shook him out of his thoughts. He grabbed the receiver as his mother wiped her hands. "Hello?" There was silence, and then a click. "Hello?"

"I'm calling for Beth Flannigan." The voice had a bulldog's snarl. A cop, maybe? For a second, he allowed himself to hope.

"She's busy."

"I need to speak with her right away."

His mother looked over. "Who is it, Robert?"

"May I ask who's calling?"

"Ace Credit Reclamations."

His mother took the phone. "Who is this?" she asked in the tone she only used when she thought someone was messing with her children.

She was quiet for some time after that. Whatever the man said turned her to marble. She said "yes" and "yes" and "no" in turns. Then, "We don't know where he is." Another long pause. She repeated it: "We. Don't. Know where. He is." Later, more hushed, she said, "We couldn't possibly come up with that kind of money." She grew whiter as the man on the phone continued to talk.

When she finally hung up, she moved as if strings pulled her arms and legs.

"What did he say?" Robert asked.

Her hands quavered as she lifted the knife, but she couldn't seem to decide what needed to be done.

"Mom?"

"Sean owes money."

"That's no surprise."

"If he doesn't pay, they'll collect from us."

"Collect what? We don't have any money."

She turned away.

"Can they do that?"

"How should I know, Robert?"

"I don't think he can."

"He said he could."

"But if Sean was the one who charged things—"

"I co-signed the credit card."

"What?"

Her eyes were fixed on the vegetables.

"Why?"

"When he started school. For emergencies." She covered her eyes with her shaking hand. "Your father thought it was dumb, but how could I send him across the country without some way to protect him?"

Robert put his arm around her shoulder like Sean would have done, but on him, the move felt unnatural. He had no confidence to lend. His arm gave no support or comfort. He was just another burden to carry.

"I guess babies count as an emergency," he said.

"We have two months."

"That's something, at least. How much does he owe?"

She shook her head, not looking at him.

"Can we pay it?"

He wanted to bite back the question. The funeral was expensive, the move was worse, and she'd been unemployed for too long.

For hours that night, Robert lay in bed, staring at the ceiling, the football from Sean's state championship clutched in his hands. The ball had been the last thing Sean gave him before leaving for college, and in the two years since, Robert hadn't wanted to change even the air it held. In the video from that game, Sean gleamed in the stadium lights. The team had been pushed back practically to their own two-yard line. Beneath his helmet, Sean scanned the field for an open receiver, the other team's defensive line surging. He didn't show even the faintest sign of hurry as he cocked his arm.

Though the video did not pick up the sound, Robert always imagined he could hear Sean's fingers as they flicked off the laces, spinning that perfect spiral. The video footage slowed at this moment, Sean's arm falling in slow motion as the ball rocketed into darkness and fell again into the sodium lights and then into Seth Sorensen's hands as he crossed into the end zone. CHAMPION flashed in the school's purple and blue over a freeze frame of Sean's distant, smiling face.

In the deep of the night, the ball's leather was cool against Robert's hands, as if it held all those autumn afternoons when Sean tried to teach Robert to throw. His brother would line up Robert's fingers over the laces, showing him how to slide his skin across the leather's grain as he released. Somehow, all

Robert's throws came out wrong. He studied every move Sean made, absorbed every word, replayed the advice in his mind every night as faithfully as prayer, but when Robert threw, the ball was nothing more than a wobbling duck. Sean would laugh and ruffle his hair. "You'll get it."

He looked out the window, casting his mind down the street and into parts unknown, not sure where even to start—assuming Sean was still in the city at all.

Robert walked out of the apartment the next morning to find himself face-to-face with the biker. Or, rather, face-to-chest, his nose grazing the t-shirt that stretched over the man's bulging pecs. "Scuse you," the man grunted.

Robert froze, mumbling an apology with a tongue that wouldn't work. The biker would have fit in well with the unemployed loggers that filled the bars back home. He had arms like they did, biceps that put the high school linemen's to shame. Robert hadn't seen the biker's girlfriend since the night he'd yelled through the walls. Maybe he killed her. He had a killing kind of voice.

"You guys have company?" the biker asked. "I been hearing babies."

"Y-yes."

"No shutting em up, huh?" the biker snorted, then turned away, bouncing down the steps with more spring than Robert would have given him credit for. He waited until the man was out the door before following him down the aging stairway to find Jerome outside.

Garvey High loomed like a fortress over Frankfort Avenue. It towered behind the thick-trunked Willow Oak and Beech. Its bricks were dark and somber, as if they were mourning the death of summer. Half the neighborhood kids loitered on the sidewalks out front, drifting under the leafy green canopy, shouting insults at each other and laughing because somehow calling someone a bitch or a fuckhead showed you were friends if you knew how to shout it right. That, at least, was just like Herman.

Robert and Jerome followed the taped papers marked "REG" which lead them towards the cafeteria. In the crowded halls, their shoulders knocked everyone else's shoulders. Robert was not the only white kid, but he was definitely the whitest white kid, pale enough for freckles. Even after a summer off, the smell of food hung in the air around the plastic chairs and tables, a stomach-turning blend of Salisbury steak, canned green beans, pizza, and peaches.

They split to get in the lines for their last names, Jerome heading to AAA-CAZ for Anderson and Robert to FAA-HEZ for Flannigan. Robert's line was shorter. In under twenty minutes, he had a locker assignment, a schedule, and a five-dollar combination lock. After, he waited on a bench, staring at the walls. Sea turtles swam in the murals along with fish, both vertebrate and jelly. The shadow of a shark loomed, murky, in a corner. He imagined scuba divers swimming for the surface, their air running low. Everything was cold and blue under the fluorescent light.

Two girls walked by, heads tilted towards one another in conversation. Their jeans rode low on their hips under midriff t-shirts and Robert sat up a little taller, ready to say, "Hey." Maybe even "What's up?"—or was that trying to hard? These were city girls. He smiled and nodded his head at them, trying to muster all his inner cool, remembering too late that smiling was the least cool move of all, remembering that he should look stoic and confident and above-it-all. But it didn't matter. They didn't cast even a glance his way. They just walked down the hall into some alternate future that didn't include him.

"Something down there?" Jerome asked. Next to him

stood a big kid in oversized basketball shorts that danced a hula around his calves with every step. The guy couldn't stop talking. His words had a lilt to them, the speed and rhythm of Spanish even though he wasn't speaking Spanish. You could float on that language, Robert thought. It would be an ocean below you, bobbing you along its waves. He realized that he recognized the story the guy was rattling off, the attack in Strawberry Mansion.

Jerome shrugged the gossip away like a fly from his shoulder. The kid's eyes flicked towards Robert. Robert wondered if he would be an added news item, the *new white kid*, or if he wasn't worthy even of that little bit of interest.

"Where you from, dawg?" the kid asked.

Robert shrugged. "Around."

"Not around here, that's for sure."

Jerome rolled his eyes and turned, leading Robert away. "Forget Ricky. That guy's always in everyone's business. What classes you got?"

They walked Robert's schedule three times, making sure that he wouldn't look lost or hopelessly new. They didn't have a single class in common. Even their lockers were on different floors. With each trip through the schedule, the halls were a little emptier. "Hold up," Jerome said as they finished the final round. "This is my locker. You got to remember it so you can catch me between classes."

"What are your digits?"

"1167."

"All these numbers—your locker number, my locker number, the combination, the classrooms. I'm never going to remember."

"It's easy. Eleven, six, seven. It rhymes. My locker's a poet."

"And it didn't even know it. Man, that joke's tired."

"Nah—not tired. An oldie but a goodie. Anyway, you'll remember it now." He clapped his hand over the metal label. "What is it?"

"Eleven something seven."

"See? You almost got it. Eleven sixty-seven, which is easy because six is one less than seven."

"I got it, I got it. Eleven sixty-seven. I won't forget."

"Better not, else I'll come whoop your ass."

They laughed and had turned to walk home when Jerome suddenly stiffened. Dropping his voice, he said, "Let's go the other way."

Robert followed Jerome's stare to a group of guys rounding the corner. "Who are they?"

"Maurice."

They walked with the swagger of popular kids, moving in an orbit around a tall, light-skinned guy. His dark hair was cut close to his skull with a part so straight it looked like it was cut in with an axe.

"Well, well, well. Looks like Gay-rome has a new boyfriend this year."

His ultra-neat hair would have made him look studious, but his lip was split where he'd been slugged. The unmistakable shadow of knuckles darkened his chin. His shoulders were broad and straight and his waist so athletically thin that Robert wondered if he had to have his t-shirts custom cut to fit so well. Maurice held his head tilted back, looking down through the galaxies that separated him from lesser men.

The two guys flanking him were taller, and they shared a kind of skinny scrappiness. They were lean and powerful and their baggy jeans hung low on their narrow hips as if to suggest that only total manliness held their pants up at all. They reminded Robert of kids he knew in Oregon, the kind who surprised you with dirty aggression, who believed fair fights were a sign of stupidity or weakness.

Jerome wavered like his legs had been sawed in half. Any wind and he would topple.

Maurice shifted his gaze to Robert, his chin tilting higher to punctuate his words. "This kid try to touch you yet? Cause it's only a matter of time. Caught him in the janitor's closet last year rubbing his dick all over some kid. How old was he? Eleven? Twelve?"

"That never happened."

"Saw it my own self." Maurice's cut lip pulled open, and he licked the new blood away as if nothing could hurt him, as if the taste of his own blood were some magical delight that only made him more powerful. "You wear those tight little jeans to please your dark-ass boyfriend? Got yourself some jungle fever? You know, if you're chasing big dicks, you picked the wrong guy."

"Leave him alone," Jerome said. "He ain't done nothing to you."

"Heard your mama's sleeping with the garbage man now. Sucked his dick and, next hour, the man's dick turned green. Some kind of toxic shit she picked up somewhere. Heard she came home smelling like those rotten-ass dumpster fish and your sister got all fuck-crazy and ran right out to find that garbage man and banged him too. Smell reminded her of her own twat, I guess. Couldn't resist. Must've been, what? Two, two and a half hours since she last got laid? That's some kind of record for her."

Jerome's face gave everything away: the hurt, the anger, the inability to do a damned thing about it.

Maurice leaned in so close that Robert could smell the salt of his skin tinged with the iron of blood. "Guess sucking dicks runs in the family. Can't help yourself. Just got to suck any cock you can find. White cock, though? That's a new low. His thing be thin and stumpy as a used up pencil."

The hiss of Maurice's voice was as intimate as anything Robert had ever known, and he rooted his feet to the floor to keep from running. His penis felt hot and small and shameful in his pants. He hadn't even started school yet, and already they had smelled him out as a loser. If there was an opportunity to reinvent himself, he'd missed it. No matter where he went, Robert couldn't escape himself.

Blood smeared Maurice's white teeth. He smiled and bulldozed his way through. Every muscle in Robert's body was taut and humming. Cooled by the air conditioning, the gloss of sweat clinging to his neck and face made him clammy. They stood together, frozen by shame, listening as Maurice's footsteps faded.

Outside, Jerome pulled himself up onto the wall in front of the building. Seeing him sitting there, head hanging, in the full glare of the sun, Robert realized what he should have known all along. Jerome was a nerd. A sci-fi-watching, comic-book-reading, girl-deprived, run-of-the-mill nerd.

Robert hadn't known that a black kid could be a nerd. That seemed silly now, but it was true. He'd thought Jerome and every other black kid for that matter had some kind of innate cool. He'd thought Jerome, with his street talk and oversized shorts and knowledge of hip-hop, would help him navigate this new school. Now, Robert knew this wasn't true, and to his surprise, what he mostly felt was relief.

Jerome swatted a tear from his nose. "I hate those guys."

Robert hopped up onto the sun-warmed brick. Jerome's hand lay next to his; their thighs were inches from touching. Maybe the whole thing had been a come on. Maybe that's why Jerome came to Robert's apartment in the first place. Maybe he was looking for a boyfriend, or at least some new fling. There wasn't a reason in the world that Robert had to stay friends with him.

Robert said, "That kid with the bruise. He get that from fighting?"

"How am I supposed to know?"

"Cause you do."

"Maurice doesn't get caught. Could be, he got that from fighting. Could be, his brother's home and on the shit again."

Robert watched the cars pass. A rusty Honda, a pink Pontiac, a Caddy with chrome hubcaps on the front wheels and a failing donut on the back. His mother sold their car, the faded blue Buick, to pay for the U-Haul truck. Too bad. It would have fit in here. Robert remembered long drives, falling asleep in the back, its bench seat wide and soft as a sofa. If they'd stayed in Oregon, he would have learned to drive this year rather than relying on the train or the trolley or the city bus. A car went anywhere there was road. A car was solitude and space and freedom. A car was the opposite of a city.

A bus roared past followed by a hatchback that looked like it was more Bondo than car. Everything was passing him by these days, and what had he done about it? Nothing. Hid in his room, plucked a banjo, buried his head. Life came at him anyway, bearing down like a logging truck on a narrow, gravel road.

He thought of his father, coming home from work, tired in the way only work made him tired. His dad would lean into the fridge as if he had the entire state of Oregon pressing on his back until he cracked open his nightly Coors. "Some days, you're the windshield," he'd say. "And sometimes, you're the bug." He never said this on windshield days.

There had to be more to life than accepting things as they were. There had to be more than just standing on a pile of crap, waiting for the next pile to land on your head.

"I gotta go," Robert said, his own words surprising him.

Jerome looked at him with eyes that ached. His braids were immaculate and his jeans spotless and the collar of his shirt must have been ironed to stay so flat. "You think they're telling the truth," he said. "You think I'm gay."

Robert was the bug. He might be about to launch himself into a windshield.

He said, "Can you meet me at my house in two hours?"

"Where you going?"

"Just be there." He broke into a run, pausing only to turn back a few steps in and shout, "I'll see you in two hours."

"Watch your back," Jerome called back. "You don't know Philly."

THE EMPTY APARTMENT

The air in the building suffocated him. Judging from the reek of sweat and mildew, the air conditioner had been broken for a while. How had this escaped him the last time he was here? A sharp scent of urine rose under the mildew. Stink must grow with the heat. These were afternoon smells.

On the elevator buttons, a dark, sticky layer of grime obscured the up arrow. A dark-skinned lady entered and stood next to him, prim in her flowered housecoat and wire-framed glasses, a canvas bag of groceries and white handbag dangling from her forearm. Robert wondered about the manners of the place. Perhaps he should say something, nod hello. He just stood there, staring at the lettuce poking out of the bag like some kind of freak.

A white man entered behind her, shirtless and continuously whispering something Robert couldn't hear. His hair was long and bedraggled, his chest dirty. Robert looked everywhere but his direction. Lock eyes with a guy like that and he could pull you into his world. The man's arm flung out and hit Robert's sleeve at the start of each fresh rant. He hissed, the volume dropping and rising like a man in an argument with himself. The lady only stared forward, waiting for the doors to open.

Aside from the hissing man, the only sound was the

squeaking and rattling of the elevator as it descended. Robert tried again to make out the man's words, but they all blurred together in a hot fuzz broken only by the occasional curse word. Those, for some reason, were loud and clear.

Robert could run now, before the elevator arrived. He could save himself from being trapped in a box with a maniac. No one would care. No one would even notice. Running was the smart thing, really. He'd come back later, this time letting Jerome know where he went so his mother would at least have a place to look for the body.

Robert's fist clenched as he felt the sting of the madman's fingers once more against his arm. He wouldn't even be here if it weren't for Sean.

"Whatever," his brother would have said. "You came here on your own. I had nothing to do with it."

The doors screeched open, the gate clattering behind. Robert watched the lady, waiting to see if she would step inside. You didn't get to be her age without being smart. She adjusted her bags and pulled the metal gate the rest of the way open. Robert followed her and the man into the flickering lights and stale air of the murder box.

Bridget's green man would hiss just like this guy. His hair would be as ragged and greasy and insane. He would smell as gamey. Robert pressed the button for the seventeenth floor and silently prayed that the elevator had the stamina to make it. As the lady reached to pull the gate closed, a fourth person squeezed in, a thin girl with a nose ring and purple hair. She nodded to the woman. "Sup, Matilda?"

The older lady nodded back as the floors dropped below them.

The girl turned to Robert. "Haven't seen you here before."

"I'm, um," Robert faltered. He stared at the silver charm that hung on a chain around her neck, trying to make out what exactly it was, before realizing she would think he was trying to look down the wide scooped neck of her torn t-shirt. "I'm looking for my brother."

"OK, I'm Um.'" She grinned, and Robert blushed. She was a little younger than Angela with a thin waist but a chest large enough to stretch her thin shirt tight, the lace of her bra patterning its surface. He was staring again. He jumped his eyes up to find a nose sprinkled with freckles, her brown eyes laughing at him through purple bangs and thick black makeup. "Who's your brother?"

"Sean. Sean Flannigan."

Her smile dropped. "Sean, huh?" She looked him over, sizing him up, counting all the ways he fell short. In the corner, the black lady shifted her groceries. The girl stepped closer, her breast brushing his chest as she breathed. Robert stopped breathing altogether. His eyes dipped to her cleavage again before he caught himself. His head spun, and he inhaled sharply, the cinnamon scent of her gum burning in his nose. The ranting man had stopped ranting. He and the black woman were watching them. The purple-haired girl narrowed her eyes, stopping time. Robert felt pinned to the elevator wall. The elevator lurched and settled. She tilted her head, then turned towards the doors. "Haven't seen him."

She pulled the gate and stepped out. "Catch you later, I'm Um,'" she said, not bothering to look back.

The man was hissing again, burbling into a crescendo. His arm flung out and hit Robert's shoulder, and Robert faked like it was cool, like he hadn't flinched at all, like he couldn't already feel the bruise building itself under his skin, like he got hit by crazy people in moving murder boxes all the time. No bigs.

As the elevator lurched upwards again, he stared at the graffiti on the walls. A lot of it was unreadable. The letters curved in scimitars and ended in arrow points. What he could make out was mostly profanity, some of it misspelled and some not really all that profane or imaginative. "Eat me" or "suck it." Sometimes, an adverb added color, "suk me hard." With an elevator this slow, you'd think they would have time to come up with something cleverer. And how did they do it, these ghost people, these phantom writers? Did they always carry black markers? Did they wait until the elevator was empty? If he were to pull out a marker now, write, "fuck you, Sean" on the panel near the door, would the lady or the shirtless man say a word?

His eyes travelled the walls, reading note after note, until he saw it there in the corner, the tight, cramped writing he'd known since childhood. "The pilot is dead and we're all going down," Sean had written. He had stood just over there, stooping, scrawling the words at waist level. Robert could almost see him, bending to hide the pen. Sean always cocked his elbow awkwardly when he wrote, so different than when he threw a football.

The ding of the elevator as it reached the seventeenth floor startled him. He blushed—he needed to stop being so nervous—but the grocery lady pretended not to notice and he was grateful. She got off in front of him, pressing the button for the nineteenth floor before sliding the gate closed for the ranting, shirtless man. She waddled down the hall, unlocked a door four apartments down, and left Robert to confront Sean's door alone.

Robert wondered if it made the rent cheaper, having an apartment directly across from that decrepit, clanking elevator. Probably not. Sometimes, you're the bug. He knocked on the door, knowing no one would answer. He tried the knob, but of course it was locked. He pulled his new school ID from his back pocket and tried to work it into the space between the door and the frame the way they did sometimes in movies, and then tried putting a corner in the lock and wiggling it around, but nothing worked. He tried the key to his own apartment. It wouldn't fit in the hole. He knocked on the door again, harder this time, frustrated at knowing that no one was inside, no one was coming, no one was ever going to come. His mother had a key, but that didn't help him now. He'd been stupid to come here, stupid not to devise a better plan. It didn't matter that he'd come all this way alone on a bus. It didn't matter that he'd braved the shirtless, hissing man or the salad woman or the purple-haired girl who laughed. It didn't matter that he'd done all this because he loved and needed his brother. It didn't matter because the door was locked and no one was home, and there wasn't a thing he could do about it, and he should have known better than to try.

He sunk down and stared at the door. If you were the bug, you were the bug. There wasn't a damned thing you could do about it. He would go meet up with Jerome, who might or might not be trying to come on to him, and tell his friend where he'd been and that it all came to nothing but a wild goose chase. They wouldn't find Sean, now or ever, because there was nowhere else to look. Jerome would nod, knowing that of course that's how it would be. What else did Robert expect?

Robert rose and rested his weight against the door, giving it a final knock, softer this time. He wondered how close he was to the neighborhood of the sinking houses. He wondered if some ash-filled creek was gurgling away under this building, like the ones on the news, the old backfill slowly pulling away, the foundation starting to cave.

He imagined the morning Sean left, the babies crying as he pulled the door shut; their diapers, already full; their stomachs, already empty. Had Sean tied the corners of the sheet down, or had Angela? Had they left together or separately? Who was the last to go? But he knew the answer to that final question.

Sean. That's why he'd called: to make sure their mother was coming, to know that she would take the babies so that he could walk away.

Robert began to turn back towards the elevator but was stopped by the eyes of the salad lady peering at him from her doorway. "They're not home," she said. "Haven't been home in days."

"I know."

"Then what you come looking here for?"

Robert gazed at her, feeling stupid, trying to find the words that would explain. Finally, he said, "This was the only place I had."

The words were dumb and empty, but she nodded. "Your folks take them babies?"

"My mom did. We're looking after them."

"That's fine," she said. The word *fine* filled like a balloon the way she said it. It held hope.

"I thought if I came here, I might be able to figure out where they went."

The woman considered this, then nodded again. They were separated by yards, but her quiet voice filled his ear without her ever seeming to raise its volume. "Child," she said, her low voice cracking a little as she spoke. "Oh child, child, child. You know, if they wanted those babies, they would have stayed."

Robert swallowed. "We can help them. I don't think my brother ever really knew that. He always thought he was the one who had to help us."

He was telling her too much, he knew. His mother, if she'd been there, would have given him a hard look and shook her head, just once, to silence him. But silence didn't work here, where babies got left tied under sheets. Maybe that's why strangers were always starting conversations. Here, you needed help from skinny black boys and women with skulls topping their canes. You had to talk and trust.

The woman disappeared for a moment and returned carrying her white purse. She locked her door behind her, even though she was only coming out into the hallway. "Can't be too careful round here," she said.

From her handbag, she drew another, larger ring of keys. "So happens," she said, "that I'm the manager." She fitted a key into the lock. "So happens," she said, "that I'll help you look. Only for a few minutes, you understand. I don't believe in going through other people's affairs, but as there's babies involved, I'm going to make an exception this time."

He wanted to offer her something in return, but he had nothing to give but his name. "I'm Robert," he said.

"Matilda." She held out a small, wrinkled hand, and they shook. "Pleased to make your acquaintance, Robert."

If the lobby had smelled bad, it was nothing to the stench of Sean's apartment. Matilda cupped a hand over her face as she hurried to open the window at the far end of the room. The breeze only pushed the heavy funk towards Robert. A bin of dirty diapers erupted with flies as Matilda passed. "I'll take this to the incinerator," she coughed. "Give you a chance to look round. Got to get Scott in here to clean out the rest. Get it ready for new tenants."

Robert nodded, afraid to open his mouth for fear the smell would invade. He worried the smell was working its way into his skin.

A pair of cockroaches scurried along the skirting board of what passed for a kitchen, the thin strip of linoleum running along the far wall, a half fridge, three-burner stove, and pair of particle board cabinets separating it from the rest of the room.

Pieces of a broken dish lay unswept on the floor. Under Robert's feet, the brown carpet was so old and gummed together that it no longer qualified as carpet at all. It was more of a sludge from which a few stray carpet fibers threw themselves up like the arms of the drowning.

He couldn't imagine Sean putting up with this. But then, he wouldn't have. His brother wouldn't have been able to stand the idea of Angela's beautiful feet touching that filth. He would've gotten an area rug on credit. This apartment was cheaper than the two that had come before it, but he could still hear Sean talking about its river view. Through the grime-dusted window, a thin strip of water shimmered distantly in a narrow gap in the buildings. Each glint of sunshine had a price tag. Bile rose in Robert's throat, but he choked it down. He'd found a way in. He wasn't going to throw it away because of gross carpet and a bad smell.

He picked his way through the shards on the floor of that sad kitchen. A plastic cutting board had melted to the back burner. The strip of counter, barely as wide as the thin stove, held a teetering pile of unwashed pots and a stack of unpaid bills: the rent-to-own place, electricity, gas, credit card, water. "Final notice" was stamped in angry red.

As Robert shoved the MasterCard bill in the back pocket of his jeans, something caught his eye, something barely recognizable wedged under the half-sized fridge to steady it on the uneven floor. He pulled at it, knowing what it was but not wanting to believe. A small testament, the kind they hand out free on street corners. Years ago, their father, a lapsed Catholic, had tossed it to Sean one afternoon as a joke, but football was a game of inches. Sean made a game-winning touchdown pass that night, and he had had it tucked under his hip pad when he threw the championship Hail Mary. Now, the edges curled and browned with sweat and drips from rotten vegetables. Sean might as well have shoved their dead father under the fridge. It wobbled as Robert gave one last tug and yanked the testament free. In the center of the living room, the crib stood alone. The thin cotton sheet lay crumpled where his mother had thrown it back. Robert swallowed the ball of whatever it was that was growing in his throat.

The bedroom held almost nothing. Sean and Angela had taken nearly all their clothes. Robert stepped around a pool of red fake-silk bed sheets and pulled open the drawers of the nightstand. The knob came off in his hands, pulling through the chipped particleboard. Empty.

Angela left two sweaters in the closet. Moths fluttered out as Robert touched a sleeve. A pair of shiny yellow pumps, the left one missing its heel, lay tossed in the corner.

Matilda was back when he returned to the living room, her head leaning out the window for fresh air.

"You find what you were looking for?" she asked.

Robert hadn't known what he was looking for, but whatever it was, it wasn't here. "Thanks for letting me in."

"You welcome," she said. After a pause, she added, "Hope you find him."

UNDER THE PLYWOOD

Jerome sat on the concrete steps outside Robert's apartment, his face hanging like a beaten dog's. "Where you been?"

Robert glanced at the open window of his family's apartment. His words would carry. He didn't want his mother to know he'd been looking for Sean. "Let me handle this," she would say, but she couldn't handle it. With work and the babies, she didn't have time to handle it.

"Come on," Jerome said, pulling himself up.

"Where to?"

"Just come on."

The testament held the envelope in place in Robert's pocket. They were only paper, one bill, one little book, but they weighed on him. The envelope nudged his back with each step like a finger poking. *See?* it said. *See? See? See?*

Nothing *to* see. Chances were, the bill wouldn't tell him anything more than the apartment did. It'd be just another dead end. He was no detective.

Jerome walked next to him, not saying a word. He pulled him down an alley, continuing three narrow row houses down. Each was boarded up, but Jerome slid his fingers under the plywood where a door had been. The graying board pulled back. The nails that had held it stood in the doorframe, rusted soldiers. Jerome disappeared under the wood and it slapped back into place. Robert was alone in a city alley. If he hadn't seen

Jerome go in, he would never have known anyone else had been here. Jerome was house-swallowed. Behind the plywood, there could be a roomful of gang bangers. Maybe they had Jerome. Maybe they had taped his mouth so he couldn't scream. Maybe they were psychotic killers who had already slit Jerome's belly open and were washing their hands in his stomach blood, using his friend like some kind of demented basin.

The plywood rattled and Robert fought the instinct to run like hell.

"Come on," Jerome called from the other side. "Don't be a chicken."

Robert sighed and looked at the sky, which might be the last piece of brightness he saw in this world. He tried to imagine his dad's strong arm wrapping around his shoulder. Which was dumb. His dad couldn't protect him even when he was alive; he'd only gotten himself shot.

The splintery edge of the plywood bit into his fingers. The board shoved him forward as he ducked under, like his mother's hand at the funeral, pushing him towards the casket to face the way things were. In the house, the air was musty and velvet black, broken only by the weak beam flickering from Jerome's dollar store flashlight. "I keep this by the door so I can see when I come."

"We shouldn't be here."

Already, Jerome's beam was bobbing away ahead of him. "It's cool. My brother found it first, a few years ago. I come here all the time. No one cares."

"What if some crackhead decides to move in?"

"Man, if you were a crackhead, would you choose this place?"

"Yeah. Why not?"

"You don't know nothing about nothing. You couldn't see the cops roll up—and where would you go if they did? Crackheads want the corner house. Ones with side windows. More ways to see and get out."

Robert wondered if Jerome was making up this reasoning to give them courage. His eyes followed the flashlight beam over the walls. Pineapples, he noted, surprised. The wallpaper was patterned with small, gold pineapples so worn and dirty that he could just make them out over the dark wainscoting. There was something solemn about them, their regularity, the rigid flop of their leaves. "This must have been some place back in the day."

"Come on," Jerome said, shoving the flashlight into Robert's hands. "Help me pull off some of these boards and we'll make a fire. Brighten the place up a bit."

"We don't need to do that."

"Shine the light so I can see."

"It's too hot for a fire anyway."

"No, I almost got it." His voice was desperate, angry, verging on tearful. If he'd come here all the time, like he said he had, he'd never done this before. The wainscoting hadn't been touched. Now, it shrieked, popped, and splintered.

"Stop." Robert pulled Jerome back firmly by the shoulder. The flashlight dropped and rolled in an arc, shining its weak beam in a line that divided them. "We don't need it," he said, softer now. He had no idea why it was so important to him that the board stay untouched or why it was so important for Jerome to pull it down, though he knew somehow Maurice was a part of it. Maurice, and maybe Sean.

Jerome's expression was unreadable in the dark. "This place is condemned. The whole thing would be torn down if anyone gave even half a rat's ass. They don't. It's just like all the Chum—no one cares. Stuff's probably all full of termites anyway. Best thing to do is burn it."

Jerome was right—he always was. If anyone cared, they

would've stripped those parts they cared about, taking door-knobs and cabinets and paneling and tubs to put in some rich man's house. Strange that they hadn't done that here. Robert wanted the house left exactly how it was, forgotten and uncared for. Even rotting, the house had a quiet dignity. The bill nudged his back again, as if reminding him that he had to make a decision. Trust Jerome, or don't.

"I can't believe you're such a mama's boy," Jerome said.

"This place is awesome."

"Yeah?"

"Yeah."

"Can't barely see it. This flashlight don't work for jack."

"How'd you see when you came before?"

"A little fire and we could see it all."

"We're not even supposed to be here, and now you want to send smoke signals to the cops? Hey officer, here we are. Just follow the smoke. We got to be smarter than that."

"How we going to see then?"

"What we need is a lantern."

Jerome bounced the flashlight's beam over the wall, connecting the pineapples.

"What do you think is through that door?"

"Kitchen, maybe," Jerome said.

"Let's go see."

"No way."

"Why not?"

"Why you want to go in some dark old kitchen?"

"You scared or something? I thought you said you came here all the time. You're telling me that you've never checked out anything but this one room?"

Robert sunk onto the bottom step of the creaking wooden staircase. Jerome sat next to him, his shoulder knocking

Robert's. Robert didn't want to believe Maurice. He didn't want to think that Jerome had brought him here because it was more private than a broom closet, but he also knew Jerome was lying when he said he'd come here all the time. Their arms brushed, the little hairs tingling against one another.

Rumors. Robert had to be stronger than words. Every crevice of the Chum was a test, even this old house. If he passed, this dark, quiet place would be theirs—his and Jerome's. But you didn't get to claim a place just by skirting under a flimsy bit of old wood. You had to trust. You had to trust when trust was hard.

"I went to Sean's apartment."

"I thought you said he'd cleared out."

"He did."

"And?"

"I didn't find much." Robert drew out the envelope. "Only this."

"You can't open it. It's illegal."

"Since when do you care about legal?"

"We're talking a federal offense."

Robert pulled out his pocketknife and slid the blade under the flap. Illegal was leaving babies in cribs. Illegal was getting a manager to let you in to snoop. Illegal was trespassing in an old row house.

With one quick jerk, the envelope was open. It felt good, cutting something that couldn't feel pain. Robert smoothed the page of figures on the wooden step. Sean hadn't bought much before they'd cut him off. $22.06 at Kmart, $6.57 at Burger King, a handful of smaller charges, a fine for not meeting last month's minimum payment. Even this bill was two weeks past due.

Jerome whistled low and slow. "Fifteen large and then some. Your brother was maxed *out*."

Robert blinked in the face of all those numbers. This

wasn't even Sean's only credit card—just the one he'd still been allowed to use. Robert had no idea what his brother made in a year, but even with two jobs, it couldn't have been enough for all he bought, the oversized TV, Angela's trendy heels, his mother's silk shirts. Sean always wanted to treat everyone to the best. When he went pro, he could pay it all back.

"Whoa. Your brother went to Floatilla last month! Spent sixteen dollars and ninety-five cents!"

"What's Floatilla?"

"You're kidding me, right? I mean, I know you're not serious."

"Of course I'm serious," Robert said, sick of Jerome knowing it all.

"Floatilla..." Jerome's voice grew distant and dreamy. "I can't describe it."

Robert punched him in the arm, and Jerome snapped back to the present. Robert said, "Start trying."

Jerome rubbed his shoulder. "What's gotten into you?"

It's not what's gotten into me, Robert thought. *It's who's left.* But what he said was, "I'm just sick of not knowing anything, and of people reminding me that I don't know anything."

"No one can be told what Floatilla is. You have to see it for yourself."

"What are you saying?"

"Let's go."

"Now?"

"Saturday."

"Whatever."

"It's the only way."

Jerome's long fingers were inches from his own, the heat of one hand mingling with the heat of the other.

Robert looked away. "I've got to help my mom."

The air changed. Heavy. Jerome looked at the bill again,

pretending nothing was any different. "You see anything that helps you?"

Robert focused on the numbers. He'd been hoping for something solid, a hotel room maybe, an address.

"You said your brother had a job, right? You try his work?"

"Two jobs. Neither boss has heard a thing."

"How do you know?"

"That's what my mom said."

"Shit, man. If we're detectives, we got to do the asking. We can't rely on second hand knowledge. We should call ourselves. What's the place called, the main one where he worked?"

"Goss Vending." His mother was going to kill him. He could hear her now. *I'm not spending good money on Miss Martha so that you and your friend can traipse around the city.*

"Goss Vending," Jerome said. "That's our next step then."

"Our?"

"Of course 'our.'"

Robert could say no. He could walk out. Weeks from now, Jerome would just be that one kid he knew for a few minutes before school started and he made his other friends. Or, if there were no other friends, Robert would be that weird kid on the edge of things. There, but not in any kind of way that mattered. Not important enough to be a target. All he had to do was walk away.

Darkness folded in. Neither moved. They huddled together in the weak pool of light staring at a paper that had no more to tell.

"My mom's working the phones. We'd have to go there."

LIFE SCIENCE

The first day of school started with a warm mist. Robert stood by Jerome's stoop, trying to talk down his nerves. School was school, no big deal. He couldn't walk in all cowering. If he did? Blammo. Guys would smell his fear. Maurice would flatten him. Could you make a banner from a flattened kid? Robert saw himself, fabric-thin, snapping in the wind, his hands tied in bows around the end of a pike.

His mom surprised him that morning with a blue-striped polo shirt. She'd found it on a sidewalk sale rack on her way from the office and thought "it would look nice." Robert was fairly certain that, in the Chum, *nice* was that last way a fifteen-year-old boy wanted to look. Nice people were targets. He needed to look tough, hip, streetwise, something—anything but nice. But he wore the new shirt until just before breakfast when Sammy spit up all over Robert's shoulder. His mother had the phone in one hand (the collector) and was wrestling with a thrift-store stroller with the other. Her face fell as Sammy unleashed, but Robert was never so happy to be puked on. His faded red t-shirt was wash-softened and he liked its fit, the seams of its shoulders lining up precisely with his own, like something Kurt Cobain or Chris Cornell would wear.

The sliding step of the mailman brought Robert back to the present. "What's the word?" the mailman asked.

"Nothing."

"Nothing?" The mailman laughed without slowing his stride. "No word at all?"

"I'll let you know if I think of one."

"Strength, my brother. That is your word today."

"Strength," Robert said, but the mailman's attention was now on the lady sweeping her stoop two houses up.

Jerome bounced down the concrete steps. "You talking to yourself?"

"The mailman."

"LeRoi." Jerome followed Robert's gaze to where the mailman stood flirting. "Best point guard to play for Garvey in twenty-five years—least, that's what my mom says. My sister had a huge crush on him."

"He didn't like her back?"

"He likes *everybody* back."

Three girls now crowded the stoop in front of them, laughing and smiling like they were in heat.

"Dude is a serious player."

"You say that like it's a bad thing."

"Bad? Does it look bad to you? Shit, man. I want him to give me some pointers. What other mailman you know got game like that?"

Maurice didn't know a thing about Jerome. As they walked, Robert cast his mind ahead of him, thinking about the girls they would meet, wondering whether they would talk to him. Jerome's shirt was almost identical to the one Robert's mother had plucked off the sidewalk. She had gotten it right. Everyone would be wearing new shirts. He should have been more careful, laid a towel over his shoulder, not let Sammy drink so fast. He didn't have the game God gave a five-year-old in his first tee ball season.

Garvey loomed before them, all brick and concrete. Robert hoisted his backpack further up his shoulder. *Strength,* LaRoi had told him, but he didn't know where to find it. A breeze lifted. The chain to hoist the flag tapped against its pole, ticking like a clock or a bomb. Maurice was there, standing by its base, his back to them. Robert's lungs emptied and filled. He'd always been fast—he could thank his mother for that. He could run if he had to.

His breath faltered. They were walking closer. Neither spoke, which meant Jerome had seen Maurice as well, but he wasn't stopping or running or changing in any way except in his silence, as if, by being quiet enough, maybe they could make themselves invisible.

Maurice wore new basketball shoes: Fila, the ones Grant Hill would wear this season. Who hadn't drooled over the ads? Maurice had flattened each lace into a series of perfect Xs. Surely, he could feel them now behind him. Their fear was something physical. It reached out a sparking, electric hand, and tapped Maurice's shoulder. He glanced back, locked eyes with them, but turned to keep talking to his audience.

A whole group of beautiful girls. Hair curling and lips kissable and jeans tight on their thighs. Girls whose beauty made Robert fold in on himself with yearning. Bubble-gum-smacking, pager-checking, luscious, smiling, hip-tilted girls. Dark girls and light girls, tall girls and short girls, girls with big boobs and girls with small. Hard-muscled girls and soft-dimpled girls. Girls who, if Maurice said so, would think Robert was gay.

Maurice didn't even bother to smirk their way. He threw his arm around a slender girl in a small, strappy top. She had café au lait skin and a mouth as red as Robert had ever seen. Maurice whispered something to her and her laughter was like hiccups and Robert was suddenly so electrically alive that he couldn't hold a single thought. His mind buzzed and reverberated. Maurice's hand slid down the girl's back and into the pocket of her jeans, his fingers massaging the round curve of her ass, letting them envy what they could not have.

The decision of where to sit was never to be taken lightly. From the biology lab doorway, Robert stared at the tables, already gagging on the stench of formaldehyde. The front row was for nerds, which he was, but he didn't need to advertise it. The back row, on the other hand, would sniff him out at once. Already, juniors and seniors, those who had put off science or flunked it, lounged across those tables, owning the room.

Ms. Scarborough, thin and wrinkled in her pale blue sweater, fluttered like a moth around a cage of small, white mice. When Robert was first tracked into accelerated science, Sean warned him that the senior AP class dissected live frogs and aborted fetal pigs. "They use the baby pigs," he'd said, "because they're so much like people, all skin and bone and fat. Kind of messed up, don't you think?" Robert wondered vaguely if the mice would live through the semester, and whether he himself would for that matter.

A dusty stuffed owl perched on a fake branch over the mouse cage, an irony seemingly lost on Ms. Scarborough. The mice, too, were oblivious, running over her hand, sniffing out food pellets. The owl had lost its left eye and stared from a hole filled with tufted white cotton like some kind of zombie owl fit for *Slayers*, ready to ruffle its feathers and swoop from its branch. Robert wondered what it would take for a zombie owl to turn a person into the undead. A scratch of the talons? A bite?

Some guy in a varsity jacket knocked Robert as he slid into the middle row. He didn't bother to apologize. Robert was just another foreign specimen, no more interesting than the jars lining the walls. They could split him open in a tray, pin his skin back against the cork, pull everything out, and know nothing more about how he worked.

Ms. Scarborough was still fiddling with the mice, stroking them and speaking softly. Her hair was curled and sprayed in place but so thin that he could see the outline of her skull. By the whiteboard, a sun-faded kitten stretched for a tree branch with its claws. "Hang in there" floated above it in bubbly purple letters.

She turned to the class, not daring to look anyone in the eye. "I want to welcome you to the wonderful and fascinating world of life science." Her voice quavered, too timid to carry weight, as she spoke the words she'd memorized over years until any sense of wonderment or fascination had long ago faded. Something warm and wet slapped against Robert's neck, a feeling so familiar he didn't have to look to know what it was. A spit wad. The back row broke into quiet laughter, but Robert didn't look back. The wet mush slid to rest in his collar, cooling against his neck. He knew that to flick it away would only invite more laughter. No matter what he did, there would be another spit wad. He couldn't win this game.

Ms. Scarborough rattled on about the Miracle of Life Science. If this class was a food chain, she occupied its lowest rung. Robert might have been happy that someone was actually lower than him, if only she were not the one person who might have protected him. She walked them through the class rules by rote, ignoring the students breaking them around her. She explained that they would not be checking out their textbooks because in years past too many had been damaged. Instead, she wrote an assignment on the board, page numbers to read and questions to answer before the bell. She turned again to her mice.

Robert had pictured high school science as a series of

experiments, bubbling with beakers and Bunsen burners. He had seen himself in goggles pouring the colorful contents of one test tube into another, little pops and fizzes and puffs of steam as the elements reacted. Instead, he hunched over stained and crumpled pages reading other people's hypotheses and theories.

The guys in the back row, however, believed in practical experiments. They grabbed aluminum dissection trays and a jar of dead fish, sliding it down the long black counter, timing to see who propelled it the fastest. Some guy in a varsity jacket leaned his arm against the wall over Ms. Scarborough, his head bending towards hers. She wouldn't meet his eye, as if she felt something sexual in the way he looked at her, so terribly bold and direct. Robert imagined him running his free hand down her cheek, allowing his fingers to brush through the curls of her hair, though he stopped short of that. Something was being negotiated, perhaps a grade or the number of days he would be allowed to skip. His posture was as gentle as the hero on a romance novel, but she flinched away. She shook like she might turn to powder for the janitor to sweep away in his metal dustpan.

Robert struggled to focus on the words swimming on the page under his eyes. His ears filled with the scraping of metal on laminate as he waited for the jar to shatter.

The only good thing he could say about the day was that he had gotten through it. He stood by Jerome's locker after the last bell, his jaw and teeth aching from being clenched. Apart from lunch, he hadn't spoken to a single person all day.

Jerome broke through the throng of students shuffling towards the exit like sunshine coming through clouds. He beamed, waving a slip of paper over his head. "I got her number, man. I got it."

"Whose?"

"Keesha Bates. Have you seen the butt on that girl? Damn."

"Butt?"

"Tell me you're not serious."

"What?"

"A girl's butt is the first thing you check out."

"Legs, maybe. Boobs for sure."

"And butt. That's the most important part."

Maybe he did sound a little gay.

"You can't *not* look—especially when it's Keesha Bates."

Or straight.

"She's the finest woman in the class. And I have her number."

"You going to call her?"

Jerome turned the combination of his lock idly, as if he had no idea what number to settle on and wasn't in any rush to find out. "Course I'm going to call her."

"Tonight?"

"I don't know about tonight. Why's it got to be tonight?"

"How'd you get her number?"

"She just handed it to me."

"You didn't say anything?"

"Guess she just couldn't resist the power of the J-Dawg. This is my year."

"Let me see." Robert took the note with the round loopy numbers. He squinted at her writing, disbelieving the words. "'I'm going to lick your candy cane slowly and suck all the sugar from it.'"

"I am so in."

"Jerome, did you look at the back of this?"

"Why would I look at the back? Her number is on the front."

Robert held the note for him to read: TO JAVIER. PRIVATE.

"Since when do you go by Javier?"

Jerome grabbed the note, staring at it as if his eyes could bend the letters, make Javier into Jerome. Something flexed in the small muscles around his eyes, the pain of knowing that this was the way things were and would always be. Robert knew those muscles. If there were a gym just for them, they would be champion lifters.

"Were you supposed to pass this?"

"She slid her fingernails up the side of my arm. How am I supposed to be able to read with her fingernails on my arm?"

It was a fair point. Robert dug in his backpack for the address of Goss Vending. "Any idea where this is?"

"South Philly. We'll take the Broad Street Line."

GOSS VENDING

Robert had never ridden a subway. He'd only ridden buses, and on buses, the drivers glared. They glared as he boarded and glared down the road and glared in the mirror when people laughed. Robert decided that they were like the mastheads on ships or gargoyles on buildings. By grimacing, they kept bad luck at bay, keeping the bus safe and strong. The Broad Street Line of Philadelphia's subway was different. Robert barely glimpsed the driver in her yellow cardigan as she slid the train to a stop, but one thing he knew for sure: gargoyles didn't wear cardigans.

"I can't believe you don't check out the butt. That's some kind of serious oversight." Jerome plopped his backpack down and slid into an orange plastic seat. "What are you going to tell your mom when we get there?"

"I have no idea."

"Better come up with something."

Darkness rumbled outside the window. Garbled sounds hiccupped from the speakers, but it was impossible to put those fragments of sound into anything meaningful. They slowed for the next station.

"Too bad you don't have some chocolate. You could say it was an early Mother's Day. You're just coming to appreciate her."

"Then she would *know* something was up."

"She would?"

"Wouldn't your mom?"

"Maybe, but she'd be too busy eating chocolate to care."

Did his mother even like chocolate? Now that Robert thought about it, he couldn't remember ever seeing her eat it. Surely, this should have come up. He searched his memory for anything, an M&M, a Hershey's Kiss. He shuffled through birthdays and Christmases and all the times he'd drawn her a picture to tape to the wall or pooled his money with Sean for a bottle of perfume to sit on her bureau with all the other unused bottles. Maybe she hated chocolate. Maybe that's why they'd never gotten it. Maybe she was allergic, or afraid it would make her fat and slow, or perhaps she worried over unfair labor practices in Latin American chocolate-growing economies or was anxious to avoid high-fructose corn syrup and artificial preservatives. Had his father and brother avoided buying her chocolates at her request, or had they just never thought of it? Robert had lived with the woman all his life, yet when it came to chocolate, she was a mystery.

Jerome sighed. "You don't have chocolate, and you can't say you need help with Sammy and Deacon cause that would make her worry, and you can't use Sean as any kind of excuse cause no one knows where that mofo is or we wouldn't even be here. You can't ask her for help on homework cause that would look bad, and you can't use me as an excuse or she might say we shouldn't hang out. Man, you got a ton of things you can't say."

"And nothing I can." The subway smelled of cheese, cinnamon, and cleanser. He was starting to think this trip had been a terrible idea.

"Maybe we can just sneak around her."

"I don't know."

"But she's the receptionist?"

"Yeah."

"Probably can't skirt her then." Jerome bounced a pencil

against the seat in front of them, tapping out a drum rhythm as he thought. He stopped suddenly. A smile spread over his face. "You've never been there before. Not ever."

"Are we stuck in some kind of time loop? Didn't I just say that?"

"We been thinking way too hard. Check it: you've just come to see where she works."

"Would she buy that?"

"Why not? You're in a new place. You want to know where she is when she's not at home."

"I guess."

"Don't guess. You got to *know*. You have to believe it or else she won't. And it makes sense anyway. You're responsible for the babies and your sister. You need to know where she is."

Jerome grinned, pleased with himself. It did make sense. So much sense, in fact, that Robert wondered why he hadn't already visited. "So why are you with me?"

"Why not? I'm here because we're brothers, brother." He punched Robert's shoulder, and Robert filled with love for him.

"Yeah," Robert said. "Yeah."

The confidence he felt during the rest of the ride vanished the moment his mother turned her eyes on him. Her cheeks went so suddenly pale. Fear. That was fear in her face. In her mind, he might as well have carried her walking papers. Professionals didn't bring their home life to the office—not if they wanted to keep their jobs. He could see every weight she had stacked on her small shoulders. One small paycheck and four kids to support. Her last job search, so long, so failed. Only Sean had saved them, and now he had skipped out. Her boss owed them nothing. Less than nothing. For all they knew, he might be looking for a way to cut ties and be rid of the Flannigans once and for all.

Robert's mother stood, coming, he knew, to usher him right back out the door, but before she could clear her desk, a red-faced man stepped from the thin door behind her. He stopped, looking up from the stack of papers he carried, a kind of happy confusion blooming over his face as he looked at the boys. Robert felt caught. His mother's jaw was tight as she bit out the words, "Mr. Murphy. This is my son Robert and his friend Jerome, and they know full well that they are not supposed to be here."

"Ahh, Bobby!" the man said, all enthusiasm and smiles, as if this were the hundredth time they'd met rather than the first. Mr. Murphy was inches shorter than Robert with graying blonde hair gel-combed back from his flushed face and a lilting Irish accent that made every word float. "Sean's little brother and the mirror image. He told us all about you, how proud he was, how you stepped right up to help when your father passed, God rest him. Tell me, Bobby, my lad, do you throw the pigskin like your brother? Going to be a football star?"

"I don't throw so well."

"Never you mind, son. Never you mind. It'll come."

The reception area was less fancy than the one Robert constructed in his mind. The room was little more than a few quick walls, their beige paint scarred, thrown together in the front of a warehouse. A plastic spider plant, dyed a color of green not seen in nature, threw dusty tendrils over the chipped edge of his mother's shabby desk, and behind her, two filing cabinets leaned against one another for support.

Mr. Murphy prattled on. "I hear there's no word, but not to worry. Sean'll come round. Just sowing some oats is all. Tell me now, you boys coming to work for me after you finish high school? I always need good drivers for the vans. Once you're licensed, that is."

"These boys are going to college," Robert's mother said in

a voice that brooked no argument, as if college were only a matter of will and not a matter of money.

But Mr. Murphy only said, "Your ma's right," as if she had expressed exactly his own thoughts.

"Are you busy right now?" Jerome said. "We'd love a tour."

Robert's mother closed her eyes. "I'm sorry, Mr. Murphy. These boys have homework that they should be getting home to. They won't take up any more of your valuable time."

"Nonsense, Beth. You worry too much. There's nothing on my schedule that can't be delayed for five minutes or so. This'll give me a chance to stretch my legs."

The phone on her desk rang, and though her eyes never left the boys, she answered it before it had a chance to ring again. "Goss Vending," she said, her voice low and briskly efficient. She didn't chirp. She wasn't falsely friendly or stupid. She merely picked up a pencil and took note of the conversation.

"A machine'll be giving someone troubles," Mr. Murphy whispered, already in tour guide mode. "Your ma will dispatch one of our boys and we'll have it right as rain. I tell you, she's a gem. Slid right into that chair on day one as if she were born for it."

He turned them through the doorway and into the warehouse. "We may work with machines, but at the end of the day, we're still a people business. Sure we rent machines and we fill them up, and I can see why people think the machine does all the work, but when their Snickers gets jammed or it's run out of crisps, we need a man straight away, not just to fix things up but to put them at ease. Someone courteous and respectful who will put things to rights."

"Is that what Sean did? Fix machines?"

"A fine lad, your brother. A wonder with machines, and better with people. Sure, restocking is the bulk of the work, but even then, it pays to have a friendly smile. Sean was a great one for smiling."

"Yes," Robert said.

"Your ma tells me that you haven't heard a thing." Mr. Murphy pronounced the word "ting"—a blip on the radar. A location. Robert felt the sweep of a long green line of light crossing over them all, lighting each in turn. And distantly, Sean's little blip would be lit as well. Somewhere. Robert wished Mr. Murphy would say it again (ting, ting, ting) until it lit him all the way to his brother, but the man's tongue ran headlong in its own direction. "Strange that. Unlike him. Never missed a day. Never a moment late."

They rounded a corner and Jerome let out a long, low whistle. "Are those really all Fritos?"

"Crisp packets on the left. Chocolate bars on the right. We used to do more business in gum, but that's been dying off a bit. People are looking for healthier offerings. Granola bars, if you can believe it. Even cola is dropping off a bit, but we're starting to do a great business in water. Water! When it's free from the tap. Not that I'm complaining, mind."

Robert could see why Sean had loved this man. He had a warmth you could bask in.

"Smallboy," Mr. Murphy called, leading them towards a van. It bounced on its hinges as the driver laid another flat of Powerade in the back. "I want you to meet Beth's son Robert and his friend Jerome."

From behind the white van emerged a man who looked exactly like Rocky. Not the Rocky from the later movies, cut and polished as a human diamond, but the early Rocky. The one who drank raw eggs and punched frozen meat and ran the museum steps in nasty old sweatpants. Robert sometimes imagined himself a houseplant raised in the light of Sylvester Stallone. Friday and Saturday nights, his father would kick back with some favorite film in the VHS, cracking a beer.

Movie stars were supposed to be smaller in real life. Not this guy. Smallboy was more Italian Stallion than the Italian Stallion himself. He towered over them like he'd walked straight off of the movie screen. "Any word from your brother?"

Brudder. Even the voice was the same. Robert shook his head.

Their father loved every Rocky, but neither Sean nor Robert cared for the man who KO'd Apollo Creed or Mr. T or Drago. They loved the one who went the distance, who stood fifteen rounds only to lose by decision. The one who knew how to endure without a hope of victory, who trained even after he was kicked out of his lock, who bought food from the nerdy pet shop girl for his turtles Cuff and Link. That man was real to him, though Robert never expected they would meet. Sylvester Stallone might have morphed into something half cyborg, half plastic, but here in South Philly, the real Rocky was alive.

Robert's mind flooded with questions: Why was he so desperate for Adrian once the fight was over? Would he have fought as hard without her? What did it feel like to have your eye lanced? Was it hard to hit a man you didn't hate? To hit your idol?

Mr. Murphy had stopped talking, a sure sign that their time was up. Jerome said, "Sean didn't say anything to y'all about where he might go, did he?"

The question lacked all subtlety, but Mr. Murphy was too busy checking the contents of the van against the printed sheet to notice. "Would that he had, boys. Would that he had."

"Said he wanted to go to Jamaica," Smallboy said.

"He didn't mention anywhere closer?"

"Alls I heard was Jamaica. Said they got no worries there, just rum and white sand. Said his wife would get tan as a toasted coconut."

Robert could see Angela in a small, turquoise-colored

bikini, her oiled skin browning in the sun, large sunglasses balanced on her nose as she read some trashy novel, stretching her body flat under a cloudless sky without a care in the world. Sean would have wanted exactly that. The image was the antidote to a cold, gray warehouse stacked with boxes.

"You think he went?" Jerome asked.

"To Jamaica?" Smallboy snorted as he hoisted several flats of water at once. "We was just swapping pipe dreams, but he'd a done anything for Angela if she wanted it."

Mr. Murphy glanced up from the clipboard. "Italian women. Married to one myself. Always straight to the point, she is. Honest as the rain and bright as the sunshine."

"Drive you crazy every time," Smallboy said.

Mr. Murphy bent to the van, turning Smallboy with him to consult the paper. Robert's mother appeared at the door. Business was business, and tour time was over. He wanted to thank Mr. Murphy for his time, but the man seemed to have forgotten they were there. Maybe that's how it was with men in sales. They were friendly for the immediate transaction, but their words didn't mean much. And that was fine. He had come here for clues leading to Sean, but if there was anything to learn, they had missed it.

WHAT WAS OWED

It wasn't until they were back on the northbound train that Jerome said, "Should've brought chocolates. Even if your mom didn't like them, I bet that Murphy guy would."

"For real."

"He sounded just like the guy who sells Lucky Charms."

"What? The leprechaun?"

"You think that's for real or that he's faking?"

"The accent? He's Irish."

"He's been in America for a long time to still be sounding like cereal. Tell you another thing, I bet he's more mad at your brother than he lets on."

"Maybe."

Across the car, a little girl threw a tantrum, banging her mother's head again and again with a half-sucked lollipop. A slick of red goo striped her mother's pale hair, but she only stared out the window. Tears left tracks through the mess on the girl's face. She stomped and screamed in her seat.

"Think your brother would actually go to Jamaica?"

Robert shook his head. Jamaica might as well have been the moon.

"Yeah." Jerome wiped his glasses on his shirt, oblivious to the screaming that echoed through the car. The girl's mother was clearly high on something. Her glassy eyes didn't move.

"Should we do something?" Robert nodded his head across the car.

"What you gonna do? You gonna fix that?"

The woman lurched up as the speaker squawked some new bit of noise. She tugged on the child's arm, pulling her down the aisle like a rag doll as the train came to a stop.

"Any idea where to look next?"

"Nowhere to look."

"You want to talk to his football coach?"

"Sean walked off more than a year ago."

"So that's it? We're giving up?"

"Unless you have a way to get us to Jamaica."

They sat back, absorbing the bumps and turns in the track.

"He's out there, Robert. You can't give up."

His mother bustled in an hour late with Brussels sprouts, chicken, and the traces of a scowl. He found a small, brown bottle on the counter, Lactobacillus reuteri Protectis. His mother's crunchy granola health food purchases all sounded like some magical potion.

"What's this one supposed to do?" he asked.

"Probiotics," she said. "A drop in each bottle should settle their stomachs. Only a drop though. That stuff's expensive."

He fed the babies while she heated black-eyed peas. Bridget stood on the sofa arm, jumped, and landed in its cushions.

"This is not a gymnasium," their mother called.

People said that talking out problems was a good thing. Healthy. That wasn't how his family worked. The line between her eyebrows deepened as she nipped the end off each Brussels sprout and cut a cross into the stem. The oven door squealed as she cracked it open to peak inside, but the wave of heat that should have come did not. She gasped and flung the door wide to pull out a baking sheet of pasty white chicken. "Nowhere *near* hot," she said. She checked the knobs and put her hand in the oven's center.

"Can we finish the chicken on the stove?"

"We'll have to."

"I can do it." He put a skillet on the cold burner. His mother was reaching for the handle as Bridget thundered into the kitchen, stopped breathless, and then thundered out again. "For heaven's sake, Bridget," she said. "We have neighbors downstairs."

"I'm sorry about the office."

"Those kids need more recess. I don't know how on earth they expect them to learn a thing all sugared up and trapped at a desk."

"I wanted to see where you worked. You know, in case we needed you."

But his mother was gone before his excuse was half out, off to take Bridget by the hand and sit her down. Even in Oregon where they'd had no real neighbors, their mother hadn't liked noise. When Robert was little, she sent him outside, telling him to run it off. Running was always her go-to cure.

He turned the chicken, listening to the quiet murmur as his mother read to Bridget. *The Monster at the End of This Book.* Her favorite.

YELLOW PAGES

Robert and Jerome lay on the carpet, paging through the phone book. The phone sat before them, the wall cord a winding mess. "I don't think this is going to work," Robert said. Hassler took rows and rows. "Football doesn't even have a listing."

"There," Jerome said. "It's under Athletics."

"Oh. Yeah." He listened as Bridget sang to her dolls in the other room. She never stayed at any game too long. What if she came out in the middle of his call, yelling about the green man or eavesdropping and asking questions? She'd tell. She'd tell, and he'd get the tongue-lashing.

Jerome stared at him. "You need me to dial for you?"

"Like I can't dial a phone."

"Old museum phone like that? Might be rusted in place. Might strain your fingers."

"Whatever."

"Then do it already."

Robert placed his finger on the first number and pulled it around, unsure why he'd let Jerome talk him into more wild-goose-chasing disappointment. It wasn't that he wanted to stop searching, but this felt like a wrong turn. They needed a better lead. "What if no one answers?"

"Leave a message."

"What should I say if someone d—?" He stopped short as

a woman's voice chirped in his ear. "Hi. Is this—" Robert stopped, not knowing where he was going. He could have planned what to say if Jerome weren't rushing him. "I'm, um, hoping to speak to the football coach?"

"Do you know which one you're trying to reach?"

He didn't. "The head coach?"

"He's out of the office right now, but I can leave a message." Her voice was a bird's. He could picture her flitting around the office, perching on a lamp, the rim of a pencil cup, her computer screen. She was the first person since Jerome who actually sounded interested in helping.

"The truth is," he said, "I'm not sure who I should talk to. I'm calling about my brother. Sean Flannigan?"

"Oh, Sean!" she crooned. "How is he? You know, we miss him around here."

"We do too."

If she found this reply strange, she didn't say so. "Let me put you on the phone with the quarterback coach." The bird flew from the receiver, replaced by ringing.

"Parsons here."

The voice made Robert jump. The coach wasn't wasting time. Robert spit out Sean's story as fast as he could.

"We haven't seen Sean since last fall."

"I know. I just thought, I don't know. Maybe he called?"

"You think he wants to play again?"

"Football? I mean, maybe?"

"If he does, we could certainly talk."

"You'd let him play again?"

"Let's not get ahead of ourselves."

"I'm trying to find him. That's why I called."

"Gotcha."

Robert waited, but Coach Parsons did not elaborate. He

could hear a pencil scratching away in the background, the coach working on some other project. "So..." Robert felt foolish. "Have you heard anything?"

"Sorry?"

"From Sean?"

"Why would I have heard anything?"

"I'm sorry. We—" Robert watched Jerome, already flipping through the book to find the number for Sean's janitorial job. "We just had to try, you know?"

"Sorry I can't help you, kid. Listen, though: You find him? You have him call me." The pencil scratching stopped a moment. "I'm really sorry to hear he's missing. He's a good kid, but even good kids mess up."

The line went dead. Robert was humiliated.

"Try the cleaning service," Jerome said, pushing the phone at him.

"Why don't you do this one?"

"He's your brother."

"This is dumb."

"You got any other ideas?"

Jerome pushed the phone at him. Robert lifted the handset and tucked it between head and shoulder. Again, he dialed.

"BENSON'S," a woman shouted. Whatever surrounded her was loud. It sounded more like elephant racing or an in-office bowling tournament than a laundry. He shouted his question as loud as he dared, not wanting to wake the twins. The washing machines must have been built for giants and filled with stones.

"SEAN?" she yelled back. "HAVEN'T SEEN HIM."

"Yes," he tried again. "But do you know where he might have gone?"

"DON'T KNOW AND DON'T CARE. NOT AFTER COVERING ALL HIS FUCKING SHIFTS. JULIO! JULIO, GOD

DAMN IT, THE OTHER ONE!" The woman's voice faded and he could hear her yelling in the background. He sat there, the phone hot against his ear. The yelling stopped. The machines thundered on. He watched the clock tick a minute, then two. She'd forgotten him.

That was it, then. They were out of people to call and places to visit. "Well," Jerome said, "at least we followed every lead."

Robert rolled to his back and stared at the ceiling. The cracked, stained plaster made an unreadable map. He felt his emotions swing one way and another. Now that they'd failed, he didn't want the search to be over. Somewhere, there was a path.

"Jesus," he said. "I sounded like such a dumb ass."

"Don't worry, man. Chances are, they've already forgotten you exist."

LIKE OREGON,
ONLY NOTHING LIKE OREGON

Robert was the one to suggest cutting class. He heard himself say it, but the words seemed to come from some other mouth. Cutting class? He'd never before even thought of stuff like that, let alone worked up the guts to do it. But the debt collector was threatening to garnish their mother's wages. She'd sat up the last two nights over columns of numbers, trying to work out a way to pay for enough daycare to keep her job.

"You know we'll get busted, right?" Jerome said.

"So we shouldn't do it?" Robert said.

"Oh we should do it," Jerome said. "It is, one hundred percent, the only option we got left. I just want to make sure that you know we're getting in trouble for this one. No two ways about it."

In Oregon, a cold wind twisted and stunted the coastal pine that dotted the cliff tops and braced the land against angry, crashing waves. The Jersey shore was tame, its sea a beaten dog licking at each pier before it ran and cowered. Robert inhaled the salt air. Underneath the boardwalk smells (beer, deep-fried sugar), there was a touch of home.

Floatilla was half casino, half carnival. At high tide, its maze of boardwalks stretched nearly a half mile into the ocean.

Daylight dulled the colored lights flashing over each stand, but at night, the place must have shone like Vegas. Jerome was silent as a man in church as he led them straight into the heart of things, legendary Boardwalk Number Five, and home to the third largest Ferris wheel on the eastern seaboard. They passed water ice stands and hair-braiding shops, carnies calling to pitch rings around bottles or sharp shoot tin targets. Around them, large pink rabbits and blue elephants lolled on fishing wire like hanged men in his dad's old Westerns. Everything was too big, too dense.

Robert turned and found himself alone. He stopped, the people and sunlight spinning in his head. With Jerome, he felt like he had a kind of permission to be here. Now, he was an outsider. He didn't belong in this kind of light, in the middle of city people who were tough and in your face, even in the places they relaxed. Too much humanity, too much junk. Cardboard airplanes, pot metal earrings painted gold, curving yellow plastic harmonicas printed, "I went bananas at Floatilla." Tops that didn't spin, gypsy scarves no one would wear, fading seaside prints, seashells that might have come from any other beach, machines that flattened a penny for a quarter. The shops were unnamed, listing only the items they sold. Ice Cream! Gifts! Fortunes! Not one said *Floatilla Gifts N' More*, the store on the bill, the only one that mattered. It might not be on the boardwalk at all, but rather a side street shop, adjacent to the park and banking off its name.

"Kid!" a man called from the corner. "Yo, kid!"

The man was clean-shaven with a close-trimmed haircut. He wore an Oxford shirt and khakis like someone who would be at home on a church council or charity planning committee. Robert tried to pretend he hadn't heard, but the guy came up and tugged his sleeve, drawing him to the edge of the boardwalk.

"You look like a guy who knows a bargain."

Robert scanned the crowd, desperate for any sign of

Jerome.

"I got these pictures, yeah? I think you'll like them. Hell, you'd have to be a fucking fag not to." He fanned the cards. On the top of the stack, a woman lay naked and prone on some kind of red-upholstered plank, head downwards, eyes closed, red lips parted. Her blonde hair spilled across the floor. Her open legs parted into a V, her hands at their base, pushing a soda bottle into her vagina. *Enjoy Coca-Cola* was printed in the space between her tiny, high-heeled feet. "You show these to your friends? Make you the most popular guy in your school."

Robert tried to turn, but the man moved with him.

"Only five dollars," the man said. "Or, tell you what, I'll let you take five for twenty. You can't pass up a bargain like that. Just imagine."

"I don't think—"

"Don't tell me. You're worried someone will find them. Your mom maybe. You don't want to get in trouble. But that's the beauty of the cards, right? You can stash them anywhere. No one has to know."

Robert had seen better porn. Troy had found his father's magazines, and they'd studied naked women during breaks on game night while Troy's parents yelled at each other upstairs. Lara Lynn said the photos were all fake, that no boobs were that round in nature, that you could practically see where the skin had been air-brushed and retouched if you looked hard enough, but the boys didn't mind. Who cared if the pictures were altered? They would never meet these women anyway. The point was the image.

The lady on this card was older than the magazine girls, but gravity lifted her upside-down boobs and made them pert again. Despite heavy makeup, the lines on her face showed. Sadness and laughter had etched themselves on her skin, but they also gave her beauty. The composition, the wording—

everything was so clever, like some fucked up kind of art.

"Listen, kid, buy or don't buy, but you got to make a decision. I'm not going to stand here all day like some schmuck with his dick in his hands. You buy, though? You can spend all the time with your dick in your hands that you want."

The man was long gone by the time Jerome came back with the paper plate. He held it towards Robert. "Take it."

"You just vanished on me. What the hell?"

"Take one bite of this and you'll forgive me."

"I can't believe you did that."

He pushed the plate at Robert again. "Trust me."

The hot dough smelled of fat and powdered sugar. Robert broke off a hunk. He hadn't realized how hungry he'd become—that down-to-the-bottom-of-the-gut hunger that you don't feel sleeping in you until food wakes it, bringing it roaring to life. The dough practically dissolved on his tongue.

"Funnel cake, man. This old German guy makes them. Mama says he's been here since she was a girl."

Robert took the plate from Jerome and bit directly into the marvelous cake. It was perfect, crisp to the tooth but tender and spongy inside. The powdered sugar cooled and sweetened his lips. With each bite, confidence returned.

"See?"

"Okay, maybe I forgive you. This stuff's pretty great."

"Told you."

They passed the meaningless shops. But even if those places refused to tell him their secrets, the trip was not wasted. Not now, not anymore. He'd seen the Coca-Cola woman. He learned the joy of funnel cake.

The crowd flowed past like water as he licked the last

bits of sugar from his fingers. Or not like water. They were pieces of a moving jigsaw coming almost into shape before him, only to scramble again. He tried to reconstruct the glimpse.

"We're looking at this all wrong," Robert said.

"What?"

"How could I be so blind?"

"What are you talking about?"

"The people. The guys and girls? They don't go into the same stores."

"Duh."

"All morning, we've been going into guy places, looking with guy eyes. Games, food. But if Sean came with Angela, he'd want to please her. They'd just had the babies, right? They couldn't pay their bills. They were working all the time. They wanted a break. Some little bit of peace in the middle of hell. Some fun. Sean wanted to make her happy. He didn't care about himself. We got to look with *girl* eyes. Whatever she'd be into, we should be looking at that, too."

"That's the longest I've ever heard you talk at once."

"I'm right, though, don't you think?"

"Yeah, okay. Girl eyes. But that gives us more stuff to look at."

"No, man. It narrows it down. I've been looking at this like a boy from Oregon instead of a woman from Philadelphia. There's a difference, right?"

"Let's hope so."

For the first hour, girl eyes didn't help. In his head, Robert kept hearing his mother's words: *he knows everything we have.* He would take what was owed. From them, from Sean, it didn't matter so long as the money was paid.

If he and Jerome weren't trying to cram their boy selves

into the mold of Angela's desires, they could have had their fortunes read, or shot targets to win a bear, or made themselves sick on hot dogs and ice cream. His feet were hot and the sun was hotter. Lunch had passed hours ago. They needed to get on a bus.

They ducked into a shop to grab a bottle of water only to find that they had chosen the only shop in all of Floatilla that didn't have a drink cooler. One shelf was crowded with photographs of the boardwalk in poorly painted frames, crabs and starfish in each corner. Another had music boxes and glass lamps filled with seashells. Beach towels reading FLOATILLA hung down the wall like flags. They had t-shirts and puzzles and jewelry and everything, everything, was the same price: $16.95. All day, he'd searched for that number.

Rows of necklaces swayed before him. Or he swayed before them, tired and thirsty. They all fit the same general pattern, silver angels carrying smooth, round stones. He fingered a little cherub holding a transparent blue pebble. "Very nice," the small, old man called to him from the register. "One of a kind. My wife, she makes them special. You buy that for your woman and she love you forever."

"Forever, huh?" The cherub was so weird. Round cheeks ballooned under piggish eyes, and its mouth opened round, like it was trying to catch popcorn or screaming in terror. "It's all too expensive," Robert whispered to Jerome. "We'd better go."

"No sir," the man said. "Very cheap. $16.95."

"Do you maybe have a sale rack?"

"What are you talking about?" Jerome whispered. "It's dead on."

"With sales tax, it would cost more."

"We're in Jersey, dawg. No tax."

Like Oregon, Robert thought, only nothing like Oregon. His eyes spun around the store. Anything here could be the thing. God, he was thirsty. He looked again at the necklace. Even broke,

Sean would never have bought Angela anything so tatty and cheap.

"Genuine sea glass," the man said. "Right here from the shore. No two exactly alike. A piece of art."

Jerome, having wandered away again, across the shop, held up a piggy bank. "Your brother *should* have got hisself one of these."

Robert turned a seashell lamp on and off. If Sean had bought one of these for his apartment, it had disappeared with the furniture. Or maybe he bought a t-shirt? Maybe Angela was wearing it now.

"What's the name of this shop?" Jerome called to the man.

"Floatilla Gifts."

"And More?"

"Yes. So much more."

By the time she got home, his mother had had the whole day to worry. She froze in the doorway, babies in each arm and the secondhand stroller hooked on an arm. Her lips pressed tight in angry silence. Bridget ran to her room to get her doll. Sammy and Deacon began to cry. "I can explain," Robert said, lifting Deacon from her arms.

He planned to lie. He would say he had been at school all day. The attendance lady made a mistake. The teacher called him by the wrong name. Something. Anything.

His mother turned her back on him, uninterested in excuses. Her voice was low and growling. "Your school called first thing this morning. Do you have any idea what I've been through today, not knowing where you'd disappeared?"

"I'm sorry."

Her voice sharpened its edge, cutting like a razor by the time she slashed the words: "I don't appreciate this, Robert."

She hadn't even asked where he'd been. "You don't trust

me," he said, realizing it was true as he heard himself say it.

Her shoulders rose and fell, rose and fell. "You're coming straight home from school tomorrow and you're staying put," she said. "When I call, you answer on the first ring, understood? No Jerome."

"That's totally unfair!"

"Don't you tell me what's fair."

"Sean skipped all the time. You didn't ground him."

"That was Herman."

"So? Nothing happened."

She still had her back to him, fussing over the babies. He stared, waiting for her to look at him. "The first ring," she said and walked out into the kitchen. "And get used to it because that's how it will be until I can trust you not to perform another disappearing act."

She didn't say *like your brother,* but he heard it.

PROBLEMS AND FORMULAS

Mr. Burns stared at him, waiting. Robert didn't know what the question had been or how long ago he'd been asked. His body might have skipped class yesterday, but his mind was gone today. He looked to the whiteboard for help, but all he saw were solved equations. Mr. Burns crossed his arms and his blue eyes hardened. "Bobby Flannigan, have you heard one word I've said?"

At first, Robert didn't register his own name. He'd never been a Bobby. Never. Not until he started school in Philadelphia. His English teacher called the roll by last name, and when he had raised his hand at Flannigan, she had paused and looked at him. "I hear you're new to the area," she ha said. "We're so glad to have you, Bobby." She was three names down the list before he realized he should have corrected her. Too late. When it happened again and again in each class, he realized he'd been caged in a new name. One that didn't fit. Now, he'd missed a question and looked like a dope because Mr. Burns had asked Bobby and he was Robert.

"All right," Mr. Burns said, his eyes scanning the students crowded into the small room. "Let's try again. LaQuira, can *you* tell me the formula for figuring out the length of the hypotenuse of this triangle?"

Robert blushed. The question was easy. Stupidly easy. Mr. Burns stared at him as LaQuira answered. He was a slim, birdlike man who always wore a tie and had a reputation for taking no shit.

Robert had always been good at math. He liked the way the answers were the answers. There was no fuzziness or maybes. The unknown could always be solved if you had the right pieces of information.

Every time he closed his eyes, he saw rows of lamps and banks and beach towels, all $16.95.

The math room was not built to hold this many desks. Students shifted sideways down the aisles to reach their seats. Forty-nine kids and a teacher in a room designed to hold maybe twenty. Robert blinked hard, refocusing on Mr. Burns. The clock's tick was too slowly eating the five minutes until lunch.

Mr. Burns snapped his book closed and stared at the class. The students stared back as if it were a contest, but if it was, Robert's money was on Mr. Burns. He had a way of commanding their attention without saying a word. Jerome said he'd been a New York stockbroker before becoming a teacher in the Chum. Rumor had it, he was a millionaire with a house in Merion and he worked here on some kind of self-imposed mission. LaQuira said he was trying to make up for some kind of shady insider trading deals, but she only shrugged when Robert asked her where she'd heard that. Robert's own theory was that Mr. Burns was a teacher and had always been a teacher, and people just made him a businessman because everyone worshipped businessmen, even when they ran their companies into the ground or made shady deals or spent their days on golf courses or private planes to private islands. Personally, Robert didn't see the draw.

Burnsie didn't take any flack. Jerome said he pulled apart two brawling defensive ends last year. "Mr. Burns? Man's got some kind of Spiderman strength," he said. Math was the one place where Robert felt completely safe.

Staring at his textbook, Robert's eyes glazed over, and his

head echoed with the words of the shopkeeper. *You buy that for your woman and she love you forever.* As if the dumb thing were a charm or an amulet. The more he thought about it, the more the cherub looked poised to give a blow job. His mind drifted to the Coca-Cola card, safe in his locker.

Mr. Burns's eyes were on him again as if he had Spidey-sense for dirty thoughts as well as spider strength. "Bobby Flannigan, you'll stay a minute and have a word. The rest of you are dismissed." The bell rung as he said "dismissed," and at once the students slammed their books shut on their papers and bustled to get their things into their book bags. Robert filled his own bag more slowly and carefully, waiting for them to leave before approaching his teacher's desk.

Mr. Burns, too, waited until the last kid was through the door before he sighed and spoke. "Bobby, I'm going to be straight with you." His voice had the harsh, nasal vowels of the wealthy. "You've come into this school with good grades and test scores in math. That's why they put you in this class. We're only a couple weeks in, so maybe it's too early to tell, but looking at your homework and class participation, I'm not seeing that aptitude. We may need to assess whether this class is the right one for you."

"I'm sorry. I'll do better."

"Is something bothering you, Bobby?"

"No."

"You look like your mind is elsewhere."

His life was nothing but word problems lately, missing the information he needed to solve them. Mr. Burns wouldn't really want to hear all this. *Excuses are like assholes,* Sean used to say. *Everybody's got one.*

"Tell me, did you know the answer to the question I asked you in class just now?"

"Yes."

"You just missed the question? You didn't hear it?"

"Yes."

"But nothing's bothering you." His voice was flat, skeptical.

"I, I'll pay better attention."

"You skipped class yesterday."

Robert couldn't meet his eye.

"Our first test is in four weeks. I want to see a decent score from you, or else we'll have no choice but to look at your placement. It's always hard to know who's doing what in other parts of the country. Your math class may not have been equivalent. Trust me, though. I don't think you want to go down a level if you can help it."

"No. I like this class."

"The kids in those other classes? Well, they're focused on things other than math. Things can get rough. This class you're in now? We're hoping these students will go on to college. Is that where you see yourself?"

He could. Studying what, he didn't know. Engineering, maybe? Or music? It wasn't worth thinking about. If the debt collector came, there would be no money for tuition or books or dorm rooms. He'd have to get a job to help his mom, go work with Mr. Murphy stocking vending machines, and take on the responsibility that Sean had dumped.

His mind went to Maurice and the back row of biology and what another math class would mean. He couldn't lose this one safe place. Moving to another section of the class was one thing—he could be with Jerome—but moving down a level was something else. "I can do better."

"Talk is one thing, Bobby. I need to see performance."

Mr. Burns fixed him with his gaze like Robert was a bug wiggling on its pin, but Robert thought he also saw a glimmer of kindness too.

"That's enough now. Go get some lunch. I've never known a boy yet who could think on an empty stomach."

* * *

Ricky had Jerome cornered by Robert's locker, babbling on about some girl who'd randomly gotten all sweaty and starting puking all over the gym. The kid never knew when to shut up.

Jerome was unimpressed. "Probably just dehydrated."

"We hadn't even stretched yet."

"Stomach bug then."

"Nigger, please."

"What did you just say to me?"

"The girl OD'd."

"Don't be throwing 'nigger' around. Not to me, and not around me."

"Donna thinks it was heroin, but my money's on crack."

"Don't you have class?"

"I'm giving you an education. Show some appreciation."

"If I need an education, I'll look around for someone who isn't ignorant to teach me lessons."

"Knowledge is power," Ricky said, his parting shot before he headed down the hall.

Jerome turned to Robert. "What took you so long, man? I know you can beat Ricky here, even on those skinny legs."

"Mr. Burns asked for a word with me."

"Yeah?"

"Yeah."

"What'd he say?"

"I wasn't concentrating on class." Robert spun the combination and pulled his lock open. His locker smelled like fungus. "He calls me Bobby."

"Course he does."

"Not just him, either. All of them."

"Yep."

"Why?"

"You're white," Jerome said, as if pointing out the obvious.

"So?"

"So, white boys named Robert are Bobby and black guys named Robert are Robert. Last I checked, you're white." They slid onto a bench at the first open table and dumped their sack lunches into a single pile to divvy.

"I don't want to be Bobby."

"You got an Irish last name and you're the whitest white boy in the history of white boys. In Philly, you got no choice *but* to be Bobby." Jerome tore his cupcake in half and gave it to Robert like some kind of consolation. "Or you could come up with some dope ass nickname, but that only works if the nickname sticks. I don't know if you're a nickname kind of guy."

Robert bit into the sandwich his mother had made at six that morning. The mayonnaise and tomato had soaked through the bread, but it was all the better for that. Even in the Chum, Sean wouldn't have been anything but Sean. Robert, though? He was either Bobby or I'm-Um.

He sat up, suddenly knowing where he'd seen the necklace. He could see it again now, dangling down the girl's breasts. He didn't know how she'd gotten it, but if they really were one of a kind, it had come from Floatilla Gifts N' More. "I need to go back to Sean's place."

"Now?"

"No, but soon. After school."

"You've thought of something. We're back on the case!"

"It's probably nothing. It could be a total waste of time."

"Whatever."

"Seriously, you don't have to come if you've got other stuff to do."

"B.S., man. You know I'm not letting you go again on your

own. We're in this together."

"Cool. I've got to stop at home first. If I don't answer when my mom calls, I'm done."

"Your mom's a trip."

"Once she does, we've got to hurry. We'll only have an hour and a half before she gets back from Miss Martha's with the babies and Bridget. We can't risk missing that bus."

"Sounds like a heist film, you timing it like that. I'm in."

"Man, this place reeks." Jerome's voice was little more than a whisper traced with awe. He looked wide-eyed. For the first time, Robert felt the pride in being somewhere in Philly that Jerome hadn't been.

"They still haven't fixed the AC."

"Probably never will." Jerome said it like something they both already knew. He wasn't teaching; he was sharing an observation.

He started to walk towards the elevator but stopped when Robert didn't follow. "I thought we were going to your brother's place. It's upstairs, right?"

"Not this time. There's a girl we need to find."

"Okay. Which apartment?"

"She was on the elevator last time I was here."

"You know the floor, then."

"I didn't really catch it."

"Do you know the girl's name?"

"Not really."

"Not really? Man, I thought you were in a hurry. How you know she's going to be around?"

"I told you you could sit this one out."

"What are we gonna do if she doesn't come?"

"Come again tomorrow?"

Jerome looked at him for a hard minute, his eyes filled with doubt. Finally, he shrugged and said, "All right. It's your party."

They sat, watching the door. Five minutes passed. No one came or left. Jerome said, "It really does reek in here."

"We established that already."

"What's she look like, this girl we're watching for?"

"Thin. Kind of pretty in a strange way." Robert hesitated, then added, "She has purple hair."

"You have lost your mind."

"I think she might know Sean."

"That doesn't mean she knows where he's at."

"She was wearing the necklace. The angel one, from the store."

"She could have bought that her own self."

"But it was on the bill. That's weird, right?"

"Bill could've been for anything in that shop."

"One of a kind, the guy said."

"Why would your brother give it to some neighbor, though? He'd give it to Angela, if he bought it."

"Maybe he did. Maybe she didn't like it and gave it to the girl. I don't know."

"Then how does that get us any closer?"

"Well, if they're friends, maybe Sean and Angela told the girl where they were going. They could've asked her to watch out for the babies until my mom got here. That's plausible, right? The necklace was, like, payment or something?"

"You grasping."

"It's the only clue we haven't followed up. And the last time I was here? As soon as I said I was looking for Sean, she got all weird. She knows something."

Jerome rolled his eyes. "Great evidence, Sherlock."

"What else have we got?"

"A smelly old lobby, I guess."

* * *

Robert could live with the fact that the only miracle of the afternoon was getting home before his mother. They had waited and waited before sprinting for the last-chance bus. He dashed up stairs four minutes before his mother walked in, barely long enough to catch his breath and spread his books on the table. He started math, but the only problem that mattered was this: he had five weeks before the debt man collected.

His mother opened the day's mail. Bills, bills, bills. She was in a good mood in spite of them. The expensive formula and the probiotics seemed to be working. The babies were napping and only waking once in the night. It was amazing the difference sleep made, like some kind of magic that returned their smiles. On top of that, Mr. Murphy told her that she was the best secretary he'd ever had and that, if she kept it up, he'd think about giving her a raise, and even though that didn't exactly do them any good *now*, Deee-Lite was on the radio singing "Groove is in the Heart." His mother moved her hips along, nodding her head in time as she opened the mail.

"I'm going to go hang out with Jerome."

"You seem to be forgetting that you're grounded."

"I thought that was just while you're at work."

Her hips stilled. The groove left her heart. "You never cut class a day in your life. I'm guessing he had something to do with yesterday's little adventure."

"Jerome?"

She paused over a handwritten envelope, the only one in the stack, looking at its front and back. Only their own address was scrawled on the envelope, no return.

"Mom, he tried to talk me *out* of skipping. For real."

"'For real?' You even sound like a hoodlum."

"Jesus, Mom. It's not like we were dealing crack."

"I didn't say that."

"Is this because he's black?"

"Of course not. Don't you dare put that on me."

"Then what?"

"This isn't Herman. You could get yourself into some real trouble."

"That's why I need a friend. This isn't the kind of place you want to fly solo."

"Fly solo? Do you hear yourself?"

"He's a good guy, Mom. You know he is."

She looked at him frowning before sliding her fingernail under the envelope's flap. She peered in, and paused.

"What is it?"

She didn't answer. Three twenty-dollar bills slid into her hand.

"Who sent it?"

"It doesn't say."

"You think it's from Sean?" He took the envelope from her hand. The writing was larger than his brother's and not so blockish. "Or maybe Angela?"

"Angela?" His mother snorted. "If that girl had two twenties to rub together, she would have blown it on makeup or some over-priced t-shirt."

"What's the postmark?"

"Philadelphia. Real helpful, huh?"

"Well, considering we hardly know anyone here..."

"It's Murphy I bet. It seems like something he'd do, doesn't it? A little help but nothing obvious."

"Murphy?"

"Who else do we know with spare money?"

Sixty bucks. Nothing in terms of what Sean owed, but he

knew his mom could stretch it at the grocery store. It seemed like the right time to press. "So, can I go to Jerome's?"

Her eyes were still on the postmark, a smile playing over her lips. "Twenty minutes. Don't be late."

A POCKET IN THE WORLD

The air in the abandoned house reminded Robert of his father's flannel shirts. It wrapped around him, soft, warm, scented with dust and wood. In the darkness, his father's mellow eyes seemed to rest on him. "You and I?" he once said. "We're cut from the same cloth." They'd been washing dishes, but Robert couldn't remember what they'd been talking about, what similarity they'd shared.

Memories of his father slipped away faster than he could stop them. It was like trying to catch creek water in cupped hands. He tried to picture his father's face, but the image was hazy and wrong. He couldn't remember the thickness of the bridge of his father's nose or the angle of his eyebrows or how far below his ear lobe his father's sideburns dipped.

He didn't say any of this to Jerome. Instead, he said, "This place reminds me of the woods."

"This place? A building?"

"My brother took me camping once. Only once because he had to borrow all the stuff and it was a real pain in the ass."

A half-truth. Sean had gotten the idea when he found an old backpack at the Goodwill. It didn't fit him right, stabbing his kidneys with each step, but he didn't say so until afterwards, and only jokingly, as if it were no big thing. He made sure that Robert had the good stuff. His buddy Chad, whose dad was a doctor, lent him the rest of the gear. Everything Robert carried was light and technical and packed together perfectly. Chad adjusted the pack so that it nestled right in the hollow of Robert's back and barely seemed a burden. Chad scoffed as they packed the stuff Sean bought for himself, the lumpy sleeping bag, the dented tin pans. He didn't even have a bedroll, but Sean just laughed along with Chad. He carried the gear and food for both of them, acting as if his pack were as light and comfortable as Robert's.

With his toe, Robert pushed the house's dust into a little hill. "We hiked all day up Mount Hood until we got to this little lake. It was so quiet there, like we were the first human beings ever to see it. At night, the darkness was warm and soft, just like it is here. Like a little pocket in the world where no one could bother you."

They sat silent. Their thoughts roamed the room like moths.

"Why does Maurice hate you?" Robert knew as he asked that it was a stupid question. Ignorant. People hated other people all the time. Hate didn't need a reason. So he was surprised when Jerome's voice broke the darkness:

"I was the last person to see him and his brother before his brother got shot."

"Why would that make him mad?"

"His brother was stone cold kicking his ass."

"Huh." Robert sat a moment with that information. "Hard to imagine anyone kicking Maurice's ass."

"He don't want you to imagine it. He don't want *anyone* to imagine it. My ass be breakfast if he knew I said anything."

They sat, listening to small, clawed feet scrabbling in the walls.

"That scar on his head? That's where his brother split it open."

"Jesus."

"Violence begets violence. That's what the Bible says and that shit's for real. Police beat the gangs and the gangs beat each other and the bangers beat they brothers and the brothers beat all us all."

Shit rolls downhill. That's what his father used to say. Why could he remember that when he couldn't remember the man's face? Robert thought of those kids in Jonesboro who'd shot up their school: Mitchell and Andrew. Normal names. Normal guys. He could imagine them in class, the two guys no one wanted anything to do with. Shit rolled down on them and down on them until they'd had enough and push the shit back on everyone else. It wasn't so hard to understand. Strange, that you could kill someone with a touch of a finger.

"Who shot his brother?" Robert asked.

"No word."

"He die?"

"Naw. Lost an arm below the elbow. Homeboy's even meaner with one arm than he was with two."

"What's his name?"

"Andre."

The scurrying stopped. Robert's mind wandered to the girl with purple hair, living in one of those apartments, on one of those floors. He wished he could remember where she'd gotten off, but if he'd even known, the floor was long gone from his mind.

"I want to go there someday," Jerome said. "Mount Hood. When we're grown, maybe. We'll save up, get a couple of train tickets. That's where we'll go."

Robert wanted to tell him that the trains that ran through the city didn't stretch all the way to that mountain, that you couldn't always find a magic bus with the right number to take you where you wanted to go. He wanted to tell Jerome how, that night by the lake, he couldn't sleep for hours, how every time the wind lifted a branch, he worried that a bear was lumbering over to rip them to shreds. He wanted to say that when he did sleep, it was deep and sound, like the world was a television and he had clicked it off. And that when he woke, bleary-eyed, and looked out the tent flap, the sun rising over the lake lit a rippling path to paradise through the dark and pointed trees. Everything was newer and fresher than he'd known it could be. Jays flitted with little brown and gray songbirds, and the jays gave the morning color and the songbirds gave it sound, and he and Sean watched them for a good hour through the tent flap, not wanting to disturb them, even though they were hungry. He wanted to tell Jerome how good bacon tasted when they finally got the fire going again, and how they sopped the grease with their bread. He wanted to say how a trip like that could stay with you your whole life, that it was there any time you needed it, that all you had to do was close your eyes and there was that mountain, that sunlit path over water, that birdsong.

Robert only said, "I'll go alone tomorrow. No sense both of us waiting."

"You might not ever find her. It was only luck you did the first time."

"She lives there."

"How many times do you walk in and out your front door in a day? A few times. That's it. What's the chance she going to walk in during the littlest part of the hour you have to be looking?"

They sat there in the dark together, letting it cover them. Like the mountain, the house invited silence.

"Shit." Jerome grabbed Robert's shoulder, his voice hoarse with panic. "Did you see that?"

"What?"

"What do you mean, what?"

"Just what I said. You going to tell me?"

"How could you not see it? He was huge!"

Darkness crawled towards them, drawing in like breath.

The plywood over the door hadn't creaked or rattled. Whoever it was had been with them the whole time, watching, listening to every word they said. Jerome's arm shivered against his own. Robert searched the room for an addict or murderer or Maurice or whoever it was Jerome saw. "What was it?"

"Biggest goddamned rat I ever saw."

"Good grief."

"What?"

"All that fuss over some little rat? You nearly crapped yourself."

"That thing was huge! Like some old lady's lap dog. That thing get ahold of you and you'd be done. Probably carrying the bubonic plague or something." Jerome pointed the flashlight to a hole in the baseboard. A big one, sure, but Robert didn't care. The house in Oregon was full of mice, and what was a rat but an overgrown mouse? Rodents he could handle.

"Let's get out of here," Jerome said, not waiting for Robert to agree. "Fore that thing bites us and we end up with rabies and tetanus and all kinds of other badness."

The sun was always brighter after the darkness of the house. Rows of boarded doors stretched before them, reminding Robert of the game shows his father sometimes watched. Behind one door, fabulous prizes. Behind the other, shattered dreams.

"It's not like I have other options. I just have to keep going back until I find her."

"We need information. Information, and jumbo-sized rat traps."

"I don't think we could ever set enough. That whole row is probably crawling with rats. Even if you got them out of that house, another bunch of rats would just move in from the next one over."

"We could make something to scare them away."

"Like what?" Robert pictured a fake machine gun with a row of shining bullets feeding into its side.

"They make scarecrows to scare off crows. We could make a rat-crow."

"You mean a scare-rat?"

"Whatever."

"First we're detectives, then we're rat farmers. Why's a rat going to be scared of a fake person when it's not scared of us real people?"

"We'll make it bad ass. He'll be a big old G.I. Joe scare-rat or something."

"Maybe we should just get a BB gun."

"How we going to get a BB gun? This isn't Oregon, boy scout." Jerome scowled at the horizon. "I can name you ten guys with guns to unload, but ain't none of them BB guns."

Robert glanced back at the plywood door as they rounded the corner, wanting again to squeeze into the place no one wanted. Forget the scare-rat. Forget the gun. He wanted to sit in darkness and breathe in the musty, rotting wood. It wasn't an Oregon forest, but it wasn't a hot sidewalk either. It held no crying babies. It wasn't a numbered bus filled with the angry and catatonic traveling unknown routes. He'd entered the first time thinking they were trespassing, but he didn't think that now. They had claimed that one small rejected piece of the Chum as their own.

"What you need," Jerome said, "is someone who could tell you where she lived."

Robert stopped mid-step. "A manager."

"Yeah. A manager would know. No sense waiting around forever, not knowing if she'll come. Not if there's someone you can ask."

Robert stood, stunned by his own stupidity. Of course.
Of course.

A MANAGER

Matilda took a long, slow sip from her china cup. The lip had once been gold-rimmed, but only traces remained. Her cup, like her apartment, was decorated with faded, secondhand class. The yellowing doilies of her end tables were starched and ironed. The tables themselves suggested antique store elegance, their varnish polished away with years of care.

"You asking me to meddle in people's business," she said. "That ain't right."

Robert put on his reasonable, responsible face. "We only want to talk to her."

"That's none of my affair." Matilda's lips pulled in, her mouth holding the number of the girl's apartment. Robert knew he owed her gratitude for letting him in Sean's apartment in the first place. He'd only gotten this far thanks to her help. The girl's apartment number didn't seem like a big deal. It wasn't like he was breaking and entering. Frustration licked its way up his throat. Nothing had changed, except now rather than letting him knock on one little door, she turned prim and proper sipping from her old cup, sitting straight-backed as the queen of England on her throne.

Jerome smoothed his jeans, his hand an iron for wrinkles that didn't exist. "We don't want to bother anyone, ma'am. That's why we came to you. We don't want to knock on a bunch of doors and disturb people. We knew you'd point us right. We could ask the girl our one little question and then we'd be out of everyone's business."

Matilda laid her eyes on him for a long time. In his crisp new polo and ironed jeans, his glasses, his braids in neat rows against his head, Jerome looked—every inch of him—like a guy you could trust. That's what Robert saw. Matilda, though, looked afraid. Her lace collar trembled against her throat. She sipped quietly, as if to calm her nerves, while the air conditioner ticked time in the corner.

"I don't like being threatened in my own home," she said.

"Threatened?" Robert glanced at Jerome, who looked as baffled as he felt. "Who's threatening you?"

"Tell us the number or we'll disturb all your tenants. That's just what he said, and if that ain't extortion, I don't know what is. Don't you go thinking you can manipulate me."

"We didn't mean," Robert started, "we don't want—"

"You can leave."

"We just need to know if she saw him."

"You got no cause to ask her that."

"He's my brother. Isn't that cause?"

Matilda didn't answer.

"She might be able to tell us where to look. He might have said something."

"You just stirring things up. Upsetting people." For all her flowers and lace, Matilda's voice now was as level and firm as a two-by-four. "That's not right. It ain't going to help nobody. And I'll tell you something else: you come round her knocking and bothering the whole building, I be on the phone to the police so fast your head will spin. They won't stand for you disturbing people's peace like y'all disturbing mine."

"I'm sorry," Robert said, but Matilda was already escorting

them to the door. "We didn't mean—"

"You go on now. The authorities ought to take things from here."

"But we tried them." He could see it now, the misunderstanding. He would clear it up. "The police haven't done anything."

"Then there's nothing to be done."

"They have too many cases. They don't care. It's low priority for them, but it isn't for us." The words flooded from him, but the knob clicked shut against all he said. He stared at the greening brass number on her door, and then dropped his eyes to the splinters that fringed its base.

"Sorry, man," Jerome said. "Guess I should have let you have this one on your own."

"She was so kind before."

"She still might be." They waited for the elevator, Sean's empty apartment at their backs.

"She looked terrified. Seriously, what did she think we were going to do?"

"It's not her fault. Just another generation."

They pulled the elevator's gate open and shut themselves in. Every floor gave way under Robert's feet. "Wait, you think she's prejudiced?"

"Everybody's prejudiced. Can't help it."

"How can you be so calm?"

"You think this is a new thing?"

The door slid open. "We were so close. She was the one who gave me hope in the first place, and now she's snatched it right back."

They climbed onto a bus and watched the trees skim past the windows. A group of girls talked and laughed on the sidewalk. Water ices, each a vivid red, green, and blue, dangled from their hands like delicious but forgotten fashion accessories.

"What do we do now?" Robert asked.

"Well, you still got plan A. Wait in the lobby til the girl shows up. Wait on the sidewalk if the manager gives us grief."

"But you were right. It was a stupid plan before, and it's even stupider now."

"Sometimes, the stupid plan is the only plan you got."

THE STUPID PLAN

The thing about Jerome was, if you were going to be stuck in a hotel lobby with anybody, he was the guy you wanted to be stuck with. During those waiting afternoons, he bounced through a long list of conversation topics: strategies for dressing like a player, strategies for getting your mother to trust you, strategies for running from a cop, strategies for passing a math test, strategies for maximizing the amounts of snacks you could buy at Wawa with a five-dollar bill. He zigged from *Slayers* to Maurice to Keesha Bates to his bitch of a sister. If one topic edged towards becoming stale or depressing, he shifted.

The first afternoon, they watched for Matilda, planning routes to run if she caught them. When, by the second afternoon, she had not appeared, they worked on a new theory; she wouldn't look for them so long as they could find the purple-haired girl quietly. No one needed to be disturbed. It was almost like she'd agreed to it.

Only when the elevator hit the ground that fifth and final afternoon did they realize that no one had let Matilda in on that deal. Her lips folded up like a church lady's handbag, something clutched. She stared at them a full minute, the weight of her eyes growing so heavy that neither Robert nor Jerome could stand its heft. Her footsteps, when she finally moved, were emphatic against the grimy floor.

"We talked about this. You need to leave."

"We're just sitting here," Robert stammered as he and Jerome scrambled to collect their papers, stuffing them into their backpacks.

"I told you you can't be bothering no tenants. This is the only warning you going to get. I'm out of my mind not to be calling the authorities this instant."

"Ain't no law against being in a lobby," Jerome said.

Robert closed his eyes, wishing he could pull Jerome's words back out of the air and stick them in his pocket, somewhere deep and quiet where no one would ever know they had existed.

Matilda dug through her handbag. "You so sure about that?" For a moment, Robert wondered if she was looking for pepper spray or a Taser or a gun, but what she pulled from her bag was nothing he would have expected. Matilda had a cell phone.

He'd seen them before, of course, but not in the hands of anyone he knew. In Oregon, there wasn't much reception outside of Portland, and cell phones were for rich people, not people like them.

"Robert," Jerome said, his voice full of urgency.

Robert shook himself out from his own surprise and scrambled, the papers jamming in his zipper as he yanked it closed. Matilda had already pressed a number, something speed-dialed. Not 9-1-1 but something that bleeped a string of digits. Robert dashed for the door, looking back for Jerome. He didn't see the purple-haired girl until they crashed.

She wore a short skirt, ripped tights, black boots cracking over the toes, and an expression that told him to watch it. Her eyes were rimmed with black and she hardly glanced at him before shoving her way forward, her breasts brushing his bare arm.

She almost made it to the elevator before Robert

thought to call out, "Wait! Wait, can I talk to you?"

Matilda pressed *end* just as it started to ring. "These boys was just leaving. I told them they can't be here molesting no tenants."

The girl's face pulled into a smirk. "Molesting, huh? Tell me, guy, you going to molest me? You like things rough like that?"

A blush flamed up his neck, quick fire. "I just have a question. About Sean."

She snorted and turned away. Matilda said, "Y'all need to go home."

"No." Robert didn't know why he was pushing it. Matilda held her phone ready again. He was burning every bridge to Sean, pouring gasoline instead of water. He wasn't even sure he was right about the cherub. "He gave you the necklace. He left, but you're still wearing it. That's got to mean something."

Matilda hit the speed dial.

"What makes you think I got it from Sean?"

He met her gaze like it was a dare, a showdown he could only win by refusing to draw.

"You been talking to Angela or something? She tell you that?"

"Angela?"

"I know you know who Angela is."

"Yes, hello," Matilda said. "I'd like to report some intruders."

Jerome tugged at his sleeve, "Come on, man, come on," but Robert stood his ground. Let the police come. Maybe, if they did, they'd actually start looking. Do their jobs.

"I need to know where my brother is. I need to know why that necklace is the last thing he bought before he took off. You know something, and whatever it is, it might help."

"Kid, you really need to stop talking."

"What I need is to find Sean."

Matilda gave the building's address.

Robert said, "I'm not going anywhere until you tell me

something."

Tears pricked in her angry eyes as she glared back. Her teeth set against one another so that, as she spoke, the words half seethed and half sobbed out of her. "Fine. He left because of me. Angela found out we were sleeping together, okay? That what you wanted to hear?"

Robert reeled. She could have said anything, anything else. Jerome stopped tugging. "You and his brother?"

"What's it to you?"

"Nothing." Jerome lifted his hands to show that they were empty, harmless. "Nothing at all. It's only, why's he messing with you when he's got a wife and babies?"

"Guess a guy can have a family and still be lonely."

Her words twisted in Robert's belly like a nest of snakes. He'd asked for them. The girl was exactly Sean's type, the kind he always used to go for. Small waist, big boobs, fearless attitude. She was every punked-out goth girl he'd dated in high school, every girl that made their mother cringe. Angela had changed all that. From the moment he met her, Robert couldn't see any other girl. Surely, it was the same for Sean. Angela was a girl you gave up everything for.

"He didn't sleep with you," he said. "He loved Angela."

"He did, God knows why." Her quick laugh brimmed with bitterness. "He loved that bitch, but he still slept with me."

Matilda moved to the door, looking to see if help was coming. The police car might be there any minute, or it might never be there. Was this the "9-1-1 Is a Joke" kind of neighborhood or the other kind?

"People fuck up," the girl said.

Anger was a body inside of him. He wanted to split his skin, to get away from here. The lobby smell burned in his eyes. "Sean didn't hurt people like that."

"We got to go," Jerome said.

All the hardness melted from the girl's face. "Maybe he didn't used to hurt people, but he sure as hell broke my heart. Broke yours, too, from the look of things."

She was so pretty when she looked at him like that. It wasn't fair.

"I'm sorry, kid. I didn't know what I was doing. If it makes you feel better, I don't think he did either."

Two bodies inside him pushed in different directions. One wanted to run, leaving everything she said here on the lobby floor with all the other grime. The other wanted to pin her to the wall, crushing her under his forearm until she told him everything. Each pulled with equal force, rooting him to the ground.

"He needed people, your brother."

"He had us."

"Eventually he had you, but there was a long time before that. Then, he only had me."

"And Angela. And his sons."

"What does it matter? A few months of getting what he wants and the bastard takes me to Floatilla. We spend the whole day there with his fucking kids, and then he dumps me. Gives me the necklace and says he can't keep doing this to Angela. Like he can buy me off with some cheap carnival shit. Like I'm some little girl he can placate with a trinket. I told Angela everything. Next I know, she's gone, then he's gone, then your mom's walking out with the babies and you coming here looking. Like I said, I don't know where he is. I'm the last one he'd tell after what went down with Angela."

Jerome had his sleeve again. "Listen, man, you know what you came to know. Cops catch us here, and neither of our moms is letting us out of the house for a month. Sean will still be gone. He's more gone every day."

Robert's eyes never left the girl. "You wrecked everything. You tore my family apart."

"Sweetheart," she said, stepping into the elevator and pulling the cage door behind her, "they'd torn themselves apart long before I got there."

THE GENETICS OF LEAVING

Robert and Jerome sat on the couch and stared at the blank wall. It stared back, unmoving and imperturbable. Something was rising in Robert's throat. A sob, he guessed, but it felt bigger than that: a golf ball, a grapefruit, a world. Only, if Robert had a world waiting to be coughed up, this world would be smaller than the one he had lived in, small and diminished because it was missing Sean, its brightest star, because the Sean that had always lit this world had collapsed under the weight of his own heat and gravity.

He wished Sean had never left Herman. He wished his Dad never stepped out of his car that last day.

"Well," Jerome said, "what's next?"

"There is no next."

"There's always a next."

"I just wish I was home."

"You *are* home."

"Home is a country away."

"But now you got this home, too."

Robert didn't want pity exactly, and he certainly didn't want to be told how to feel. He should have never let Jerome anywhere near the purple-haired girl. No one outside that apartment building needed to know what his brother had done. Alone, Robert could have hidden her words away. "We were a family."

"You're still a family."

"Bullshit."

"You've still got your mom. You've got Bridget. You've got Sammy and Deacon. And, man, you got you. Sounds like a family to me."

"You don't know. You never met him." Robert hated himself like this. He hated Jerome for being here, bringing it out of him. He didn't want to feel better. Better was the least honest way he could possibly feel. "Sean was the one who mattered."

"I don't know him, but I know you."

"So?"

"So? You matter."

"Whatever."

"Who else is holding your family together? Who else takes care of the babies while your mom's buying groceries, or helps Bridget tie her shoes when your mom leaves for work? I don't see Sean doing those things. I see you doing them."

Jerome had no right to lay that on him: the family. Robert was never strong enough to carry that weight. He heard himself sneering, "Like you understand."

"You think I don't?"

"You don't know shit."

"What the hell has gotten into you?"

"You. I'm sick of you sticking your nose into my business all the time. You think I don't see? You think I don't know what you're doing? It's just too much fun watching a white boy suffer. You're not going to miss one little minute of it."

"You think that's why I'm here? Cause you're so damned entertaining?"

Robert just stared at the wall, refusing to utter another word. They had wasted a whole month looking for Sean already, and all they uncovered was pain. Matilda had known, he realized. She would have kept him back, protected him from himself. Jerome, the one who was supposed to be his friend, had pushed him deeper in. But Jerome wasn't the one about to have some debt collector down his throat. Jerome wasn't the one whose life was teetering into uncertainty. Robert wasn't about to try to explain.

"You need to check yourself. You really do." Jerome snatched up his backpack and slammed his way out the door. The emptiness expanded around Robert, pressing steadily from his gut into the evening. Outside, a siren grew louder, louder, then faded away.

Robert stared at his homework, but he couldn't get his mind off Jerome long enough for the problems to make sense. Fucking know-it-all. Knew everything about Philadelphia. Knew everything about the Chum. Knew everything about babies. And now? Knew everything about Robert. Knew everything about Sean dodging his debts and running around on his wife. He sat there talking like his stupid words could pull Robert through this mess, like he knew how. Probably could whiz through this math too, since he knew so much.

Sean always gave everyone anything that would make them happy. That's what Jerome didn't know. Sean never cared if that giving hurt him. The girl probably threw herself at him, desperate for his affection. And he'd given it to her because giving was what he did. Generosity was supposed to be a virtue.

The math book stared blankly back. All the angles were incongruous. "Right" had lost meaning in any context. He felt like Mr. Burns was standing—no, looming—just behind his shoulder, waiting for him to prove he could do it, watching him fail. Robert needed to get out of his own head for a while. He needed to silence the incessant noise of his thoughts.

Beside him on the couch, Sammy rolled from belly to

back. Robert caught him before he rolled himself off the couch altogether. He sat Sammy on his lap and looked into his eyes. "How is it that you guys are twins, but you can roll over and Deacon can't?"

Sammy bounced and smiled back at Robert. He wasn't a snuggler. That was Deacon. Like his father, Sammy was always moving. He had Sean's nose, too. Robert hated himself for noticing, but there it was, plain on the boy's face. Sammy might be pudgy, but his nose was long and straight and narrow without any trace of Robert's hook. What else had the little guy inherited? The charm? The selfishness disguised as selflessness? He was a baby. He hadn't done anything. Yet there it was, the genetics of leaving, passed down from father to son.

Robert laid Sammy down again and looked at his math. His mother clattered in the kitchen, frying up a quick dinner of eggs, bacon, and canned baked beans—things that didn't need their broken oven. In a minute, he'd get up to fix the toast, but first, he wanted to solve at least one problem.

As if Jerome had the right to be mad! The numbers blurred. *He* was the one who butted in. He was the one who had forced Robert to take him along when he wasn't needed, always so sure Robert couldn't handle a thing on his own.

"We're doing triangles in school, too!" Bridget leaned over his book.

"Yeah, well, somehow I don't think it's quite the same thing." He looked up and read the hurt on his sister's face. He was too hard on her. Too hard on Jerome, on Sean, on everybody, maybe. Robert sighed and threw his arm around her. "What are you learning about triangles, Bridget?"

"They have three sides," she said, her voice small and hesitant. "We look for them around us, but they're harder to find than rectangles."

"Do you see any in this room?"

"The ones in your book, silly."

Robert smiled in spite of himself. "Those ones are easy."

"There's some." She pointed to the quilt draped over the back of their lemon-colored couch hiding the darkness on the sofa back, so many years of resting, oily heads. "Tell me about your triangles," said Bridget.

"What do you want to know?"

"What's your homework? What do you have to do with them?"

"I don't know if you're going to understand it. There's a lot of math between what you're learning and what I'm learning."

"Tell me."

Robert caught Sammy as he tried to roll himself off the couch again and sat him in his lap. The little guy looked pleased with himself. Sean's touchdown smile dimpled his chin and cheeks. Robert moved the book from his knee to the coffee table to make more room for Sammy. Bridget plopped herself next to them, and he told her about triangles, hypotenuses and legs, angles and formulas. He realized, as he spoke, that he knew the answer to the first problem. Why had it even seemed hard? He helped Bridget solve the angle, talking her through the steps, multiplying and adding for her.

"I guess they better clear the desk next to me," he said. "You're ready for high school math."

Bridget beamed, and her pride made Robert laugh out loud. "Come on, turkey. Let's help Mom."

Deacon had curled himself in the corner of the crib, gumming his little finger. "You been awake this whole time, little man?" A string of drool fell down Robert's shirt as he lifted the baby to his shoulder. "I think he's got some teeth coming in," he called to his mother, carrying him into the kitchen.

"If he does, he's being awfully quiet about it." She put her arm around Robert's shoulder. When he leaned in, she pecked him on the cheek. It felt nice. It felt like family.

A thudding knock startled them all. Jerome, maybe.

"I'll get it," his mother said, wiping her hands the rest of the way dry on her skirt. "Fix something for the boys, will you?"

In a minute, he would go apologize. He owed Jerome that. He got out a can of green beans for each baby and handed Bridget a spoon. "You want Sammy or Deacon this time?"

"Sammy. Deacon always bites and won't let go."

"That's because he's part velociraptor."

Bridget rolled her eyes, too old for that joke, but he saw her smile too. He listened for Jerome's voice, but someone else was speaking, the voice too deep to make out clearly from here. He'd have to save his apology, but it would keep. The twins looked happy. They ate quickly, Deacon taking longer because, like Bridget said, he always bit the spoon.

His mother hurried back into the kitchen. "Who is it?" Robert asked.

"Our neighbor."

"The biker?"

"Shush." She rifled through a cabinet. "He's still there."

Robert had almost forgotten him lately—and the girlfriend that had disappeared weeks ago. Robert lowered his voice to match his mother's. "What's he want?"

"Flour."

"Flour?"

"Flour."

"No one borrows flour. That only happens on TV." Robert fought to imagine any reason a murderer could need flour. Could you cut drugs with it? Sell them for a higher profit—could you do that? Or maybe it was a trap for another murderer who had been trying to spy on him! The biker would sprinkle flour on his floor. Anyone sneaking in would leave footprints, and he'd know he'd been infiltrated.

Afterward, his mother said nothing more about their neighbor. She called them to the table to eat while the twins thumped on their high chair trays.

"Do you think they miss Sean and Angela?" he asked.

Their mother froze, a spatula full of eggs still in her hand, hovering over a plate. "What do you mean?"

"The boys. They're happy. Do you think they know their parents aren't coming back?"

"Sean will come back."

"It's been a month, Mom. A month."

"Bridget, come to the table."

"What if he doesn't?"

His mother turned to the beans, flicking spoonfuls onto each plate. Everything about the way she held her body told him to stop talking, but he couldn't seem to shut up.

"Do you think we're a family—a whole family, I mean— even if Sean and Angela don't come back?"

"Robert, I don't care to discuss this right now."

Bridget said, "A family is a mommy, a daddy, a boy, and a girl."

"That's only one kind of family," Robert said. "We're another."

"I said, that's enough. Sean will be back."

"But, I mean, we *could* be a family, even if he doesn't come back."

"One more word and you skip dinner."

He fell silent. For a long while, there was no noise but the scraping of plates and the banging of baby fists. Robert's mind, though, would not be quiet. "You know, we don't have to stay in Philadelphia. We could go back."

"Sean will look for us here."

"Or not."

"He will."

"He's not coming, Mom."

"I'm not entertaining this discussion."

"You're not facing facts."

"That's it." She swept his plate away. "You're done."

"Why is it so hard for you to deal with reality?"

"Because it isn't reality, and you're scaring your sister." His plate clattered in the sink. "If you want to be in this foul mood, you can go do it in your room."

"Fine." He shoved his chair back under the table. It must have driven his father crazy, her silence, the way she sealed her lips tight as an oyster. As if everything that needed to be said had been said.

He couldn't think of one time his parents had argued. His father always just smiled and joked. Except maybe in those moments late in the evening when he concentrated all his thoughts into the banjo, his fingers digging down into the strings to pull the music out.

Maybe his father had liked his mother's silence. Maybe he had loved it. He'd been gone less than a year. Robert hated himself for not paying enough attention to know. It was impossible, now, to imagine him into the Philadelphia apartment. Impossible to know how he'd react to Sean's vanishing, what he would or would not say. His dad left that final morning like he always did, not saying goodbye or I love you or any of that crap because why would you say those things when you'd be back? He just hopped in the old Buick with his lunch sack, cranked it up, and went to die.

FRONTS

Their mother was reading Bridget her bedtime story when, again, the door began thudding. Robert busied himself with English, trying to make his way through some poet who twisted words into puzzles only their teacher could solve. His mother could get it. Probably could use a break, since she was so busy facing reality and all.

More thudding.

"Get the door, Robert."

He threw himself off his bed, displaying the maximum amount of annoyance as he undid the bolt so he wouldn't have to admit that he was maybe just a little scared to open the door at night.

The biker stood with a loaf pan wrapped in a checkered dish-towel. "Banana bread," he said. "Thought you guys could use some."

Warmth seeped through the cotton into Robert's hands. He should say something, he knew, but every word in his head had scurried away like cockroaches from the light. He should smile, at least, or offer his hand, or maybe a handshake would be weird? And anyway, just because a guy made banana bread, it didn't mean he was safe.

Except maybe he was.

The biker turned and unlocked his own door. "Thank you," Robert finally remembered to say.

"Don't mention it."

ANGELA

That night, Robert lay in his bed thinking of Angela. She was like a beautiful gun. It never took much for her to go off. After the move, Sean and Angela had called to ask if Robert wanted to go to the mall, not to shop but to hang out. They figured he'd be bored now that the family's few boxes were unpacked.

Robert had never been to a mall without a shopping agenda. Before school each fall, their mom would take them to JC Penney for two pairs of jeans, four t-shirts, a hoodie, and a flannel. They went in, found things in his size, bought them, and left. He thought everyone shopped that way, with a plan and an exit strategy. Why go look at stuff you couldn't afford and didn't need? And why, in a city so large, did they have to travel so long to reach a mall? It must have been an hour on the bus from Center City.

The Gallery Mall was a modern-day palace with a soaring glass ceiling and mosaic tile floors that were open in the center so that you could see everything at once over the iron balconies. Each level stretched endlessly, filled with light and sound, connected by escalators that seemed to extend right up to heaven itself. Some of the stores sold normal stuff, but others were dedicated to things Robert couldn't imagine anyone buying. They took turns trying a three-thousand-dollar massage chair and laid their hands on globes filled with lightning.

Afterwards, Robert waited at the bus stop with Sean and

Angela thinking about how, if you had enough money, you could be a wizard or a king.

They had laughed at him, his brother and sister-in-law, because he didn't know about bus numbers and he'd stepped on the wrong bus. If they hadn't pulled him back, God only knew where he'd have ended up. "You think you can just hop on any bus and it'll take you wherever you want?"

"Go easy on him," Angela had said. "We just have to show him around. He'll get it."

Robert loved how, when she laughed, her face crinkled and her nose scrunched up over the bridge.

"*There's* the one we want," she said, but as Robert was about to step on board, an elderly white man cut in front of him, not bothering even to say excuse me.

Robert wouldn't have made an issue of it. The bus had plenty of open seats. If he'd noticed the man waiting, if he'd had eyes for anyone other than Angela, he would have stepped aside out of respect for the guy's age.

Angela didn't see it that way. No. Angela considered it rude, a slight. She took it personally. Her eyes narrowed, and in that instant, Robert felt something inside her building. She grew taller than the five foot one she was. At the same time, she grew in, condensed, became potent, and then—

"What the hell do you think you're doing?" She grabbed the old man by the elbow. He must have been in his seventies at least—thin and unsteady—but none of that mattered to her. She pulled him back off the bus step. His thin, white hair, so carefully combed back, fell forward in greasy strands. "You," Angela told him, "can wait your turn like everybody else."

Shock filled the old man's eyes. More than shock, he realized. Fear. Robert, too, was shocked, but also strangely flattered and grateful. She cared enough to stick up for him. Even as the old man shrugged his shoulder out of her hand, took a step back, set his jaw, straightened his windbreaker, and made a sarcastic "after you" gesture, something was missing. The old guy simply wasn't man enough for her.

Angela never gave an inch. She stepped up after Robert, scanned her bus pass, and walked down the aisle like a queen. The plastic seat was a throne with her glowering in it. She stared down the old man, the last passenger to board, and, as he looked for a place, she wrapped her arm around Robert's shoulder, the side of her breast kissing his bicep. "Some people," she said as the man walked by, "have no fucking manners."

They knew how to live here, Sean and Angela. They fit in. Robert remembered the shirts Angela picked out for him to try on that afternoon—garish, expensive, and three sizes too big. Sean wanted to buy them. He'd just put them on the plastic, he'd said, but Robert refused. The kids in the neighborhood? Their clothes seemed to enlarge them, but in the store mirror's reflection, Robert saw only a gangly kid drowning in fabric. His neck looked thinner, his elbows more awkward, and his skin more fish-belly white. It was a relief to return the clothes to the racks.

He had to be eight inches taller than Angela, but sitting next to her on the bus that day, it hadn't felt like that. She seemed to look down on him kindly from the height of years as she cupped his chin in her hand and ran the side of her thumb down his cheek. "You're going to break some fucking hearts when school starts," she said in her lispy, working class accent.

Strong and beautiful as she was, Sean couldn't have cheated on her. He couldn't have, but he did.

THE FLAGPOLE

Robert arrived early the next morning, ready to eat crow. "I'm sorry," he would say. "I was a jerk," or maybe "an asshole," "a dickweed," "a turd." He tossed around possibilities as he waited on Jerome's stoop. And waited. The stone got harder by the minute. At this rate, they were going to be late. LeRoi passed and nodded his usual good morning but, being behind schedule himself, did not stop to talk. His mailbag thumped his thigh with each dipping step. Robert was just about to get up and knock when Jerome's sister put her head out the door. Large, stiff curls fell over her eyes. "You know Jerome left already, right?" she asked.

"No."

"Well, he did," she said, and shut the door.

For the first time, Robert walked to Garvey alone. September was almost gone. In a month, his dad would be dead a whole year. The morning was dull and gray, humid but not hot anymore. Grass broke through the cracks in the sidewalk. No one cared. If anyone gave the Chum a thought, then men working for the city, men like his dad, would be here with shovels and herbicides clearing it up. They would spray weeds and patch broken edges or, better still, replace the damaged concrete slabs altogether, and everything would look cared for and clean.

Robert was glad they left the weeds alone. He appreciated the grass for its determination. Philly had slowly paved over every green piece of itself, but the grass would not be denied. There was something to be said for persisting where you weren't supposed to be. The Chum might not have some green canopy of trees or soft dirt underfoot, but nature (crows, squirrels, pigeons, rats) survived here anyway, on whatever terms the city offered. Funny how people saw these things as weeds and pests. That was how people felt about what they couldn't kill.

Robert walked a little straighter and faster. The others at school could say he ate farm boy bread. They could ask where he kept his horse and boots. The turkey on whole wheat that he once again carried in his backpack was now a badge of honor. He and Jerome were weeds, pests, things that persisted.

The air around Garvey was humming. A crowd pressed so thick that Robert couldn't see his way to the steps. Once he found Jerome, he could apologize and tell him his new theory, but the entire school swarmed. Perhaps someone had pulled the fire alarm or called in a bomb threat. Maybe the metal detectors flanking the doors had malfunctioned. He scanned the faces, thinking at least he could find Ricky, who would know what was what, which was when he noticed that the crowd's attention was focused in the wrong direction.

Whatever was going down, Robert wanted no part of it. That kind of laughter was always at someone's expense. He pushed his way up the stairs towards the entrance when he overheard a guy ask, "Who is it?" and another answer, "That one sophomore faggot."

Robert froze, the crush of bodies pressing him one way, then another, moving him like kelp in the tide. The guy could have been describing any number of sophomores. He looked towards the flagpole, but all he could see through the crowd were the hats of two police officers forging their way in. Robert, too, turned into the current. He couldn't see anything, but he pushed deeper, submerging himself in the crowd.

Ahead, he heard Dr. Turner shouting for everyone to go inside—or trying to. She was a small woman whose mouth was too wide for her face, and her voice was thin and reedy. He could hardly hear her through the wall of people. She yelled like someone trying to stay calm in the center of a hurricane. Her poorly veiled hysteria only excited people, calling them to the storm's eye. "Inside!" she pleaded. "I need you to go inside. Come on now."

The crowd was thicker here, so thick Robert had to force his face between shoulders and shove his way in. He felt his backpack stripped from his body, but he couldn't worry about that now. His ribs were crushed on every side so that he could barely breathe, but he had to know. Ahead, he saw a small circle of daylight and made his push. He caught a glimpse through elbows, and again shoved his way forward.

Jerome was handcuffed to the flagpole, his pants puddled around his ankles, revealing his tighty-whities. Where they were still clean, their bleached cotton glared in the sun, but the hips and butt were grass-stained and dirty. His legs looked thinner unclothed. Black and blue eye makeup ran in blurred streaks down his face, and his lips were smeared with a violent red lipstick. A blonde wig rested on his shoulder, presumably where it had fallen from his head, though it refused to shake off. Some of his own braids remained neat, but others were torn out, his hair sticking up, a patchy, bloodied mess.

Someone's arm clocked Robert's cheek, and he blinked his vision clear.

Under the limp flag, one policeman stooped to pick up Jerome's glasses from where they glinted in the dirt, remarkably unbroken. He pocketed them as he fumbled for the key for his cuffs. Jerome jerked again and again against the pole, tears shaking down his face with every convulsion.

Around Robert, people trembled with laughter, charged with the sight of a nearly naked boy. "It's not a flagpole," someone said. "It's a *fag*pole. Get it? A *fag*pole."

The officer unlocked the cuffs, but Jerome only fell to the ground, refusing to move. Dr. Turner lifted him by the armpits, but he only sagged in her arms like a sack, unable to hold the weight of so many staring eyes. And so she let him fall again. She struggled out of her sunflower-patterned blazer, wrapped him in it, and tried again.

Her jacket was the wrong kind of cover. In sunflowers, Jerome was only more gay, only more broken. Robert felt his breakfast coming up, and for a moment, he was certain he would puke all over everyone around him. When he didn't, he felt half guilty. Puking was the one thing he could have done that would have taken the focus off Jerome.

Above, the flag cracked like a whip, startling Robert into focus. Jerome hadn't seen him, and Robert couldn't get away fast enough. He couldn't stand the idea of himself as another bystander who did nothing but stand by—no, worse, who added weight to the crowd. Better for Jerome to think that no one who knew him had been a part of that hateful crowd. Better to think that none of his friends would have the memory of him crying in sagging, dirt-marked underpants. Better that this all be private, unspoken. That way, he would be allowed to pretend to forget.

Robert shoved his shoulder between two fat girls, forcing his way through their huddled, fast-lipped gossip. "Don't touch my boob, perv," one shrieked, but Robert didn't stop to apologize. Now that the police had penetrated to the center of things and Jerome was covered and uncuffed, the crowd loosened. Robert found his backpack, trampled flat and covered with dusty shoe prints, and made his way to biology.

At lunch, Robert sat alone and inspected his sandwich. The turkey had slid to one slide, the tomato to the other. The bread had practically disintegrated. He bit into it and chewed. All his big theories about the resilience of pests were crushed. Jerome had to be in hell.

Some kid was laughing about the lipstick. "Fool be mugging like a fucked up clown."

Robert couldn't bear to eat even a bite. He threw his lunch, uneaten, in the trash. At his locker, he stared at the spines of his textbooks, trying to think what he would need. To his right, he could see the guy from biology, the one with the varsity letter, pressed up against Keesha Bates, who never passed Jerome a note. The guy's hand was under her thin shirt, cupping her breast openly as he kissed her neck. She groaned, her body grinding against his. Robert looked again into his locker. The words on his textbooks had no meaning. A warning bell rang, but he continued to stare as the hallway emptied around him. World History, Biology, Economics: they were all just combinations of letters. They didn't make any sense. None of those books held anything he needed to learn.

The final bell. Still he stood. There was a right thing to do, and whatever it was, it occurred to him that this wasn't it.

He jammed his backpack in the locker and slammed the door. Someone should stop him, demand a hall pass, something, but no one even noticed. He walked with his head up through the metal detectors, wondering why he had taken so long to find the courage to leave.

Robert banged on the Anderson's front door, wanting to make himself heard over the television talk show that blared through the old oak slab. Jerome's sister answered, a baby on her hip. "You supposed to be in school."

"I need to see Jerome."

"He's sick."

"He can see me."

Her eyes rested on Robert for a long minute, and he realized, to his surprise, that she didn't trust him, and he wondered if it was because he was white. "Come back tomorrow," she said, and swung the door.

Robert's foot stopped its swing before he knew what he was doing. His mouth wouldn't form a single word.

Their eyes rested on each other.

"Okay," she finally said, turning back to the TV. "You know where his room's at."

Jerome lay on his bed, staring at the ceiling. He didn't look over as Robert walked in. He didn't smear away the tears drying on his cheeks. The whole world's cruelty pressed into the room, the entire thing shoved into a space barely bigger than a closet. A weight so heavy Robert felt his chest might be crushed, no way to breathe or speak.

"Guess you heard," Jerome said. When there was no answer, he added, "Guess everybody heard."

Robert sat on the floor and leaned his head against the solid side of the bureau. The enormity was too much. They sat in its presence as vampires watched from the walls.

Finally, Robert asked, "You know who did it?"

Jerome didn't answer at first, then said, "You sound like the cops."

Robert waited.

Jerome dashed a fist across his eyes. "They wore masks."

"Masks?"

"Yeah. You believe that shit? Like we were on TV or something. They didn't say anything the entire time. Not even one word. They just laughed."

The detail seemed off. Surely, they would have had to say something, at least to one another to coordinate their actions. "You think it was Maurice?"

"Did you not just hear me? How am I supposed to know?" He crushed his eyes closed until he grew calm. "They jumped me from behind."

"If they jumped you from behind, when did you see the masks?"

"You come here to interrogate me?"

"It's just, if it *was* Maurice—"

"It wasn't."

"But if it was?"

"Leave it be."

Robert stared at dripping fangs. The dead rose again and again. Against any one of them, you had to go with a wooden stake and a steel gut and kill those fuckers all the way or they only came at you again and harder. They brought backup and laid elaborate plans. All the garlic and crosses in the world didn't matter after that point—he'd seen it on *Slayers* with Jerome every week. Cross a vampire, and you were doomed.

Only, Maurice was just a guy. He might look all mythic badass with his muscles and his smooth t-shirts, but so had Sean and look how human he turned out to be.

"You didn't wait for me this morning," Robert said.

"So it's my fault now?"

"No. It's not your fault." Robert closed his eyes and willed the aching smaller until he could speak again. "I'm just—" He stopped and restarted, "I'm just saying that if they try it again, they're going to have to deal with both of us."

"There were four of them. You think two can take on four? Four who fight dirty? Four who are strong? Four who ain't doing this for the first time? Four who got friends and can make themselves twenty-four if they need to? After all you seen, you still don't get it."

"But—"

"We put our heads down and lay low. Understand? That's how to survive."

Robert could see it was the right advice, even if it didn't feel right. If his father had just stayed in the car, they would still be in Oregon. "You watching *Slayers* tonight?"

"Duh."

Robert lifted the model plane Jerome had displayed on his shelf and examined its perfect seams. "What would you do if the police caught them?"

"Nothing."

"You wouldn't say anything even then?"

Jerome turned his face to the wall.

That night, under the new moon, Robert's room was dark and the streets outside were as silent as they ever got. Only the faint glow and the dull, wet rush of the occasional passing car leaked in through the window glass to mark the flow of time. A few hours ago, after another phone call, he had thought he'd heard his mother crying.

He had no idea what the hour was, but it was late. Deep in the middle of the middle of the night, he thought, and rolled the words around in his head, wondering if the line would work as a song lyric. His mother was quiet now, having gone to bed, and he should have been sleeping too, but his mind would not shut down. It skipped from one thought to another so that he felt like an engine revving rather than slowing to a stop. *Busy brain*, his father called it when work stress had him pacing the floors in the late night or early morning. He would get up and watch one of his old movies with the volume low. No point to staying in bed not sleeping.

But in their small apartment, Robert had no choice but to stay in his bedroom. He pulled the banjo from under the bed and pressed a pillow against its neck so that he could touch the strings in silence.

Jerome's sister had re-braided his hair that night as they watched Slayers, her red nails parting his hair, her fingers quick and nimble. She'd been at it for an hour before Robert arrived, and he wondered now how many evenings she spent doing his hair so that it looked so neat. She was gentle with the comb and murmured to him as she worked, letting Jerome know when there was a knot she needed to tease out. He'd never before seen her tenderness. Watching, Robert wanted to be a little brother again. He missed the feel of his own brother's strong hands mussing his red hair, the motion saying there were larger forces in the world, and that if you were small, so much the better: they could carry you.

When Jerome came back to school, the boyfriend talk

would begin in earnest. Tomorrow or the next day, they would walk into Garvey, Jerome's hand knocking his, and it would mean more than it had yesterday. Because he was gay and now everyone knew.

No. Robert's fingers bit harder into the muffled strings. No! Jerome had been excited to get Keesha's phone number. He wanted to play football to make the girls love him too much.

A helicopter passed over the head, its searchlight briefly illuminating the room.

Maurice would sneer at these thoughts. Of course, Jerome said all the right things, but only a fool bought in to all that fronting. Robert could hear Maurice talking to him now, *Just how big a dumb ass are you?*

But then, wouldn't he be just as big a fool to buy what Maurice said? Robert picked faster, and the tips of his fingers stung against the strings.

One of them was lying. That left two possibilities: Jerome was gay or Jerome was not. If he was not, nothing anyone said mattered. And if he was gay?

Robert stopped playing and stared at the walls.

If he was? Could Robert really walk out on his only friend? Say that everything Maurice said was true. Say that Jerome was lying awake at this very moment, just across the street, thinking of the boys he liked, dreaming of them as Robert dreamed of Angela. Jerome was still his friend. Okay, yes, if Jerome made a move on him or something, then they would have to deal with that, but he never had so far. How was being friends with a gay guy any different than his friendship with Lara Lynn had been? He wasn't interested in romance there, either, but if she had been, then he would have figured things out. There wasn't any point in trying to stop a problem that didn't exist.

None of this thinking solved the problem of appearance,

of Maurice, of the things people said. There were places in the world where a gay guy and a straight guy could be friends and it wouldn't have mattered. Seattle, Portland, Eugene—there were surely even places like that in other neighborhoods in Philly. Places where people were open-minded and accepting and cool. He just hadn't lived in any of those places.

In Herman, one of the marching band (the flautist?) was tackled in the locker room and some guys shoved a stick of deodorant up his ass so far he'd had to go to the ER to have it removed. The school could say "tolerance, tolerance" all it wanted, but that kind of thing taught a different lesson. In Herman, you adopted a logger swagger. Here, you carried the street. Either place, people saw being gay as a kind of weakness, but now that he thought about it, Robert couldn't imagine anything more fierce than being exactly and honestly who you were when everyone around you expected some other kind of act.

So he would never be cool if he hung out with Jerome. So what? He'd never been cool anywhere. Gay or straight, Jerome was the best friend he'd ever had. Robert again saw Jerome crumpled at the base of the flagpole, synthetic hair sticking to his smeared lipstick. Robert saw himself there.

He let those thoughts settle like dust. Deep in the middle of the middle of the night—he plucked one combination of strings after another, searching for the rhythm and sound.

THE DAY AFTER

Robert stared. His skin hung so tired and heavy that it felt like it might slide off his skull and leave a puddle of face on the sidewalk. GAYROME had been spray-painted on the stoop in large blue letters.

Jerome was late, and when he finally came out, he had the drooping look of someone who hadn't slept either. He barely glanced at the words. His expression didn't change, not a flinch, not a flicker. He simply turned his feet towards school and said, "Just so you know, I don't want to talk about it."

"Okay."

"My sister's been going on nonstop, telling me how much better I'll feel if I just let it all out. Bullshit. I don't need to go on reliving it."

"There's other stuff to talk about."

"There is."

They walked several blocks not uttering a word. There may have been other stuff to talk about, but Robert couldn't think of a single thing. His mind kept circling back like a buzzard to a carcass. He couldn't remember now whether the flag had been raised or what the police officers looked like or whether their voices were kind. He wondered who had been the first person to arrive and what they had done when they saw Jerome, whether they laughed or called for help or fled, and, after that first person saw, how fast the crowd had grown. He wondered where Maurice—or, he reminded himself, whoever—had jumped Jerome and how much it hurt when the shining metal handcuffs slapped across the thin bones of his wrists and just how long Jerome was bound, but he knew the answer to that last question. Eternity. Nothing less.

Jerome said, "You still want to find your brother?"

Robert stole a glance, trying to read his friend's face. After everything, he couldn't believe he was bringing up Sean now. They had hit the wall. There was nothing more to learn. It was over. "He's probably clear across the country by now."

"You sure?" Jerome's voice was dead level, full of the steady authority of a teacher who's letting you know that you got the answer wrong, but wants to give you another chance.

"It's not important anymore."

"Because of yesterday?"

When Robert didn't answer, Jerome grabbed his arm and dragged them both to a stop. His fingers dug into the meat of Robert's arm and his eyes fixed on Robert's, the desperation in his stare commanding full attention. "Look, man, you got to give me something else to think about. I don't got any more space in my head for yesterday."

Robert replied as gently as he could. "There's nowhere else to look."

"I've been thinking about that girl." Jerome paused as if Robert would follow this statement with some kind of epiphany, but Robert didn't want to think about her.

"Look," Jerome said. "Break it down. You said Angela left."

"Her and Sean. We've talked this to death. They could be anywhere on the planet."

"No. That's where we messed up. That girl didn't think Angela was gone. She thought you'd talked to her."

"So?"

"So, Angela's here. She's in Philly."

"Mom already called Leona. She'd know where Angela is if anyone did."

"Knowing and saying are two different things. What if her mom only *said* she was gone? What if Angela went home?"

"Home?"

"That's where my sister went when her man cheated. Straight home. Now we got to live with her."

The bottom dropped out of Robert's stomach. It slid into his feet, sloshing against his toes. "You think she's that close? And she hasn't visited her own kids?"

"She wouldn't be the first mama to leave her babies and not look back."

"But her own family covering for her?"

"It fits what we know."

Robert kicked a broken bit of concrete, sending it skittering down the sidewalk.

Jerome kept talking: "Saw a show on stray cats last night—crazy what shit you find on TV at two a.m. It's what got me thinking. It said, when a cat goes missing, most people can't find them because they're looking too far away. The cat's usually close. Under a porch. In a drain. They're scared and don't know what to do, so they find a hole and stay put. I think maybe Angela holed up just like one of those cats."

Robert's thoughts settled and arranged themselves like a kind of brain furniture. They were oddly comfortable. "You been thinking about this all night?"

"Beats thinking of other things."

"Hidden in plain sight."

"You think I'm right? You think she's at her mom's house?"

"Only one way to find out."

No one said much to Jerome that day. They stared, and their stares enforced some kind of quarantine zone. Through it all, Jerome kept his eyes up and level and refused to notice, though of course he did notice. Like Robert, he felt the staring in his gut, a bottomed-out, sunk-stone kind of feeling. They didn't talk about this.

On the way to pick up Bridget, they strategized. Robert didn't know Leona's address, but it would be in his mother's address book. And then what? A stakeout? The cops on TV always had cars or empty apartments for their stakeouts—not to mention money for Cokes and hoagies.

Bridget waited on the front steps of her school, scuffing her sandals and sighing in a full display of showy boredom. She pretended not to see them until they were inches away, treating them to the whole performance. "You're always late when you come with Jerome."

"It's only five after."

"I can walk by myself. I know the way."

"Mom says to wait for me or Miss Martha."

"Mom's at work. She'd never even know."

"She'd find out. And then she'd kill you, and then she'd kill me. I don't know about you, Bridge, but I'm too young to die."

Bridget surged ahead for the rest of the block to show them she knew what she was doing.

"You run too far ahead and the green man will get you," Robert called.

"Like you know about the green man," she replied, but she slowed.

At Jerome's, Robert and Bridget waited near the door while Jerome rummaged through the cabinets for chips. His older sister was on the couch, flanked by two of his younger brothers, her baby sleeping on the recliner. She stared at the high heel that dangled from the ends of her painted toes, the shoe as liquid red as the nail polish. The television's cartoon colors danced across the surface of each. "You get beat up again today?" she asked her brother, not bothering to pull her eyes from the screen.

Jerome ignored her. With the thick curtains drawn across the windows, the dark room was lit only by the flickering blue glow of Batman fighting Sandman in a city not so different from Philly.

Once, Robert had shocked himself on a hot wire fence. For days, his hand buzzed electric, as if his skin couldn't figure out how to dispel the energy it had absorbed. The room felt like that now. Every corner sang with charge. "Let's get out of here," he said.

But Jerome's sister wasn't done. "You can't let them treat you like that. You got to fight back."

"Everybody knows so much about what I *got* to do and how I *got* to be."

"Beat 'em up, man," one of his brothers said, his eyes not leaving the TV screen.

His sister nodded. "They only be picking on you if they think they can."

Bridget was tapping Robert's hand furiously, as if sending him code that it was time to leave, but Jerome was rooted to the floor, his fist so tight on the chips that it looked ready to burst at any moment. "You don't know nothing about it."

"I was in high school."

"You dropped out of high school. Don't you go telling me how to make it through."

"I dropped out to get a job and support your broke ass. Nobody beat me up and chased me out."

"You dropped out cause you're too stupid not to get yourself pregnant."

The electricity zinged louder; the chip bag strained at the seams. Robert threw open the door, allowing the harsh afternoon sun to light its tractor beam through the depressing darkness to his friend.

"I'm trying to help you," his sister called as he walked out.

"Everybody's got advice."

Bridget walked slowly for a while, stealing glances at Jerome. Robert supposed it was good for her, seeing that not all families worked the same way. Their own might not talk, but maybe that wasn't so bad compared to all the words filling the rooms around Jerome, shoving him this way and that.

They dropped Bridget at Veronica's and were making their way to the plywood door when they saw the car at the alley's end, an old, black Mercedes that oozed a kind of tempered class. It idled or purred or growled there, low on its tires, as an arm shot out and tossed a paper bag that clattered on the pavement. That done, it slunk away.

Robert and Jerome looked at one another. They didn't need to say a word to know they would find out what was in that bag. They dashed to grab it and pushed their way under the plywood. Its creak provoked frantic scurrying in the darkness. Robert scrambled to find the flashlight, praying his hand hit it before it hit something furry, warm, and toothed.

"I hope those rats don't like potato chips," he said.

"They'd be some kind of fool rats if they don't."

Robert shoved a handful into his mouth. The chips were broken and greasy, over-salted and delicious. He said, "So what is it?"

Jerome unfolded the top where the paper sack had been crushed shut. The flashlight made the sack into a luminary like the ones Robert's mother made every year until his father died, lining their driveway on Halloween even though they lived too far out for kids to trick-or-treat. Only, this paper lamp kept a shadow whose shape Robert could make out without Jerome saying a word. "...Is that?"

"Fuck, man."

Jerome drew a handgun from the bag. It looked nothing like the pistols in Robert's father's westerns, pearl-handled six-guns slung low on the cowboy's hips. It wasn't black or silver, but the dull, brownish color of dog turds. Neither Dirty Harry nor John Wayne carried a gun like this. No, this was a street gun, a back-pocket gun, small and square-barreled. Its presence was its own kind of silencer, and Robert's voice came out as a whisper. "Is it real?"

Jerome's fingers suddenly pulled back, dropping it into the paper bag. "Probably got a body on it."

"A body?"

"Why else dump it unless they used it to murder someone?"

Robert grabbed the bag and pulled the gun out. He stared at it, turning it over in his hands, then wiped it furiously with his t-shirt as to polish it.

"Careful," Jerome said. "It could be loaded."

Robert fumbled, almost dropping it. "How do we tell?"

"Do I look like I know?"

Robert caressed it now, stroking it as softly as he'd once imagined stroking Angela's hair. He liked the hard lines of it. He rested it in his hand, holding its weight. It was deadly, but it was in his hands. He could control it.

"We should turn it in," Jerome said.

"It's probably the right thing to do."

"You sound like you don't believe it."

"It's just..." Robert sighed. "Maybe we could put it away for a while."

"Put it—what if some kid finds it? You want that on your head?"

"We'll hide it. No one has to know."

Jerome looked at him sideways. "Pass me the chips."

They passed the chip bag back and forth, the gun sitting between them, until every crumb was gone and they'd licked every crystal of salt from their fingers, and then they eased back against the wall in the small halo of the flashlight.

The rustling edged closer. Jerome turned the light on a fat, gray rat in the corner. The beads of its eyes glinted, looking anything but frightened. Robert grabbed a hunk of concrete from the pile they'd made. He would throw the rock at the rat's feet, scaring it back to its hole. He felt the hunk's weight and balance, enjoying the grittiness in his palm. His body acted of its own accord. As he cocked his arm, he lost the awkwardness he'd always known and the muscles coiled and uncoiled in a vicious whip that sent the rock flying at a speed Robert could not believe he had produced. It hit the rat squarely in the middle of its skull, and the thing dropped.

They watched half-expecting it to pop up any moment, angry and hissing, but it didn't move and would never move again. Jerome let forth a slow, steady "Daaaaaaamn." He shone the light on Robert's hand and the rock pile and then again on the rat. "You should try out for baseball."

"I can't throw," Robert said.

"That's not how it looked just now."

"Is it dead?"

"Has to be. You wonked the crap out of that thing. His brains be pudding."

Sean's arm was Sean's arm, not Robert's. Only now, Robert's arm was possessed, his brother invading him. If he had this, what else did he share with his brother? He could have the cheating gene, the-walking-out-on-his-wife gene, the abandoning-his-family-gene. Robert stared at his hand wondering if it was still *his* hand.

"Throw like that? You should try out for pitcher this spring. I'm serious."

A moment ago, the rat had a life. It might have rat babies waiting in the wall, wondering when their dad would be home. "I don't even like sports."

"Think how it would change your status. You ever see an athlete take crap? No. And you won't. Jocks are immune. And the girls hang on them. They don't even have to try."

Before Sean had an arm, their mom had fretted over the clothes he'd worn and his punk music and the way he spiked his hair and the eyeliner he used to mark his face. He'd been a different person. Once he started football, it didn't matter what he did. He might have a preppy haircut and jock clothes, but he got his girlfriend pregnant and their mother still saw him as perfect. Maybe Robert should be glad to find he had that same potential, that same gift. Instead, he wanted to find a hacksaw, press it to his shoulder, and cut away its infection before it spread to his heart.

They should turn the gun in. Jerome was right. He couldn't trust himself with that kind of power, not if he was going to go around killing innocent animals when armed only with rocks.

Even so, he could hear the gun whispering to him from the bag, promising protection, promising power. He had said it himself: they didn't have to decide anything now. Besides, the rock only killed because he threw it. The gun would only do harm if he fired it, and he wasn't going to fire it. He'd just hold it now and then.

Jerome asked, "So where we going to do our stakeout?"

"I don't know. I've never been. Maybe we should check it out first. See if there's some place we can hang out unnoticed. A bench or a bus stop or something."

"You mean we go to stake out our stakeout?"

"You got a better idea?"

The house was quiet around them, muffling the distant city noise. Jerome nodded to the rat. "You got to move that thing."

"I thought we were working on a stakeout."

"Its eyes are watching me, dawg. Sides, you leave that rat in here, this place will be all maggots and flies."

The thought of picking it up, feeling its dead weight in his hand as fleas and whatnot jumped from its dead flesh to his living flesh, made Robert's stomach flop. He slid the gun bag over his hand, using it like a potholder to pick up the dead rat. Its body was still warm and its head drooped towards the floor. With the rat in one hand and the gun in the other, Robert felt like some kind of fucked up old scale. He imagined himself teetering, trying to balance. The weight of the gun was the opposite of the weight of the rat, the difference between power and powerlessness.

He was sick of being a victim. He pushed the gun into the rat hole, knowing no man or child was likely to dare put his hand there.

"We're going about this all wrong."

"The rat?" Jerome asked.

"The stakeout. We don't need to hide."

"Don't wave your hands when you're holding that thing. I can see its teeth."

"Everyone's hiding lately. It's dumb. I'm Angela's brother-in-law and her babies' uncle. I have a right to ask. I'm going right up to Leona's door and knocking."

"If she's been hiding Angela all these weeks, why you think she'll talk now? You think she's going to just hand her over?"

"It doesn't matter what Leona says. It matters how she says it. We'll know."

The biker thundered down the old wooden stairs as Robert entered the building with Bridget that evening. The man's shirt read *Fuck You Numb Nuts* and his expression read *get out of my way* and his jeans were splattered with something that might have been rust or might have been blood. "Hey," he said.

"Hey," Robert managed to reply, pushing Bridget to the other side of him to shield her. The biker pushed his way past and out the building's door, his body as unyielding as the blade of a highway snowplow.

Inside, their mother juggled both babies on her lap and made goo goo faces. Deacon giggled and Sammy smiled around the side of his hand, which he gummed steadily as a long string of drool stretched from his mouth towards her skirt. Robert plopped on the couch next to her and took Deacon.

It was wrong to have favorites among babies. You were supposed to love them all the same—and he did love them, both of them, completely—but there was something different between him and Deacon. Maybe this was how his mom felt about Sean. Maybe, even when he was an infant, she felt his baby self respond to her in a way Robert's baby self did not. Maybe there was something deep there, something different than love, that connected them. Deacon giggled as Robert again and again blew zerberts into his arm.

"You miss me or something?"

"He loves his Uncle Robert."

"He does, doesn't he?" Robert felt taller. Not that a baby's opinion should matter, but then again, why shouldn't it? Who better to decide you were all right than an unbiased baby?

Bridget brought her doll out and sat next to them, an entire family crammed on one small couch. Their mother shifted Sammy, sitting him up on her other leg. "Do you have homework?"

"Mom, it's Friday."

She worried too much. Homework, homework, homework, because someone needed to go to college, someone needed to finish, someone needed a decent job with a decent paycheck so they weren't always scrambling, and by now even she had to accept that that person wasn't going to be Sean. Robert leaned his head on her shoulder and let it lie. He noticed her economizing, regular lettuce and apples instead of organic, generic Cheez Bitz instead of organic veggie chips. He hadn't mentioned anything, afraid to disturb whatever trend had led her to buy normal people food for the first time in his life. He figured she was offsetting the price of the babies' probiotics, diapers, and formula, but there were still the daily phone calls. At meals, she offered him and Bridget seconds, but her own portions were getting smaller, and her cheeks had started to hollow.

"I'm not going to let you down," he said, but even in his own ears, his voice sounded too much like Sean's.

PAPER HOUSES

It had been easy to be sure in the darkness of the abandoned house.

It had been easy to play detective and concoct plans, easy to imagine stakeouts and confrontations. It had been easy until that Monday came, and they boarded a bus heading south through city center towards Leona's.

Even in their decay, there was something stately about the row homes in the Chum. The houses in this section of south Philly were different. The neighborhood outside the bus was like some cheap, cardboard storefront version of his own. It reminded him of a movie set designed to be torn down after the film was shot. The neighborhood hadn't weathered well. Outside the bus, every window was barred. Angry red and black graffiti scarred not only the walls but the iron and glass; painted letters claimed every crumb of turf for *la confraternita mostro*. Mismatched roofing shingles peeled like dark petals straining for light. The houses' exterior brick had been stripped and replaced with some kind of thick, brick-printed tarpaper.

These could have been the houses on the news, the ones with hidden creeks underneath nibbling at their foundations until they were too weak to stand.

The paper houses peeled in long strips. Jerome double-checked the address Robert had given him, cursed quietly, and pulled the bus cord. They had arrived. Robert didn't dare meet Jerome's eye. Alone, he doubted either one of them would dare leave the safety of the bus. Not here. Danger beat through them like blood. He could feel the neighborhood coming at them, its chest pumped out and arms spread. "You think you can fuck with me, homeboy?" Robert stepped off the bus first. A man lay against the side of the building, his eyes vacant and a thread of spittle stretching from his mouth to the pavement. Robert stopped, trying to process this fact: he was staring at a dead man. The glue of the man's trailing stare fixed Robert's Converse to the pavement. A dead man lay on the sidewalk and no one cared enough to spare even a glance. Robert felt he should do something. Feel for a pulse, locate the bullet hole, call for help, something.

The dead man blinked. It was so quick and gone that Robert couldn't make himself believe that he'd actually seen it.

Jerome tugged at his arm. "Junkie. Probably kicked out of the shelter." He nodded to a squat, olive-colored building across the street. There was a hive of them, then, ready to swarm the way only killer bees and zombies and junkies could swarm. The bus rumbled away in a cloud of black exhaust. Too late to turn back, their only hope was to blend.

You could talk yourself into courage. Robert reminded himself that this was Angela's neighborhood, and if she had survived a whole childhood here, one little stroll down the street wouldn't kill them. Still, he wished he'd brought the gun, just to have it in his pocket.

Robert glanced again at the living dead man. "Should we get someone?"

"There's no help anyone can give him now. He's got to make his own help."

"People are walking right over him."

"You think that's the first addict ever laid out on the side of the street in this city?"

Jerome was jumpy as a cat, his head tucked low into his neck, his eyes constantly shifting to see what might be coming. Maybe—no, probably, there were neighborhoods like this up in north Philly. Maybe Maurice lived in one. It would explain. Grow up in this kind of place, and every day was a confrontation. You fought or you were devoured.

Robert felt like a curtain had been suddenly thrown back. He saw now what he should always have known: the Chum wasn't a bad neighborhood. It was a city neighborhood, a working class neighborhood, maybe even a poor neighborhood, but that was all. It looked nothing like Herman, so he hadn't understood. The people in his neighborhood were doing okay. They rolled out to work in the morning. Their houses were small, but they had bay windows and stoops to sit on and, once, the walls had been hung with pineapples. The neighborhood they were in now was a whole other thing. Squalor: the wet flimsiness of that word soaked into everything. Even the concrete here seemed moistly rotten with it.

Leona's house was two blocks from the bus line, but they seemed to move into a new, upgraded world with each block. Tatty lace hung in the windows and flowers grew from old coffee cans. Leona's house wasn't anything fancy, just an old, narrow, flat-fronted row home, but at least the brick was intact and the porch was swept.

He hadn't realized he was hanging back until Jerome nudged him. "Come on, man. Ask, and then let's get out of here."

Still, Robert hesitated. He didn't know if he was more terrified that he would hit another dead end or that he'd find her, find Angela, knowing she'd left her own babies, or if it was that, once he rung that bell, one of those possibilities would be gone forever.

He lifted heavy feet up the steps to the weathered door

and rapped timidly. A car coasted down the street, its stereo's bass rattling the rib bones of his chest. He kept his eyes trained on the door, but even with his back turned, he could feel the driver's eyes.

Robert tried again, his knock louder now, desperate.

"Don't tell me no one's home," Jerome said.

"What do you want to do?"

"I don't know. I don't really want to come back here again."

With no sound, the door swung open, and Robert jumped as if it were a gunshot. The woman glowering in the doorframe was thin and small and thrust her chin out to show she was a woman who would not take any crap. Her face was coated in makeup that deepened the lines on her forehead. "Yeah?" she barked.

"I'm..." Robert realized he had never settled on what to say. He should have had a plan. He should have rehearsed it. "I'm looking for Angela."

Leona's eyes flashed dangerous as lightning under a high, dark cloud of hair.

"I'm Sean's brother," he stammered on. "I thought she might be here."

"You thought wrong."

He flinched, his gaze falling on her gold high-tops and their hot pink laces. He tried to picture his own mother—or anyone's mother—in those shoes. Leona was ready for a disco to break out or a basketball game or a disco-basketball showdown. Her gold shoes glinted with the wink of a guy who was going to win the fight and wanted you to know ahead of time. Lace-fringed socks folded down from firm calves. He told himself that women in lacy socks were never dangerous, but his heart beat the word *crazy, crazy*. She was a woman capable of anything.

"I—I don't want to bother her. I just need to know if she knows where Sean is."

"What makes you think I seen her?"

Robert reached and found nothing. He could hardly tell her that he'd heard it from Sean's mistress. *Fake it til you make it,* he told himself. Mustering every bit of false confidence he could find, he said, "It doesn't matter. I know she's here."

"Little Mr. Detective here," Leona said to no one. "Look, your mom's got the babies. Everything's fine. Why don't you just leave well enough alone?"

"We promise not to bother her," Jerome said. "We'll be quick."

"Yeah," Robert agreed, too enthusiastically. "She can forget we came as soon as we talk to her. We just want to find my brother. I need to bring him home."

"You and your skinny henchman here?" Leona tapped lacquered nails against the fringed hem of her miniskirt and Robert tried not to notice her bare thigh.

"There's a debt collector. He's been calling my mom. If we can't find Sean, we'll have to pay, and my mom can't afford it. Not with the babies."

"Sounds like your problem."

"He's called you, too," Robert said, as the fact dawned on him. "That's why you don't want us to know she's here. She'd be responsible for his debts. You're protecting her."

"I didn't say any of that."

"Only, we're not trying to get her in trouble. We just want to find Sean."

Leona sighed. "I gotta be honest. Angela's very upset with your brother."

She'd seen her then. Angela was here, or somewhere nearby. Leona knew where.

Leona shook her head. "Ang wants a fresh start. I feel bad about them babies—I told her that. But she needs to forget about them if she wants to move on, and she definitely needs to forget about your brother and all his debt. She doesn't? She'll be just another neighborhood bimbo who went and got herself knocked up by some guy who couldn't keep his dick in his pants. Ang has more potential than that. What's past is past. She needs to move on."

"But Sean?"

"Your brother did a shitty thing by her. A real shitty thing."

"I know, but he's still my brother."

"He's a regular bastard is what he is. Sorry, hun."

Leona had some kind of gorgon power. One more glance would turn him to stone. Robert could feel her hand on the door, ready to push it shut. A sob rose in his throat, but he willed it into one last magic word. "Please."

Leona had already stepped back into the darkness of the house, but she hesitated and frowned. "You want to find your brother," she said, "you try St. Anthony's. Last I heard, he was skulking around there."

The door clicked shut. Robert stared, stunned, but Jerome grabbed his shoulder and shook it. "You got a lead."

"What's St. Anthony's?"

"I don't know, but we'll figure it out. You did it, man. You did it!"

Deacon was crying when Robert got home. His mother was trying to get the baby to drink the new, downgraded formula. He'd spit up a good portion on her work-wrinkled blouse. She held on to patience by her fingertips.

"Where were you?" she said. "Jerome's sister said she hadn't seen either one of you all afternoon."

"We were just hanging out."

"I'm sick of not knowing where you are, Robert."

The phone rang.

"I don't know why I'm spending money on Miss Martha just so you can disappear."

"I'll leave a note next time."

"I'd appreciate it. I'd appreciate it even more if you were home taking care of your schoolwork like you were supposed to be."

Schoolwork, schoolwork. It was the drum she kept beating. The phone rang a third time. "Are you going to answer that?"

"Dinner will be ready soon."

"It's that guy again, isn't it? The one about the money."

"Spaghetti. I hope you're hungry."

"What exactly will he do if we can't pay?"

"Don't be so dramatic."

"But we need to start thinking about that, right?"

"I would've made garlic bread if Wallace would ever get around to fixing the oven."

"Mom!"

"What else do you think I think about Robert?"

The phone's domed bells seemed to be hammering in his own head, but then they stopped short, and silence opened around them that wasn't really silence. There was no real silence in Philadelphia. Cars hushed by outside, the refrigerator ticked, Sammy added a bahbahbah, and in the kitchen, the timer beeped and beeped.

JAWN

Robert listened for his mother to go to bed. If he could snag the yellow pages, he could at least figure out what St. Anthony's was. But Bridget had had another green man nightmare and his mother had spent the last hour sitting with her on the sofa. The lights blazed in the living room so that Bridget could see there was no monster, and the babies were fussy again.

Robert didn't realize he'd dozed off until he woke to sunlight. He'd slept too long—they all had. His mother bustled through the kitchen like a windstorm, uprooting sandwiches and dashing them into lunch sacks.

"I'm afraid it's just cheese again today," she said as she handed Robert his. "I haven't had time to get to the store."

"Swiss?"

"American."

It had been days since there was turkey, days since she'd switched to store-brand wheat bread instead of making her own. Lack of time explained the bread, but the turkey was something else. She'd been to the store that week, he remembered. Turkey just wasn't on the list anymore. Cheese was cheaper.

Jerome waited for him on the sidewalk that day, the light rain pebbling his jacket. "You get a chance to look up the address?"

"No. You?"

"No."

"It's too early to be this tired."

"Tell me about it. Stupid Jacquie came home with her babies and her loud-ass boyfriend. I swear that guy's voice goes through walls. They were up all night. Every time I was about to fall asleep, he'd start laughing or yelling at the game or whatever. No wonder their babies are always crying. I'd cry too if I had to put up with that jawn all the time."

"John?"

"John? Please." Jerome snorted. "You need to develop some Philly vowels. *Jawn*. You never heard that?"

"Around, yeah, but not from you."

"It's the best kind of word. It means whatever you need it to mean, but mostly, it means you're from Philly. You gotta start working it in."

Robert wished he'd thought to grab a raincoat. His shirt was clinging to him. "How long are they staying, Jacquie and her man?"

"God only knows."

They turned up the sidewalk towards the school and straight into Ricky Gutierrez, his whole body bouncing. The kid thrived on being the center of excitement, so long as it was other people's excitement. His cheeks beamed and he took a moment to catch his breath and let the tension build before saying, "You got to watch out today."

"What now?" Jerome said.

"Maurice says the cops asked him about the whole flagpole thing. Says you put them on to him. Says he wouldn't lower himself to touching Jerome. Says he wouldn't risk catching AIDS or whatever other shit you could catch from messing around with fags."

"That's some serious ignorance. It doesn't even make sense. He doesn't want to touch me but now he's going to beat on my face? What kind of logic is that?"

"You want to ask him, go right ahead."

"No one needs to tell the cops anything anyway," Robert said. "We all know he did it. He's just too chicken to own up to it."

Jerome shot him a look that said *shut up*. The last thing they needed was Ricky passing along that precious piece of gossip.

Ricky blabbered on. "Man, I'd be scared as hell. You scared?" Jerome only rolled his eyes, so Ricky shifted gears. "You see the new girl yet?"

"What new girl?"

"If you saw her, you wouldn't need to ask. She. Is. Smoking." Ricky's face was round and red as an apple. "Maurice already tried to hit her up, but she just blew him off. Total ice queen, he said. Not worth his time."

"No wonder he's looking for someone to punch."

"Seriously, you ever seen a girl yet who could resist Maurice's game?"

Robert said, "You act like she doesn't have any control over herself, like all Maurice has to do is cast a glance and any girl comes. Maybe she's just not into him."

"I heard it was an absolute stone wall. Not even a hint of future action. Girl's totally frigid."

"Well," Jerome said, putting on his G Master Smooth act. "Once she lays eyes on my bad ass, she'll melt like sugar."

Ricky burst out in laughter that was too hard for that thin joke. He was reading Jerome through squinted eyes. That's why he was here, Robert realized. He felt like a hook fastened somewhere behind his belly button had pulled him back and up where he could see everything clearly. Ricky was fishing for intel, playing to get information off Jerome to see how he responded. And Jerome knew.

"You can't even handle her," Ricky said. "She's hot, yeah, but she's some kind of loco terrorist chica. That's why she's here. Got expelled from her last school."

"Expelled?"

"Hauled off and punched some girl right in the mouth, then kicked her when she was down. Broke a rib and everything. Guess that's how they play in her country."

"Back up. Her country?"

"You know, Iraq, Iran, something like that. One of those countries where they wear picnic blankets on their heads and talk gibberish."

"Man," Jerome said, "if you going to be so dumb, you should keep it to yourself. That's some seriously racist commentary you spouting."

"Besides," Robert added, "if she's breaking ribs and stuff, she hardly sounds like an ice queen."

"Like you know, Country Kitchen."

"Better get your story straight, else my boy Robert will call you out."

Ricky's face was red again, but now with embarrassment. "I'm the one with the information. If it weren't for me, you guys wouldn't know shit."

"You're just like your mama, biggest mouth in the Chum. That woman needs to mind her business, and you might want to start minding your own."

"Least I know what's up. You guys would've had your asses smeared clear across school if I weren't here to give you the score."

"You just keep on telling yourself that," Jerome said, but his smile was warm and he clapped a hand on Ricky's shoulder.

"It's cool, man. We still love you and all that shit, but damn. You got to get that tongue on a leash."

Only when Ricky was out of sight did Jerome's smile drop. He lowered his voice and said, "Tell me you didn't say anything about Maurice."

"I didn't have anything *to* say. You won't even tell me that it was Maurice."

"Good."

"So it was him? You going to admit it now?"

"Naw. It wasn't him."

ICE QUEEN

He didn't see the new girl for himself until math. Whatever he expected from Ricky's description, it wasn't this willowy girl with thin, bangled wrists. Ricky said her family had fled from some Middle Eastern war, that they were from one of those countries that "mangled their daughters' hoohahs" so they didn't like sex, but she wasn't wearing a burka or even a veil. Her hair hung glossy and black, clipped on the sides of her head with dragonflies that glittered in the light. Her shirt was numbered to look like a jersey, with stripes on the sleeves and dark fabric on the shoulders, every inch fitting snugly to her curves.

Never before had Robert seen someone in barrettes and bracelets look so fierce. She stood beside Mr. Burns staring over everyone's heads and through the brick wall behind them as their teacher tried to will more square footage into the crammed room. "All right, Joan," he finally said. "I think we'll squeeze you in next to Bobby for now."

There wasn't a desk next to his. There wasn't an empty desk in the entire class. Burnsie pulled a chair along the wall so she could share Robert's desktop. Joan stared at the empty chair a moment, and then settled her gaze on Robert as if daring him to react in any way whatsoever. Finally, she fell into her seat, her hair swinging over her shoulder.

"Hi," he whispered, keeping his voice low because he

figured Mr. Burns chose his desk because Robert wasn't a big talker. "I'm Robert."

She didn't say anything. Of course, she knew he was Robert. Their teacher had just told her that. He was making an ass of himself.

He tried again. "Where are you from?"

"I'm from America, asshole."

"No, I meant—" He glanced at Mr. Burns who was finishing up the roll. "I only meant, I'm new here, too. I was wondering if you're from the neighborhood?"

She turned away, her hair a curtain between them. The barrette allowed him to see only her silhouette, the angle of her straight lashes, her soft, pink lips. Her breath, he imagined, would be like raspberries straight off the canes, still cool with morning.

His life was a math problem. The measurable proximity between him and this girl was inches, but the distance between them felt infinite. What was the formula for that? If his hand traveled in a straight line to stroke her hair, how much more distance would grow in that instant?

And what about the space between him and Sean? Robert couldn't calculate any of the relevant measurements in his life. He wondered if the length was the same on one side as the other. He wondered if, with all his reasons to want his brother, he was closer to Sean than Sean was to them, or whether since Sean knew the way home, his distance shorter.

"Bobby, did you hear the question?" Mr. Burns repeated.

Robert's eyes jolted from the soft gloss of Joan's hair onto the whiteboard.

"Can you tell me how to find the vertex angle of an isosceles triangle if we know its base?"

Robert nodded, grateful for the second chance. This problem, at least, he could solve.

THE NEXT SHOE DROPS

They walked out of the building and into a perfect afternoon, the summer that year stretched into fall. Next week would be October, but the sun rested warm and gentle on his skin. Jerome was saying something, but Robert's thoughts flitted elsewhere. He wondered if dragonflies were her thing. Maybe they stood for something or she liked the way they looked, or maybe they were just some meaningless object her mom got her, like his mom got him the polo shirt he was now wearing. Maybe she didn't even like them. Maybe the barrettes were just functional, a way to keep hair out of her eyes. Why did the dragonfly drink the flagon dry? Bridget's song.

Jerome paused next to him at the top of the steps to rub the smudges from his glasses. They'd go home, look up the address, find Sean, and then Robert could give all his time to solving the mystery of Joan.

The shove came out of nowhere. Robert hadn't even seen Maurice. A fraction of a moment after Jerome pulled the glasses from his face, Robert heard the thud of arm to backpack and, seemingly at the same moment, saw the flash of Jerome's sleeve wheeling by. Time bent. Jerome ran the first three steps like a televised sprinter, replayed in slow motion, his strides impossibly long. Elegant, graceful, athletic. Robert felt the rising swell of hope that those strides would save him, but Jerome's heel caught the fourth step and suddenly he was a kettle spilling forward. His chest hit the edge of the final stair, his face skidded against the pavement, and the arm that failed to save him bounced once, then rested at his side, his glasses still clutched in his hand. His backpack split. Books skittered around him. Robert hurried to see what was broken.

"Whoops," Maurice said at the top of the stairs, but his voice held no sincerity. He dropped his feet down the steps in no hurry. "Guess it was a accident."

He hovered over Jerome, tall in his dark jeans and stainless jersey. Twelve. It was Sean's old number, Randall Cunningham's old number, and now, Maurice's number here at Garvey. A quarterback number. A lucky number. Only, luck was on the wrong side.

"Leave him alone," Robert said.

"You say something, Oregon?"

Maurice's hiking boots, still fresh from a shoebox, had touched only pavement, but they owned the sidewalk more than any boots have ever owned a mountain pass. Robert would swear that even the concrete quaked with fear under Maurice's soles.

Bridget was waiting. There wasn't time for this. Even so, he stepped up chest-to-chest with Maurice, their shirts brushing with every breath. In the light reflected in Maurice's eyes, Robert saw Jerome again on the flagpole. This should have made him afraid. In the past, it would have. Now, Maurice's gaze slid under Robert's skin like a needle. It itched. Maurice's eyes were calm but what they injected was anything but. Robert wanted to claw himself. He wanted to pull his own skin right off. He wouldn't be white anymore but something beyond color or race, something bloody and beastly. Feral. No, Robert thought, the itch wasn't a needle. It was bristling fur. His teeth wanted to gnash. His nails bit into his palms like claws.

"Feeling brave, white boy?" Maurice's voice was low and whispery.

Robert fought to make his mind work. He needed to remember what Sean once told him about fighting. He'd been in fourth grade. He was picked on. *Don't hit at the person,* Sean had said. *Hit through. You have to hit beyond the person or you'll always be pulling your punches.* But there was something else. What was it? Robert sorted through his brother's sound bites until, yes, that was it, the most important thing: *Hit first.*

Jerome pulled himself up, flinching.

Robert could feel it all growing: the anticipation, the energy, his own need to explode. Others were gathering. They craved violence. He could feel his blood pumping in his veins, ready to spill. He could feel Jerome, tense but not running. He could feel the punch building in his shoulder, but he couldn't quite feel the will to throw it. Not yet. Not now. One move, one flinch from Maurice and he was sure he could do it, but Maurice just stood cold and unworried as stone.

Jerome put on his glasses; one earpiece pointed to the sky and the lens rested crooked. He stared at something in his hand. They needed to get out of here, to ice and Advil and quiet. They needed to get to impatient Bridget before she walked alone. They needed to stand up for themselves. They needed to find Sean, and they needed to show that they wouldn't be pushed down forever. There was no right thing to do.

"This isn't over," Robert said, as if it were a threat and not a sad, haunting fact.

"Recognize."

Robert had no idea what that meant. He turned from Maurice to Jerome and helped him away. He did recognize. Himself as a coward after all. Maurice as king. The fact that he was running. The fact that the fight was still coming. He recognized the social system they were caught in and that neither one of them had any power other than the power to hurt. He recognized that the fight, when it came, would not be fair because there was no such thing as a fair fight because there was no such thing as fairness anyway.

"You okay?" he asked.

"Bruised," Jerome replied, "but I'll live. What the hell were you thinking?"

"Just that enough was enough."

"How many times do I have to tell you? You don't mess with Maurice."

"What's he going to do?"

"I know you did not just ask me that."

"Your breathing sounds weird."

"I'm fine."

"So I was supposed to leave you there with him gloating?"

"You never heard that sometimes discretion is the better part of valor?"

"I don't even know what that means."

"That's what my mama says, and she's right. Don't escalate."

"We have the gun now. Everything's different."

"You're not serious."

"I just mean if he comes at us."

"You got to know when to listen, Robert. You take this on, and suddenly you got a problem bigger than you can handle, bigger than anyone can handle. The street is the street and you can't change that. You got to trust me. You got to know I'm right about this."

When Jerome told Bridget he'd fallen down the stairs, she frowned but kissed his split eyebrow to make it feel better, then walked straight to their apartment, through the front door, and to the freezer to grab the frozen lima beans their mother always applied to boo boos. Bridget handed these to Jerome with the seriousness of a specialist prescribing life saving medicine, instructing him on their use. Now, as he pressed the limas to his face, Bridget doctored Amanda, her doll, who had suffered a stab wound in the stomach and thus jumped ahead of Jerome on the triage list and gone straight to emergency surgery.

Robert ran his finger down a column of St. Anthony's in the business section of the phone book. The nubs of old carpet fiber pricked at their elbows where they lay on the floor. The book listed several churches, a hospital, and a thrift store, each in various neighborhoods and suburbs.

Jerome winced as he rolled to his side.

"You gotta tell someone," Robert said. "Maurice just keeps pushing, no matter how low you lay. We need help."

"Let it go, already. I know this place."

"So does your sister, and she said you need to stand up."

"You want to start listening to her advice? I thought you had goals for yourself."

"I'm just saying. It's not like we can't defend ourselves."

"Stay focused. It's got to be the hospital, don't you think? Your brother can't be living in no church or thrift store."

Robert turned back to the column of possibilities. He supposed Jerome was right, at least about Sean. But if his brother had been in a hospital this long, he'd have to be in a coma or something. He pictured Sean wrapped in bandages like a mummy. He could have been hit by a car or a bus. That, at least, would explain why he hadn't been home and hadn't called. Only, Leona had said "skulking around," which implied consciousness. Robert tried to picture Sean skulking around a hospital, holding the open-backed nightgown closed behind so that no one would see his naked butt as he skulked.

Jerome rose and threw the limas back in the freezer. His elbow was bleeding again. "You coming over for *Slayers* tonight?"

"Duh."

* * *

Alone, Robert closed the flimsy pages and returned the phone book to the top of the fridge. The last time he'd been in a hospital, they had failed to save his father. He could still smell the antiseptic. His father lay in the bed before them, his skin bloodless and waxy so that he looked like a fake version of their dad. The nurse pulled a thick white sheet up to his neck even though he was already dead and beyond any need for warmth or breath or love or any of the things Robert wanted for him. Only later did Robert realize the fresh sheet was there to hide the contusions and slashes and sloppy surgeries that happen when they try to save a life that can't be saved.

Everyone at the hospital had been kind. Robert was sure they had living patients to see, other work to be done, but if that was true, they hid that fact from the Flannigans. The doctor talked through the efforts that had been made, the brief moment when they'd been able to get a heartbeat again, the moment it failed. He used the word "heroic" to talk about his team. Heroic efforts had been made, but ultimately, there was too much trauma. A fawn-haired nurse who looked more elf than human had held his hand and Bridget's. Later, she wheeled in a tray of chips and cookies and granola bars, water and juice boxes, and offered them a private moment—however long they needed—to say their goodbyes. He wondered how many death trolleys they had sitting around, waiting to wheel in to this room or that. He wondered how snack food was supposed to help you. He wondered if everyone was always so stupid about death.

Before they left, the elf-nurse caught them again and gave Bridget a small pink rabbit purchased from the gift shop. She said it was a magic rabbit and that, even though it couldn't make the sadness go away, it would always bring Bridget her father's love. She told his sister that, whenever she missed him, she could squeeze that dumb pink bunny and think of him and he would be right there.

For three days, Bridget hadn't let go of that rabbit, squeezing it so hard it looked like she was going to choke the life right out of it, but when they put their father's body in the ground, she threw the rabbit into the hole. "Bunnies live in the ground," she had said. "This one wants to live with Daddy."

As he watched the dirt sift through the plush fur, Robert was proud of her. Even at five, Bridget knew that kind-hearted nurse was full of crap. Magic bunnies couldn't make their father any less dead.

Sean lifted their sister into his arms, the dirt from her Mary Janes unnoticed on the side of his clean new trousers. She turned her face into his white collar and let it lie there. Angela rubbed Robert's shoulder as he stood there wishing she were not so achingly sexy. Not one of the Flannigans cried the whole, cold day. They stood by their stone-faced mother and, hand in hand, watched the dirt fall on the box that held their father.

What did Jerome know about how bad things could get? Robert had been there, and he wasn't about to stand at the side of another grave, knowing that this time, he could have done something to stop it.

He pulled down the phone book again. Maybe Jerome wouldn't say anything about the flagpole thing, but today, Robert had witnessed Maurice's aggression. That made this one his problem. If there was one thing he learned in Philly, he'd learned that sometimes, you had to speak.

He picked up the phone and dialed.

"Garvey High."

"Can you put me through to Dr. Turner? I need to report an incident."

LOOKING THROUGH SMOKE

When Robert imagined the blood in Jonesboro, he saw it in sheets: blood raining from the fifteen people hit, creating puddles rippling outward. He saw the blood cascading past the school steps, past the city limits, past the Arkansas borders. It thinned as it spread, becoming almost invisible, becoming so light that it floated, becoming the air that the whole country breathed like an infection.

He sat on the steps outside his apartment, bouncing a small rubber ball that he'd rescued from the gutter.

What was the difference, really, between him and them? He knew what it was like to be the outsider, the reject. He knew how fast friends forgot you. Their bodies were no different than his; he could wear their experience easily. He had the gun in the wall. Was it merely a matter of will? Did they have more courage than him? Did they value themselves more? When did enough become too much? What would it take for him to snap and become one of them?

When the biker came home that evening, Robert felt no fear. Of all the dangers in Philadelphia, one possibly girlfriend-murdering, definitely banana-bread-baking biker didn't seem so bad. He bounced the ball off the wall and caught it in a single motion.

"Looking pretty glum," the biker said.

Robert shrugged and bounced the ball again. Dr.

Turner had promised she'd look into things, but what did that mean? From what the rumors said, Joan had been expelled for doing something like that. But then, apparently Joan was caught. All Dr. Turner had to go on was Robert's story, which was one Jerome might not dare corroborate. Even if Jerome did, Robert didn't know if his friend would ever forgive him.

He realized the biker was waiting for a response, so he said, "I got some stuff to do. I just don't want to do it."

"I know how that is."

The man's Harley Davidson shirt strained over his biceps even when they weren't flexed. Robert tried to imagine the guy as a skinny kid, back before hormones and barbells and mustache growth. Failing, he tried for the high school biker, on his way to the man he was now but not there yet. Maybe that was when he had bought his first Harley, the moment defining his whole personality, though now that Robert thought about it, he'd never actually seen the man on a motorbike, never seen one parked on the block, never heard one rumbling in the street. The biker, he realized, probably didn't own a bike at all.

"I've been meaning to thank you for the bread. It was good."

"My mother's recipe. Always popular."

"If you don't mind me saying, you don't really look like a guy who makes banana bread."

"That's cause you never seen me in my frilly apron." The biker smiled through his mustache and winked. "You sure you don't want to say what's eating you?"

Robert leaned against the wall, breathing the heady odor of mildew. He squeezed the rubber ball tight in his fingers. Water stains spread through the old plaster, making shapes like countries from the maps in his old fantasy novels.

"You ever been in a fight?"

"I guess you could say that, not that I'd recommend it

or anything." The wooden step creaked as the biker lowered himself to sit, pulling a hand-rolled cigarette from behind his ear. The denim of his jeans stretched tight over his thick-muscled thighs. He radiated heat and power like a nuclear reactor. He lit his smoke, breathing deep and pausing before exhaling it, dragon-like, out his nostrils.

"But you'd do it again. If you had to."

"This city can be tough. Sometimes, you got to prove you're tough, too."

Sunlight beamed through the dirty transom, gilding the dust that hung in the air. Beneath it, the old front door stood solid and dark. Robert liked their incongruity, the lightness of the dust and the heaviness of the wood. They balanced one another. Why couldn't all things exist like that, each doing its own thing?

The air was getting heavy. He'd smelled cigarettes before, but this was different. The biker wasn't smoking tobacco at all, Robert realized. He'd lit a joint. Robert breathed deeper knowing this, wondering if he could get a contact high. His mother would kill them both if she knew. Which was flattering. The biker saw him as the kind of kid you could smoke a joint with. Robert's throat tickled a little and he wanted to cough, but he didn't dare. Not with this level of trust bestowed upon him—this level of cool.

"My point is this: you back down too many times, and they see you as the guy to pick on. You got to figure out a way to get them to see you different so you're not just some whipping boy. I'm not saying you should fight, but you can't hide neither."

"Yeah," Robert said, but he couldn't see how to make it work. If he actually fought Maurice, there was no doubt who would win. It was like Rocky and Apollo Creed; Robert's only hope was to last a few rounds.

They sat in silence while the biker finished his smoke.

Robert felt warm and hungry and a little better, even though exactly none of his problems were solved. Maybe the biker wasn't really talking about fighting at all. Sitting there with his motorcycle shirt and his aggressive facial hair, maybe what he was talking about was fronting. Robert remembered himself in the clothes Angela had picked out. He'd looked like the world's whitest, wimpiest gangster. He'd looked ridiculous, but maybe Angela had been trying to show him how to survive. What if she'd just chosen the wrong accessories? He imagined pulling the gun on Maurice. Of course, he wouldn't fire it—he didn't even know if it was loaded—he just needed to look like someone who would pull the trigger. Maurice would back off and they could all just go on living their lives.

Stubbing out the tiny butt on the sole of his boot, the biker said, "I tell you one thing, though. The people in this neighborhood? They take care of each other. You get cornered here, and you got help."

This was supposed to comfort him, he guessed, but Robert didn't want to think about getting cornered here or anywhere else.

The biker rumbled his way upstairs and into his own apartment. Alone again, Robert went back to the ball, letting it bounce off the door, then onto the tile, then catching it. He found a rhythm: throw, bounce, bounce, catch; throw, bounce, bounce, catch. He liked the way it cleared his mind as the biker's smoke settled.

Jerome flung open the door at the foot of the stairs and waved his hand to stir the air. The guy was buzzing with a weird energy that crackled in the air around him. For a second, Robert thought that Dr. Turner had already called him, that Jerome knew.

"You said you're coming to watch *Slayers* tonight, right?

Nothing's changed?"

"So long as I get my math done and my mom doesn't need me."

"Well finish your math and bring the babies if you have to. I just heard Fontina is coming back on the show. Fontina, dude. Fon. Tina."

"Who's Fontina?"

"Who's—? Are you freaking kidding me? Who's *Fontina?* Don't tell me that *you're* the one been smoking weed up in here, Mr. Clean-Cut White Boy."

"Is she good-looking or something?"

"Good-looking doesn't even begin to cover it. The woman is a total and utter bad ass. She's my favorite character ever, but last year in the season finale some ass-wipe vampire tore her throat completely open. We all thought she was a goner. People was crying for days. How can you not know this? I don't *even* know how they're going to bring her back, but you cannot miss this, Robert. You cannot."

"She's probably just another vampire now."

"What the?" Jerome looked at him sideways, his expression filled with pity. "Just don't even start if you're going to be so ignorant. There is no way Fontina is a vampire, which you would know if you'd ever saw her. She's a slayer through and through. Nothing could turn her. Now go do your math. Seriously."

"I'll be there," he said, but he was talking to an empty hall. Robert hadn't had a chance to tell him about the phone call.

Maybe that didn't matter. Jerome was the one talking about how great silence was, and wasn't he the one with the biggest secret of all? He was the one in the closet.

Maybe.

Either way, he hadn't said anything to Robert. He'd let all those rumors fly unanswered. Of all the people who couldn't judge Robert for not telling him every little thing, Jerome was top of the list.

Robert threw the ball against the door but caught it before its second bounce. Maybe he shouldn't feel bad, but he did.

THREATS OR PROMISES

They were walking to the bus stop that afternoon when Ricky told them the news: Maurice was out on a three-day suspension. They had pulled him out of class that morning in front of everyone. Each word was a needle drawing blood.

"You guys know anything about it?"

Ricky's eyes rested on Jerome's bruised and scabbed eyebrow, but Jerome only said, "Why would we?"

Robert's skin felt two sizes too small. Even if no one else could, Jerome would be able to read the whole story on his face. The bus pulled to a stop in front of them, its air brakes sighing. Ricky turned away as they boarded.

They watched the city slide by the bus window, the old stone of one block giving way to the plate glass of the next.

"Tell me you didn't say anything about the accident."

"You're still calling it an accident?"

"So you did."

Robert looked away, letting the silence hang. On the *Slayers* ads that ran along the tops of the bus windows, Fontina's face glared white against the black and red backdrop. Finally, he said, "Told you she'd be a vampire."

"And I told *you* that she's faking it. It's an act, man. She's like a double agent, but she'll be back with Jack and his crew by the end of the season."

"Or she'll be a bad ass villain they can't bring themselves to destroy."

"Fontina's no villain. People are who they are. They don't just change." The bus rumbled through Fairhill towards Bella Vista. "Seriously, why didn't you listen?"

"Look at the bright side. We've got three days with no Maurice."

"Two. One's already gone. The others will go just as quick."

"And the weekend. That's five full terror-free days."

"You feeling terror-free?" Jerome looked out the window for a block, then said, "You know how they smoke out bees to get their honey and shit? You think those bees are happy when the smoke wears off? You think they be all, 'Yes, Mr. Beekeeper, I know you stole my honey and all, but it's cool. Let's go party'?"

"Bees?"

"No, man. They mad as hell. The whole time, they thinking about how deep they can bury their stinger when the smoke clears out."

"Do you even hear yourself right now?"

"What's that supposed to mean?"

"You'd be the one to know about hiding in smoke. Smoke and mirrors is your specialty."

"Only one being opaque right now is you. My words are clear as crystal."

"You haven't once responded to what Maurice says about you. Not since I met you. Not since registration day when he first said you were gay. Not once have you told me whether he's right."

"Thought you didn't care."

"If I did, I wouldn't still be here. That's not the point."

"Then what is?"

"The point is, you should say. If you trusted me, you would tell me."

"Stop trying to change the subject."

"All I did was say what was true. Since when is that such a crime?"

"Since you decided you couldn't mind your business and had to be Mr. Mighty White Savior."

"You think I should just stand by and watch you get beat to shit?"

"You got to trust me to take care of my own problems."

"But you don't have to do the same?"

"Please."

"Don't give me that. You've been saving me since I got here. Taking care of the twins, searching for my brother. You don't see me calling you Mr. Mighty Black Savior."

"That's different."

"Because I'm white?"

"Maybe. It's not like white and black mean the same thing, Robert."

"Okay, fair, but you want me to trust you, like you always have the right answers, and yet you don't want to trust me back. You don't want to believe that sometimes I know what I'm doing."

"Maybe," Jerome said.

Robert pulled the cord for their stop, and the bus wheezed into stillness.

St. Anthony's Medical Center took up an entire block with polished white stone and shining glass. Shrubs in large pots flanked the doorway where a man in scrubs stood with an old guy in a wheelchair as a car pulled in to collect him.

"I hate hospitals," Jerome said. Everybody did. Robert understood that he wasn't trying to tell him anything. He just needed to break the silence. He needed a way for them to go back to being Jerome and Robert, together.

"We should have just called," Robert said.

"You're better in person."

"I don't know about that."

"That landlady let you into Sean's apartment because you were there. Leona talked to you when you were on her doorstep, but she didn't say jack to your mother on the phone. I don't know whether it's cause it's harder to say no to someone's face or because they respect the effort of you showing up, but either way, the phone don't work the same." Jerome settled himself into a chair in the waiting area and waved Robert on.

At the information desk, a man in red suspenders looked up from his computer screen. "How can I help you?"

Robert liked that question. He liked being asked. Maybe Jerome was right that there was just something about being in the room. The last step in the journey might not be so bad, not with this grandfatherly man here to guide them along.

"I'm looking for my brother. Sean Flannigan."

The man turned to a large black computer, hunting and pecking his way through the name. When nothing came up, he had Robert spell the name and added the extra n. Still, there were no Seans. "He wouldn't be listed under another name, would he? A nickname or alias?"

No. Sean had never been one to go by any other name but his own. Robert asked, "What about people who don't know who they are? Like if they get amnesia. Do you have any who are anonymous?"

The man shook his head. "I'm afraid I can't tell you that. Each patient has a right to privacy. HIPAA, you know?"

"What?"

"Ethically, we can't divulge information except to

those the patient has cleared."

"But what if he doesn't know who he is? What if he can't remember who to clear?"

"Amnesia happens mostly on television," the man said. "Unconscious patients are more common, but the authorities help with those."

"Which authorities?" There didn't seem to be any authorities. Authorities on what? If there were authorities out there, people who knew things and could help him, Robert wondered where they'd been.

"I'm sorry, son," he said, and he looked it, but sorry didn't help.

Jerome wasn't always right, but Robert kept that observation to himself.

A SHOT IN THE DARK

His mother was still asleep on the couch when he staggered out of bed Thursday morning. Under her fingers lay a list:

couch	50
dining set	~~100~~ 75
bedroom set	150
R bed set	100
B bed set	100
TV	35
~~banjo~~	~~2500-3500?~~

He laid his hand on her wrist and startled her awake. She snatched the paper and crumpled it in a single motion, and Robert pretended not to have seen. From her bedroom, her alarm clock bleated. "Oh God," she said, "we're late. Get Bridget."

"What's the word?" LeRoi asked every morning passing the stoop. "Strength," Robert replied in return, but at school, the word was "snitch" and he needed to lean on all the scant power of LeRoi's word. The other kids gave him a wide berth in the halls, as if snitching were a disease. In biology, a dead rat slopped across his seat, its fur sodden from the jar. Black lips curled back from its teeth as if even it found Robert revolting.

The whole thing was so dumb that he couldn't even really feel threatened, like they had grabbed their idea for vengeance from some stupid TV movie. He felt the eyes of the back row on him, Maurice's friends and teammates who only heard one side of the story, the one where Robert had made things up because he was jealous or because he was desperate for attention or because he was racist or because he was just some lying little shit.

He pushed the rat with his binder, disposing of it just like he'd done with the row house rat, dumping it into the wastebasket and wiping his seat with school paper towel, which only spread the wet.

His mother had listed everything of any value. His father's banjo, a pre-war Gibson, was the nicest thing they owned, which he hadn't known until he saw it on the paper written in his mother's hand. He had just thought it was a junky, old thing that was fun to mess around with—though as he'd learned to play better, it came to mean more. Until that morning, it never occurred to him that it had actual cash value—value that had nothing to do with the fact it was his father's.

Formaldehyde soaked into the ass of Robert's jeans, making him think of that old line from the movies, *I think I smell a rat*. Today, he knew what that smell was, and it was him. Quite a cologne he'd chosen for himself. Piquant with overtones of pariah.

Joan's eyes were on him when Robert walked into math, following him from the door to their desk, staying on him while Mr. Burns took roll, not even shifting when their teacher called her name. He wondered if she could see the decision in him. More likely, he reminded himself, she saw him in the part they'd cast him in, a death-reeking, beak-nosed, pasty-faced snitch.

The banjo was the last thing his mother had listed. He wondered how long her hand had hovered, hesitating, before she wrote it down, and how long again before she crossed it off. They were out of good formula and probiotics and no one was sleeping. It wouldn't pay the debt but it would buy time.

The folded paper tapped his elbow as he dug in his backpack for last night's homework. He secreted Joan's note in his lap, trying to look like he was absolutely riveted by every word falling from Mr. Burns's lips as he unfolded it below their desktop. He waited until the teacher turned to write on the board before reading, *Compared to your last school, how bad does Garvey suck?*

The pencil marks were so small and light that they were scarcely visible against the page, and he felt like there was something underneath those words that he couldn't read at all. Why, of all the things she could write, had she written that question, and what was the right answer? Was the note an olive branch, a trap, or something else altogether?

He wrote, *Please quantify for purposes of comparison. Specifying an order of magnitude, state Garvey's suckitude.*

He laid the note on her thigh, her fingers catching it and holding it in place. Her eyes never left the teacher until Mr. Burns turned again. She read quickly, and he thought he could detect a smile curling in the corner of her lip.

"And that was that," he told Jerome at lunch. "No response. No comment. Nothing."

"Smooth," was all Jerome said.

"But she was laughing at me."

"So? You're funny."

"Only if you're a nerd."

"Girls dig humor. What happened after she smiled?"

"Mr. Burns called on her and she said 'forty-two' like nothing had happened."

"Forty-two?"

"The right answer. If he'd called on me, I couldn't have told you the question, let alone the answer. I'm not even sure I could have told him my own name. Stop laughing, man, this is serious."

"I can't help it. Like I said, you're funny. Even smelling like some kind of fucked up biology pickles, you're funny."

Robert didn't want to feel better. "That collector guy keeps calling my mom. I think she's going to start selling our stuff if we don't find Sean soon. I don't know what she'll do after that."

"How many days we got now?"

"Not enough."

They would move again. They'd have to. Somewhere cheaper, more run-down. Somewhere dangerous.

THE STRAWBERRY ROOM

This time when they arrived in Leona's neighborhood, no dead men lay on the sidewalk. Robert and Jerome walked the blocks in silence, thinking, and then sat on the curb across from her door under a sign that read NO PARKING 7AM-7PM. A small tree struggled to grow from one of the larger cracks in the pavement. He felt the downward pull of a neighborhood like this, how it sucked at you like a drain.

Robert picked up a tiny stone, smooth and gray and forgettable in every way. A raindrop brushed his cheek. Another, his hand. He tried to make out the clouds' intentions. The drops were small and cool, but would there be more of them, and if so, how soon?

Leona was somewhere in that house, walking around in her gold shoes, ready to tell them nothing. They had talked to so many people now, and their silence felt heavy and exhausting. Robert smoothed his thumb over the pebble, its surface as blank as an empty stare, and then he let his arm do its thing again.

The stone bounced off the rain gutter, startling a pigeon. Throwing felt good this time. Nothing had died, and action, any action, felt productive, even if it didn't accomplish a thing. Rain speckled his arm. He wanted to chuck more rocks. He wanted to hurl boulders. He wanted to rock the world on its axis and make it spin right again.

"Don't throw too hard, rat killer. We won't get no answers

if you break her windows."

"I'll go easy," he said, but Robert was feeling dangerous. He *wanted* to hit a window. He wanted to hit every window. He started aiming there, not to break them but to show he could. He hit one pane after another, aiming a gentle tap on each square of second-floor glass, before working his way back down the row.

He hadn't expected anything to come of it. Later he thought that, if he had, it wouldn't have worked. But when the pebble clinked that second time against that last window, Angela's face appeared, framed by those sad, pink curtains.

Her eyes fixed on Robert, her expression shifting from confusion to worry to resolve. She held up a finger. One minute, it said. I'll be down in one minute.

"Was that her?" Jerome was on his feet now. "Was that Angela?"

Robert's stomach was suddenly alive with lizards and spiders. It shouldn't be so suddenly easy. He didn't want to think it had always been this easy, that she was always so close. He should have felt her there. He should have known, but it was Jerome who knew. She was the stray cat, hiding under her own front porch, and like that lost cat, she emerged tired and skinny. Her old t-shirt slumped from her shoulders, and her jeans sagged so low that Robert couldn't work out how they stayed in place as she stepped.

He said, "Can we go somewhere and talk?"

"Yeah," she said, gripping her purse strap as if it were a lifeline. "Yeah, it's time. I've been wanting to talk to you."

Now that it was too late to wonder whether he had done the right thing, Robert found himself consumed by the question he wished he'd asked himself from the start: Would she try to take the babies back?

He had felt the small, settled weight of Deacon in his lap

that morning as they watched his mother fill the lunch sacks. Deacon's downy-thin hair had tickled Robert's chin with every breath. If an infant crying was the sound of instant stress, then the soft stroke of baby hair was its antidote. Sammy and Deacon were part of their lives now—their *daily* lives. Robert didn't want to give that up. Not to a person who didn't feel it.

For blocks, Angela seemed to be fighting with herself. Her hair, which had, at first, glistened with rain, now hung heavy and lank. It seemed like the wrong time to mention Sean. She'd always been so strong, but now she looked like a china vase whose pieces had been fit together without glue. The slightest pressure and she would fall apart.

They were back in the block of the paper houses when she said, "You ever been to the Strawberry Room?" She nodded to a small storefront. The rain-spattered window was painted with an enormous strawberry that had faded pink with time. In the lower corner, a For Sale sign curled. "Papi used to take me here once a week back before the neighborhood got like it is."

The door opened to the warm, sweet smell of house-made waffle cones and espresso. Angela set her purse by the register and nodded to the long, glass counter, clean but scratched over time. Robert and Jerome cast their eyes over flavors while a thick-wristed man with graying hair came out of the back. "Angela, sweetheart, how you doing?"

"Getting by. You?"

"Meh. I could complain, but what's the use? Haven't seen you in a while."

In the fluorescent light, the darkness under her eyes purpled so that she looked like she'd been punched. Robert wondered how long it had been since she slept through the night and what thoughts haunted her.

"The two handsome gents with you?"

Angela nodded. "Do your trick."

"Nah. These guys wouldn't be impressed."

"Impresses me every time. Come on, Tony. For old time's sake."

"Okay, okay." The man closed his eyes, pressing his hands together as if praying. He hummed a moment and swayed from one foot to the other before becoming suddenly still. His eyes popped open, fixed first on Jerome and then on Robert. When he spoke again, his voice dropped lower, as if fueled by the darkness of one hundred lost souls. "Waffle cone men," he wheezed. He turned again by Jerome and then staggered back, as if struck. He paused again, taking in Jerome's shirt, his jeans, his glasses. "You're a raspberry brickle kind of guy," he said, then his eyes shifted to Robert and, again, he swayed slightly. "You're a little less certain. Some days, you're rainbow sherbet, but not today. Not with the drizzle and the clouds. You got a cloud hanging over yourself, if you don't mind me saying. No, you'll save those rainbows for another time. Today, you're mocha chip."

Jerome looked at Robert, who could only shrug and nod. The man was right on. "How'd you do that?"

"I been dipping cones all my life. You learn a few things."

"You were paying attention before we knew you were paying attention," Robert said. "You saw where our eyes stopped."

The man shrugged. "And there's maybe something to that as well, but that's way less fun than the swami routine. You want a dipper of strawberry, Ang? In a dish?"

"Not today." She smoothed purse-crumpled bills on the counter as Tony handed out their cones.

"Let me get you your change."

"Nah. You keep it, Tone."

They settled into old-fashioned wicker chairs by the window. The ice cream was rich and fatty. Real cream. No wonder the guy was going out of business. Who made their own ice cream anymore? Maybe if his shop was by the Liberty Bell or on the Floatilla boardwalk, he'd have a selling product, but not in the heart of a slum.

"This was me and Papi's table," Angela said. "He'd sit just where I'm sitting now, all buttoned up in his striped shirt, sipping on an espresso. Straight up, no sugar. The man is old school. Still barely speaks a word of English. Tony knows enough Italian to get by, and Papi likes the coffee here. I'd get a scoop of bubblegum in a glass dish and pick out all the bubblegums onto my napkin so's I could chew them on the way home. It would tickle Papi to no end."

She seemed to choke on that last word, and they all sat in silence for a while. Robert looked for any bridge to his brother, but he couldn't see one. He had to be straight with her, even if being straight felt brutal and cruel. Still, he couldn't quite look her in the eye when he said, "We're trying to find Sean."

"You must think I'm a monster, leaving those babies."

It was as if Robert hadn't spoken. His words evaporated, not leaving even a whisper.

"I only ever had one other serious boyfriend. Did you know that?"

Robert shook his head. With the ice cream cone in his hand, he felt like a child. Ice cream was for beaches and sunny days. It was meant to soothe cranky children or broken hearts. Ice cream was all wrong for this moment, too cold, too sweet.

"Vincent Agresta. We were together six months. That's a long time for high school. I dated other boys here and there, but nothing long term. There was something different about your brother, though. He had something about him that seemed to shine, you know what I mean? He was the only person I ever met who actually had a damned halo. Standing next to him, you felt like you had one glowing on you too. I guess that sounds pretty dumb."

"No. I know what you mean."

"He had that shine right to the end. Even when I found out what he and that little bitch were doing behind my back, he still shined like a fucking angel."

She would tell them now. That was her lead in.

Except she shifted again. "Papi was dead set on me going to college. Him and Ma both. They sent away for all these catalogues, and he'd spend the night paging through them in his easy chair. He couldn't understand a word, but he'd look at those pictures for hours. Stone buildings and green lawns. Labs with people in goggles holding flasks and whatnot. By the time he was fourteen, he was working and saving money to come to America. He didn't even go to high school. He was so proud when I got in at Hassler. *His* granddaughter, and on a scholarship, no less. Now, he just sits in the corner reading his paper. Won't even look at me except when I take him to dialysis, and then only barely."

Robert glanced at Jerome. They were, all of them, trapped in her past.

"Ma said I should get an abortion. Said the babies would ruin my life. Said I was throwing away not only everything I worked for, but everything she worked for and everything Papi worked for. I thought about it. God help me, I did. I wasn't ready to be nobody's mother."

"You don't have to tell us any of this," Robert said, but he might as well have been speaking Hindi. Whatever he said wasn't translating.

"Your brother wouldn't hear any of it. He curled me up

under his arm like he could protect me from anything. We thought I could go back to school later, that I'd have another chance, but if I got rid of the babies, there was no going back on that and things would be finished between him and me. Ironic, huh? Everything I did was to avoid getting exactly where I am now."

"Here you go, Ang." Tony handed her a steaming paper cup. "Hazelnut mocha for that sweet tooth of yours. You look like you could use a boost. On the house."

"You always know."

He shook his head and disappeared into the back again.

"So sweet. Going out of business and still giving me things. Like Sean used to be. Always giving me gifts as if buying stuff would make it all better. We couldn't afford it, but he couldn't stop."

"He was always that way," Robert said. Sean never seemed to realize that borrowed money had to be repaid. Or maybe by the time he realized it, he was in too deep. If you owe fifteen thousand, what's another ten bucks, another twenty? What if that ten bucks could make someone happy, someone you loved? Why stop? Why even hesitate?

"But," Jerome nudged in, "have you maybe seen him lately?" His voice was hopeful, but his eyes were not. Robert read in them the fear that they had hit another dead end. Angela was too far gone, too deeply mired in her own misery.

"You gotta understand—I want you to understand—we was doing our best. Daycare was out of the question, and you know how it is when you're bound to the bus schedule. The timing was always tight. Sean didn't always get home soon enough for me to get to the next swing shift. My God, how I worried. Some days, they'd be sleeping, and I could sneak out, tell myself that he'd be home in just a few minutes, a half hour tops, but some days they were awake and crying, and leaving them pulled the guts right out of me."

Robert didn't want to hear this. Not a word of it. Bad enough to think the sheet had been a one-time thing, but to think it had been a habit?

"Every day, we were further behind. That last week, we couldn't even buy diapers. Everything smelled of piss, and my god, the rashes. But what else could we do? We just stretched everything as thin as it could go so we could make it to the next paycheck." Angela's eyes suddenly went hard. "Then that purple-haired slut found me and told me what had really been going on while I was working all them extra hours. All that hell I'd gone through because I loved your brother? It didn't mean fuck all."

Robert laid his hand on Angela's, hoping his touch might coax her back. At one time, after a day like this, he might have dreamed of strawberry ice cream melting over her skin, of licking it off of her, but now, she was too naked to wish her clothes away.

"You know I didn't want to leave my boys, but between Ma working odd hours and me taking Papi for his treatments, there was no other way. Your mother's a good person. She may have been young like me when she got knocked up, but she did a good job raising you. She'll give Sammy and Deac a better home than I ever did."

That was how she'd constructed the story. Their mother, at home, raising the kids. Not their mother working all day while Robert or Miss Martha raised them. Not their mother going sleepless at night. Not their mother struggling to stretch each penny.

He rubbed Angela's hand. He could feel every bone. They were so thin and fragile, he could have broken them like twigs. "Angela, you have to tell us where Sean is. They're going to collect the money he owes. My mom can't pay it."

"The money? There is no money. We got nothing left."

"Where's Sean?"

"After everything, it's still all about him. It's only ever about him."

"It's just—"

"I gave up every dream I ever had for him and staring out from my own babies' faces is that cheating bastard."

"Please, Angela."

"I used to think I could make a difference in this world. In high school, I aced all those tests, made A's in science and math. Now I'm stuck working the register at a corner store and looking after my dying grandfather and my life won't amount to jack shit unless I do something about it right now."

She was beautiful again. Stunning. One flash of the old lightning in her eyes and all the words froze in Robert's mind, unable to move. Her beauty could work like that. You'd be talking or laughing and then she would move her lips a certain way or bend an eyebrow and it was like a punch to the gut. He couldn't breathe, and every piece of him ached.

Jerome said, "Your mother told us he was in St. Anthony's, but if he's at the hospital, they don't have him listed."

"Hospital?" She stared at them for a moment before finishing her coffee. "Wrong St. Anthony's."

"The phone book listed only churches, a thrift store, and a hospital. Figured he wouldn't be hanging out at a church or a store, so he must be hurt."

"Hurt?" She barked a short, bitter kind of laugh. "Not him. Nothing could hurt him. God knows, I would've liked to."

She tossed her cup into a nearby trashcan. Collecting her purse, she rose from her chair with a trace of her old majesty. She looked clear-eyed and wiser.

"Place changed hands three months ago," she said. "That's why it's not in the book yet. It's the church that sponsors it now, but they never put up a sign or nothing. You passed it on the way to my place, right next to the bus stop."

"By the bus stop?"

She opened her purse and laid every bill in her wallet on the table. Forty-three dollars. "You give this to your mother. It's all I got right now, but I'll send more when I get my next paycheck, like before. To help with the boys and the bills and whatever."

Robert stared at the table. He'd been right. Neither Sean nor Mr. Murphy had given his mother a thought. Angela had been the one to send the money. Of course she had.

"Jesus. Don't look so surprised. I know what your ma thinks of me, but I'm not heartless. Those boys deserve a good life. When I get my shit together, I can send more. It's the best way I can help them now."

He almost let her out the door before he woke up to the fact she was leaving. "Wait," he said. "Wait. What did you mean before, when you said that we passed it?"

"St. Anthony's."

"Yeah?"

"The homeless shelter."

THROUGH STREETS BROAD
AND NARROW

They'd passed it three times. *Three times.* They could have walked right beside Sean on either of their trips to Leona's without ever even realizing it because they hadn't been looking, they only thought they were.

Robert stared at the building, waiting for the lights to change. With a name like St. Anthony's, the building should loom over the street like a cathedral. It should have soaring arches and stained glass and statues of men in robes. Instead, the dull, olive-colored box squatted low over the dirty sidewalk.

Robert stopped at the door. He didn't have to say a word. Jerome knew. He had been there the whole journey, and he understood the weight of every step. The last few months settled in, filling Robert's feet with their sand. This close, he knew he should be running forward. That's how his mother ran her marathons: steady until that final sprint when she kicked hard for the finish and burned whatever last dregs of energy she had left. Now, he should be unstoppable, but he was only exhausted.

He hauled the door open and pushed through the artificial cool towards an empty reception desk. He looked for a bell or a sign telling them what to do, but the desk had no suggestions. The hall stretched left and right. Faint sounds of business drifted from each direction. Robert didn't know anything about homeless people. All he could think about was the dead man they'd stepped past when they first went to Leona's, a guy who'd probably come from or been kicked out of this very shelter.

Robert startled from this thought when the front door flung open behind them, a tattooed guy in thick-rimmed hipster glasses staggering through it with a cardboard box.

"You guys volunteers?"

"What?"

"You helping with dinner tonight? They're in the kitchen now."

"I'm just—"

"Follow me," the guy said, "I'll show you the way."

As he followed, Robert realized he had never really planned on finding his brother. Searching was one thing, but Sean was better at everything. Shouldn't he be better at hiding than Robert was at finding?

The building was like a Russian hospital: clean and stark and crumbling. The linoleum tiles were polished but cracked. It seemed that only their thick layer of wax held them together. The man turned again. Another hall, another left.

Just what his brother had done. Left. He hadn't asked for help, hadn't even hinted that anything was wrong. One day, he was there, and the next, poof.

The swinging door with the diamond-shaped window was fogged with kitchen steam. The man bustled through, but Robert stopped. He looked at Jerome. "Am I making a mistake?"

"Do you have a choice?"

They pushed into a bath of noise and laughter, clinking plates and running water. At a stainless steel island in the middle of the kitchen, Sean stood over a cutting board slicing a mountain of carrots, shouting some joke's punch line to a man washing lettuces in the sink. He looked the same as he always did, but with shaggier hair. His shoulders were as broad and powerful as ever, his smile as bright, his movements as energetic. Robert wasn't prepared for this. Sean should be depressed, dirty, thin. If he was the same old Sean who could handle anything, then what was he doing here?

And yet, in that instant, the familiar Sean-glow washed over Robert, unstoppable as the tide. Its wave buoyed him. It lifted and swept away his doubt. There was Sean. Sean.

A large woman with the voice of a PE coach spotted Robert and Jerome standing by the doorway. "Can I help you?"

"Those are the volunteers," the glasses guy said.

"No," Robert said, flustered by the confusion.

Jerome bailed him out, his voice clear and strong. "We came to get his brother."

Sean clutched his knife, staring. He had showered recently, and his hair was still damp, the drier pieces shining bronzy red in the harsh light. He shook his head, as if the sight of Robert were something too strange to credit.

"You two should talk in private," the woman said. "Come with me."

A faded teddy bear sticker sat on the knob where she fitted her key. "That's me," the woman said. "Just a big teddy bear."

No one contradicted her. She swung the door open and held it as they filed in. "Just close it behind you when you're done," she told Sean and left them to their silence.

Robert searched his mind for any words at all. He'd never before struggled to talk to his brother, but then, his brother had always been the one to do most of the talking.

"You're getting peach fuzz," Sean said.

Robert touched his face, surprised to find it was true. His body was constantly surprising him. Betraying him. Their dad had shown Sean how to shave, but Robert had had no one.

"Some guy's been calling Mom," he said. "A guy from a collection agency."

In the silence, the ticking of the desk clock grew louder. It was an elegant little thing, square and black with little gold hashes to mark the hours. It clashed with the well-dressed teddy bears and scuffed rainbows that decorated the rest of the room.

Somewhere in his gut, Robert felt anger starting to burn again, but he wouldn't give it oxygen.

Sean looked at Jerome, and Robert realized that they had never met. "This is my *friend*," Robert said, but friend felt too flimsy for all that Jerome was. He added, "He's been there since the beginning."

"You weren't easy to find," Jerome said.

"It wasn't always like this."

"Robert told me."

"But it is now," Robert said. "This is exactly what it's like."

"Robert—" Sean said.

"We need to start dealing with the ways things are if we're ever going to fix them."

"I thought maybe they wouldn't find her. The credit card companies. I thought, if I took off, they wouldn't know where to look and maybe they'd just lose track."

"Lose track?" Robert stared. He wanted to be kind. If he was gentle enough, Sean would come home, but he couldn't stop his tongue. "You thought, what? That they'd forget the whole thing? Like it was all just free money?"

"For a credit card company, it was a drop in the bucket."

"They call her every night."

"I fucked up."

"You think?"

"You don't even know how bad."

As if Robert would have been able to find him without having waded right through the middle of Sean's mess. Sean always underestimated him, but Robert knew that havoc Sean had made better than his brother ever had. Robert knew the exact shape of the line that grew between their mother's eyes when the collector guy called. He knew the depth of the hollow that had worn away in Angela's cheek. Sean felt the first shakings of the trouble he'd let loose—then cleared out before it really hit. Robert had been there through the quake and every aftershock.

Tell his brother this and Sean might never come home, so Robert settled for other true things: "Mom will forgive you. She forgave you when you got your girlfriend pregnant, and when you dropped out of school. She'll forgive anything you do, just like she always has, but you can't keep dumping your shit on her. You need to make this right."

"I can't."

"You've got to start trying."

The scent of nutmeg drifted through the door. Whatever they were making in the kitchen smelled good. Homey. Something with sweet potato or pumpkin. Something for fall. Robert could see why Sean wanted to stay. He could feel how little weight Sean carried when there was no one to worry about but himself. That smell said home, but had none of the responsibilities of home. No wonder Sean looked strong here.

"I talked to your coach. He said if you call him, they can maybe see about taking you back on the team. No promises, but it's something, right?"

Sean stared in the corner as if he couldn't begin to process what Robert said.

"Come on. For Mom, if not for yourself."

"It would kill her to see me like this."

"It's not seeing you that's killing her."

"Collectors. She never would have had to face those guys if not for me."

"We have less than two weeks to start paying. That's what the guy told her."

All of Sean's light flickered, and in the moment it was gone, it was as if Robert could see the thinness of the glass, its careful vacuum, the delicacy of that tiny filament that burned so brightly. Any wrong move, and the whole thing could shatter.

Robert held his breath. Next to him, he could feel Jerome holding his.

"You're right," Sean finally said. "I can't help anyone here."

Stepping off the bus, Sean's jaw thrust forward, pulling him on. It was late now. Almost dinner. Robert should have been home an hour ago.

Sean didn't slow down when Jerome peeled off for home to face a mother who, no doubt, had also been wondering where he'd been. Only when they reached the door did Sean stop, hand on the knob, every piece of him suddenly still.

Through the door, they heard one of the twins begin to cry and their mother singing the song she used to soothe Robert and Sean and Bridget. *In Dublin's fair city, where girls are so pretty, I once met a girl named Miss Molly Malone.*

Sean began to shake. Silent sobs racked his body in spite of all his strength. Robert rested one hand on his brother's shoulder. "Come on," he said. He laid his other hand over Sean's and the knob. "You've got this."

Their mother turned, mouth open to speak, but whatever words were about to be spoken died on her tongue. Her eyes locked on her oldest son, and a whimper escaped. Her legs, able to endure miles, faltered. She pressed Sammy close and he began to cry again. In all those weeks, she'd been so strong, but all that strength drained from her in an instant, and Sean rushed to hold her up.

"It's okay," he said. "I'm home."

The word *home* had never sounded so hollow. Robert watched from the door, practically invisible.

"I knew you'd come," she said.

"I'll do better."

Robert couldn't take his eyes off of the moment he had created. It shouldn't have felt so much like a car wreck.

Sean smiled at the baby in their mother's arms. "Deacon is double the size."

"That's Sammy," Robert said.

"Nope. Deacon."

"No!" Their mother was laughing. "Don't tell me that I got it wrong. I was so sure I had it right."

The note seemed sour, but no, they were laughing. It was the thing in Robert that was sour. His mother hadn't even looked at him—not to thank him for fetching Sean, not to scold him for being out late. He didn't matter at all.

"Well," Sean said, "maybe it was Angela and I who called them wrong and they needed to be set right." He took the baby from his mother's arms. "So you're Sammy, now. Was that what you were trying to tell us all those nights you spent crying?"

You couldn't just change the name of things, swapping one boy for the other. You couldn't just hug and laugh and pretend months of misery hadn't happened.

"Robert," their mother said. "Run and get Bridget. Tell her that your brother's home, and it's time for a family supper."

She split the portions that night to make enough for

Sean. Dinner felt like little more than a drop in the bottomless bucket of Robert's stomach. His mother had barely eaten. She sat bouncing babies on her lap.

"It's going to take me a while to remember which one's which."

"Don't," Sean said. "If you've been calling Sammy Deacon and Deacon Sammy, there's no reason to change them now."

Sean's things were already scattered across the floor of what once was Robert's room and now was their room, his and his brother's, like they were boys again, only it felt nothing like when they were boys.

"What will Angela say?" he asked. "You think she would be cool with you just swapping their identities?"

"Robert." A warning.

"You think they're just interchangeable like that? Little dolls you can call whatever you want?"

"That's enough."

"It's okay, Mom," Sean, the good guy, said. "The boys look incredible. They're little champs." Lifting the baby from her arms, he said, "So you're Deacon these days, are you?"

Robert couldn't take any more. He took off down the stairs. From the window, he could hear the phone begin to ring. Robert wanted Sean to answer it. That was how the story was supposed to go. Now that Sean was home, he would face the collector. He'd pay his bills and they would keep their home here in a neighborhood that wasn't the best neighborhood but was far from the worst. Sean, the hero, was supposed to save the day.

But the ringing continued and Robert turned towards the row house to sit with the rats and the gun, neither of which was great company.

The sophomore girl who sat in front of him in math always wore

ONE OF MANY
UNFORTUNATE THINGS

a biker jacket. Her name was Melody but she went by Mel, which struck Robert as one of many unfortunate things about her. He was watching the stretch of fake leather across her massive shoulders when she turned to him, the jacket making a squelching sound as it rubbed across the plastic chair.

"Heard you ratted out Maurice."

Her voice was thick and raspy and her brown hair fell unbrushed around her broad, pale, pumpkin-like face. She gazed on him with half-closed eyes as if, at eleven in the morning, she were already stoned. And maybe she was, though Robert suspected that her high, like the jacket, was costuming for some part in which she had cast herself.

"Oregon, Oregon," she said, her tone all pity. "Don't you know that snitches get stitches?"

"Guess I skimmed that page of the rules."

"He's going to be coming for you when Monday rolls around. Where you guys going to throw down?"

Joan's eyes burned on the side of his face, waiting for his answer.

"We haven't really made solid plans," he said.

Mel rested eyes on him that seemed to have the wisdom of one hundred years rather than fifteen. It was all part of her stoner look, that inner ganga soul knowledge. Nothing could phase her smoker Zen.

"Killer," she said, though there was not one killer thing about it that Robert could see, unless you counted that Maurice might kill him.

Mel said, "Heard you're hooking up with Jerome, too. A lover and a fighter, huh?"

"Hooking up?"

"What? The guy's pretty cute. You could do worse."

Robert stared at her until she turned away.

Joan didn't seem to know whether to look at him or her books. Most of the girls he knew weren't elegant, but she was. Elegant, aloof, sublime. Her chin and throat were like things that had been sculpted.

"He's my best friend." Robert's tone was tetchier than he'd meant it to be, and he hoped Joan didn't think his irritation was directed at her. "Why do people need to make it into something sexual?"

"Maybe they're jealous."

Her voice was deep and musical, like some kind of woodwind, but nothing as ordinary as a flute or clarinet. They needed to invent a whole new instrument to capture that sound.

"Are you really going to fight Maurice?"

"If I have to."

"Define 'have to.'"

"If there's no choice."

"There's always a choice."

Then explain why I'm here, he wanted to say. Explain why I'm not in Oregon with a father who's alive.

He settled for, "Not always."

"No," she finally agreed. "Not always."

Mr. Burns called roll, and Robert answered to Bobby Flannigan. As he did, he felt the brush of paper against his skin.

He opened the note carefully, shielding it behind Mel's back. It read, "Do you determine 'have to,' or does Maurice?"

Robert walked home that afternoon to find the apartment empty. On the counter, a note read: "Took twins w/ me. S."

Robert stared at the unflinching lines of each block letter. Sean had insisted on keeping the boys home with him that morning. He said it was about saving money on childcare, but Robert knew it also gave him an excuse to put off calling Murphy for another day. Sean could have been spending time with his boys any time these past weeks, but now he was acting the part of the caring father and expecting them to believe it, and Robert was done.

He crushed the paper in his fist, and then slammed a frozen burrito into the microwave. He got out his English book because he had nothing better to do on a Friday afternoon, and God only knew when the next quiet moment would be now that Sean was back. What an idiot Robert had been to believe things would be different. It was as if he'd never known his brother at all, as if, all these weeks, he'd been looking for another man altogether.

He poured salsa onto the burrito and bit in, but the molten beans burned his tongue, and he couldn't get milk out of the jug fast enough to cool it. He tried his homework again but reading was impossible. The words refused to come off of the page and into his head. Every thought filled with Sean. Robert didn't know how he could be able to find his brother but be unable to remember who he was. How could one person be so smart and so stupid?

Robert wished this anger were a wound he could lance. He wanted to pop rage like a zit, squeeze the infection, swab on some peroxide and let it heal. Instead, it swirled with the beans in his stomach like concrete in a mixer, settling to form a block in his gut.

In his room, he checked for the gun. He'd known last night that he shouldn't bring it home, but he couldn't seem to help himself. Now, he slipped his hand between the wall and the bed and felt for it tucked safely beneath the mattress.

He returned to the kitchen, smacked on the radio. The newscaster was talking about a kid in Wyoming found beaten and dying against a fencepost. He turned the tuner away until he found the local music, heavy bass punctuated with a tsk, tsk. Philadelphia's anthem. He closed his eyes and let its aggression wash into him. *This*, he thought. This was better.

He looked at his math notes and thought about Joan, picturing her waving her head to the music, how her hair would sweep the tabletop. Tsk, tsk, boom. He didn't listen to the words— he didn't need language at all. He wanted facts, cold numbers, lines drawn in the sand. He wanted what was. The whole "might be" thing was nothing but the lure in a trap. Listen to it, and the next sound you'd hear was its snap.

He still had the story to read for English when Bridget raced in. "Where's Sean?"

"Beats me," Robert replied. His mother heard from the doorway, a bag of groceries in her arms and her mouth pressed in its familiar frown. Robert's own mouth had been sealed in that same line all afternoon. He smoothed the crumpled note and slid it across the table. "He took them, Mom. He took the babies."

"He'll be back."

"What has he ever done to make you believe that?"

"Don't be so melodramatic."

She flicked off the radio, not bothering to replace it with

her own music. Her shoulders carried the old tension as she pulled ground beef and lettuce from the bag, setting each on the counter with careful deliberation. The Styrofoam meat tray and the block of cheddar were parallel to the countertop's edge. She lined up the tomatoes precisely alongside the package of buns. She couldn't control her son, but she could control the placement of each ingredient. She turned the beef into a bowl and crushed in salt, garlic powder, and pepper with firm hands.

Robert couldn't take it. He snatched his backpack from the chair and shut himself behind his bedroom door. Or not his. Theirs. Only the bed was his now. The bed and what it concealed: a banjo, a gun.

The reading for English was twice the length of their usual assignments. Melville took too long to get to the fucking point. Robert read the paragraph again, trying to make the black ink become words, become actions or character, become concepts he could care about, but they simply remained ink. He'd had enough. He lifted the book and heaved it into the corner, where it landed with a muffled thud in his brother's dirty clothes. Another failure: he'd had a chance to hurl the book against the wall, to dent the corners of its cardboard cover or, better still, break its spine, and he hadn't even done that right. He flopped to his stomach and dragged the banjo from under the bed, pulling it through his brother's crap. This time, he did not bother to dampen its sound. He moved his fingers over the strings, letting each voice its own steely, uncompromising sound. Maybe his mother wouldn't listen to him, but the banjo would, and as it listened, it spoke all he felt back into the world.

As they ate that night, Bridget chattered about school and the black cats they made to decorate the classroom and whether, this year, she would be a cowgirl or a witch or a green man or a robot. Their mom would sew her costume like she always did, wouldn't she? "Of course," their mother said, though they all knew she had no time and Sean's being home didn't seem likely to change that.

"Robert has to dress up too," Bridget gushed on, "so he can take me trick-or-treating."

He didn't know if they did that in this neighborhood or if it was dangerous, but he didn't tell Bridget that. They hadn't gone last year, not after having just buried their father. He didn't have the heart to tell her that maybe their dad's death had killed Halloween altogether. The holiday was haunted now more terribly than it had ever been by the cheesecloth ghosts that their parents used to hang in the fir trees outside their home.

Their mom had cooked two burgers for Sean, but they sat on the platter in a pool of congealing grease. Dinner felt strange, so uninterrupted. They ate without stopping to feed a baby or comfort one's cries or remove a toy from a mouth or change a stinky diaper. It seemed impossible that, until a couple months ago, they had always eaten this way.

"Did you finish that story you were reading?" his mother asked.

"Nope."

"You've been playing that banjo for an hour."

"Yeah. I guess you'll probably use that as an excuse to sell it."

"Don't change the subject."

"How am I supposed to concentrate when Sean took the babies?"

"And don't make this about Sean."

"But it is about Sean. It's always about Sean. That's how this family functions."

"We're talking about you now, Robert."

"Well, that's a first now, isn't it?"

His mother's face flashed bright with anger like a blade turned in the sun, but whatever she was about to say fell away from her lips as the front door opened. Sean strode in, his duffel-turned-diaper bag over one shoulder, the umbrella stroller on his arm, and a baby cradled in each massive hand. "Those burgers smell great," he said, smiling as if nothing were wrong or strange or his fault.

"They'll be cold," his mother said. "Let's get those babies fed too. You guys must be starving."

Robert waited for her to say more. Instead, she fixed Sean his burgers, aggressively piling on tomato, lettuce, and pickles.

Bridget's voice pitched high with excitement or relief. "Sean, we made cats today!" Which Sean would have known if he'd been there.

"That's great, Bridge." He shoved a burger into his face. Anger hung like a fog around their mother, too diffuse to land where it should.

Robert couldn't let it slide. "Where were you?"

"Around," his brother said through another enormous bite. "I went to see if I could talk to Angela."

"That took all day?"

"I thought she cleared out," his mother said, because Robert never told her how he'd found his brother. Because she never asked.

"Huh-uh," Sean grunted through a mouthful. "At Leona's."

His mother didn't tell her son how many times she had called there looking for any hint or hope. Instead, she said, "You were always too good for that girl."

Robert stared. "You're blaming Angela?"

"What kind of woman leaves her own babies?"

"Angela's nice," Bridget said.

"I was young when I had Sean, but I stepped up. I owned my behavior and found out that it didn't have to be a mistake. Sean was the best thing that ever happened to me."

Sean said, "She had good reason to go."

"A mother doesn't desert her babies." Their mom bent to kiss Sammy and Deacon each on the head, as if they needed a demonstration of what a mother's love looked like.

"You've got to be kidding me," Robert said. If he thought it would make his mother snap out of it, he would have thrown his plate against the wall, let it shatter and shatter her false reality.

Sean was softer: "She needed a clean start."

"He cheated on her, Mom, and then he dumped his kids."

"Robert!"

"It's true," Sean said.

"It's poison." Her chin was tucked and her voice low ,as if she were speaking directly to her own heart. She stood and put her plate in the sink, refusing to look at either of her sons, then clicked on her music and turned it up so that no more could be heard over the northwest grunge, clacking stoneware, and constantly running water.

Robert sealed himself in his room. Their room.

The whole scene was a replay of that one night in the fall of Sean's junior year when he stole the Buick and disappeared with his girlfriend. All weekend, their father paced and muttered, and their mother fussed over Bridget, just a baby then. The girl's parents called and, seeing the name on the caller ID, his parents didn't answer. Worst-case scenarios shrouded their faces. Without a way to get to the store, their mother improvised stir-fries from the last of the mismatched, frozen vegetables.

Then Sunday night, there was the car, bouncing up the rutted road with Sean grinning behind the wheel. As he pulled his camping gear from the trunk, their father turned towards the door with a face full of fire, but their mother stopped him with just two fingers on his elbow. "The boy needed a break," she said. "All that game pressure? Just think about it. Put yourself in his shoes. He needed a little time away."

Now, her Nirvana thrummed through the thin walls, so he played right back at it. Sometimes, the only thing in the world that made any sense was the sound of his banjo. In Robert's hands, it sounded nothing like it had in his father's or grandfather's. No doubt, he was picking it wrong. His style was hardly textbook. He didn't care. He wanted to play it every way he could think of, to find each new way to pull sound from its strings. His fingers moved in directions he hadn't known they could move, pressing frets in any combination he could conceive. When he got things wrong, they buzzed at him, but he loved even the sounds of those buzzes, their drunken excitement.

The door opened, and he looked up to see Sean watching him. "Dad's old banjo," Sean said. "I didn't know you could play."

Robert didn't want to talk. If he spoke, he would only say the wrong thing.

"Mom said to remind you to take the trash to the dumpster."

Robert glared.

"Whoa. Don't shoot the messenger. How long have you been playing that thing?"

"Since dad died."

"You're pretty good. We should get you a guitar or something."

"I don't want a guitar."

"Whatever. I just thought you'd want something a little more rock n roll. You'd be a little chick magnet."

"Get a girlfriend, huh? Maybe I could knock her up while I'm at it. That sure worked out well for you."

"When the hell did you get so moody?"

Robert wasn't moody, he wanted to say, or hadn't been,

until someone decided to dump his babies. Until his mother made him her make-up child, pouring all the parenting on him that she hadn't used on Sean.

Robert let the banjo speak. He wanted to play loud enough to aggravate his mother and drive his brother away. And Sean would leave. It was inevitable. It was what he did best.

Saturday morning. Robert snapped off the flashlight. In the darkness of the abandoned tenement, he listened to the steadiness of Jerome's breath.

"You have to tell me."

"Tell you what?"

"Whether you're straight or gay."

"You said you didn't care."

"I don't."

"If you didn't care, you wouldn't ask."

"Every day, I'm surrounded by things I don't know."

"So?"

"So I want to know this."

Jerome didn't reply.

"You know everything about me. You know how fucked up my brother is and about the debt collector and about Joan and everything. I just want to know this one thing."

He might as well have been talking to the stack of rocks.

"I guess that means you are, then. Gay. If you weren't, you'd say so."

Still, nothing.

"See? I didn't leave."

Only darkness.

"I wouldn't. I really don't care. You really think I'd leave you now? After everything?"

Silence hung again, thick as a heavy curtain in some rich lady's parlor. Not a glimmer shown through, until finally Jerome said, "I don't know."

"What do you mean you don't know? You can hear me. You can touch my hand. You'd have heard the plywood if I'd gone."

"Not that. I don't know what I am. Sometimes, all I can think about is girls. But then there's my dreams. They go every kind of way."

"So you're straight? Everyone has weird dreams."

"Haven't you been listening? I don't know what I am. Those dreams? They don't feel wrong. Nothing feels wrong, not like it should."

Now, it was Robert's turn for silence.

"Guess that doesn't help clear up any mysteries. Guess you get to be just as confused as me."

The walls were full of scurrying again. They screeched like they were fighting, and then settled.

"Do you dream about Maurice?"

"I can't control my dreams."

"Do you dream about me?"

"Robert."

"I'm serious."

"A couple of times."

Silence.

"Does that freak you out?"

Silence.

"Robert?"

"Maybe a little."

"Shit. I knew I shouldn't a said—"

"Jerome?"

"What?"

"I'm still here."

SCRAPS

Robert walked out on Monday to be washed by sunshine. The breeze blowing over the Delaware had ushered out the city's smog and the sky was a shade of blue so deep that it seemed like an ocean. The morning was crisp. After a weekend cramped in an apartment with too many people, Robert should have been in no mood for a beautiful morning. He should have wanted darkness and storms and flashing lightning, something temperamental, something enraged, but he'd been dreaming of Joan when he woke up that morning. They'd been sitting on the wall in front of Garvey, and she laid her hand on his thigh. They sat there in the sun, nothing happening whatsoever, when his clock radio went off. He thumped the snooze button, but it was too late to go back. Even so, he felt bathed in that calm.

For the first time since moving, Robert grabbed his jacket on the way out the door. The trees were wearing their finest threads, hints of gold running along the veins of their leaves, which danced on the ends of the branches. Today, all the world was flirting.

"Man," Jerome said as he bounced down the front steps of his building, "my sister is such a bitch."

"What'd she do now?" Robert asked as they fell into an easy stride.

"Just being herself. That's enough."

"She and my brother should have an asshole contest."

"This morning, she hogged all the scrapple."

Robert didn't dare ask, but Jerome knew in a glance:

"You don't know what scrapple is, do you?"

"I know it's a breakfast food."

"Not a breakfast food. *The* breakfast food."

"Sounds gross. What is it, made out of leftovers or something?"

"When you don't know better, you should at least know better than to open your mouth. You ever hear that?"

"What is it, some kind of sausage? Probably like hot dogs, made from all the nasty parts of things. Eyeballs or pig snouts."

"Just stop. There's no guessing what scrapple is. You just have to taste it, and it has to have been cooked by someone who knows how. That's all."

"In other words, it's just like everything else here. It's a secret and no one outside the city is allowed to know."

"What are you talking about? We're the most open place there is. If you need to know something, then no one's going to set you straight faster than someone from Philly."

Which was true enough. This town loved proclaiming shit. Speaking out was a point of pride that went straight back to its roots. Sean had taken their family to see the Liberty Bell on Sunday. Robert hadn't known what to expect, but he certainly hadn't expected the bell to have its own house or that the house would look so much like the rest areas they'd stopped at on the drive from Oregon. He hadn't known that arsenic was one of the bell's ingredients, along with copper, tin, and lead. He knew the bell was cracked, but he hadn't known the real break was small, almost invisible, and that the crack he'd known about was only the repair, or that the repair had failed, that it cracked again and was taken out of service. The massive, useless hunk was only a symbol, like a word but heavier.

Proclaim Liberty Throughout All the Land Unto All Inhabitants thereof it said. An order. Could you order someone to proclaim liberty? Wasn't an order the opposite of liberty? It was awfully bossy for a bell. Or maybe it was the bell itself that was being bossed around by whoever inscribed the words there in the first place, and it was the one supposed to do the proclaiming? No wonder the thing was broken. It couldn't get its own story straight.

He imagined what the bell must have looked like once it got going, the heft of it swinging on that solid wooden yoke. Once it got going, there would have been no stopping it. You just had to wait until it played itself out. That was Philly, all right.

"Maurice will be back today," Jerome said.

Strange, how people liked guys who were mean to the weak, but they did. Even the girls—no, *especially* the girls. They'd flocked to every brute he'd ever known just like they flocked to Maurice. Sean, too, though Sean never picked fights. He beat weaker guys on the football field, but that was enough. Maybe the trick to being loved was to make everyone else into a loser. No wonder Angela couldn't love Sean anymore.

Jerome kicked a broken bit of concrete down the sidewalk in front of them. It skittered along, bouncing in one direction and then another as its odd corners caught the pavement. "You got a plan for Maurice?"

"No."

"Just promise me you'll watch your back. I'm going to watch it for you, but you got to watch out for yourself, too. Where do you think he'll try to jump you?"

"I don't know."

"Might even try it on the way to school."

"Do we have to talk about this?"

"He could be packing. You need to think through your options."

Robert kicked at the concrete rock, but his angle was off. Like everything Robert did lately, it went wrong, bouncing down the storm drain. They stopped to listen to it drop.

"What would you do if Maurice had a gun?"

"I'm not going to think about that right now."

"You're not going to what? Man, you got no choice *but* to think about it."

"He couldn't get it past the metal detectors."

"You so sure?"

"He can't do anything in school. People know. They'll be watching."

"They who?"

"Dr. Turner. The teachers. Maybe even the police?"

"Oh, so now you think they can help? Cause they've been so much help so far?"

Robert looked at his feet. However fast they could run wouldn't be fast enough. "Maybe you should keep your distance today," he said.

"Like hell."

"It's me who talked. I'll say so, and I'll take the heat. You should just stay back."

"You really think that's how I'd do? After all we've been through?"

"Naw," Robert admitted, grinning. The deal was, they stuck together, even now, even after Robert messed up. He knocked his shoulder into Jerome's. "I love you, man," Robert said.

"Course you do, cause it's like I always said. We're brothers, brother."

Joan was leaning against Robert's locker, staring the wrong way down the hall, looking bored. He watched her back. Her worn blue jeans rested on her hips. He wanted to slide up behind her, sink his hands into her front pockets, and rest his chin on her shoulder. He wanted to feel her hair brushing his cheek and to turn his nose into it and smell her shampoo.

Maybe that's how that kid at her last school ended up with a broken rib.

He knew what he couldn't do, but he didn't know what he could. He needed her to move, but he didn't want her to go anywhere else. "Um," he said, suddenly back to being *I'm, Um* again, real smooth. "This is my locker."

She turned to him, languid as a cat. "I know," she said. "That's why I'm here."

"Oh." He tried to control the surprise in his voice, but he could hear it nonetheless, and her smile meant she heard it too. Jerome tapped the back of his hand several times quickly, as if Robert needed to be subtly woken up to how cool this was. Robert wouldn't look at him. He couldn't. Girls didn't wait by the lockers of guys who were surprised by their attention.

He stood, every inch of him endlessly goofy, trying to figure out what to do with his hands. He couldn't cross them in front of himself. That would look defensive. But if he put them in his pockets, he'd look like a hick. And how should he carry his eyes? A cool guy would look indifferent, but if he looked away from Joan, she'd think he didn't care or wasn't interested and might take off in search of someone who appreciated her like she deserved. Looking at her was too direct, too rude, but to look away was worse—what if she thought he was checking out some other girl and pegged him as a creeper? So he should look at her, certainly, but where? He wanted to look at her shoulder, so straight and slender and strong, but to look at a girl's shoulder was definitely creepy, and so if not there, then where?

He'd let the silence hang too long. He had no idea what

to say to fill it.

"You haven't seen Maurice, have you?" Jerome asked.

Robert shot him a look, then turned to his locker, desperately trying to remember his combination as he stood so close to Joan. He spun and spun the knob.

"You're not going to actually fight him, are you?"

"I don't know."

"Okay," she said.

The steadiness of that word, the ease with which she said it, was like a wall he could lean against. He felt stronger.

"You ready for our math test?"

So that was why Joan had come to see him. He clicked his lock open, thankful he wasn't looking at her because he knew he had no poker face. He said, "I guess."

"Oh. Then, I don't suppose you want to study with me."

She focused on adjusting the strap of her backpack. If he hadn't known better, he'd have sworn that she was nervous too, but come on—that was ridiculous. She brushed a stray hair from her face and looked off down the hall. Jerome shoved Robert hard in the back.

"Study?" Robert said.

"For the test."

"Yeah. Absolutely. I mean, you can never be too prepared, right? Studying sounds fantastic!"

Yes, Robert told himself. All he'd needed to say was yes, but he'd turned into a babbling idiot.

"I was thinking maybe the library?"

"That's the perfect place."

They stood there, her looking at him, neither of them moving.

"So," she said, hesitating, "would now be a good time?"

"Absolutely."

"Y'all go study," Jerome said, grinning like a crazy person. He gave Robert a look that meant he expected to hear all about it later. "I'll see you at lunch."

"You'll be okay?"

"Me? Damn. *You're* the one with the mark on your back."

Robert fell into step with Joan as they headed to the library. She just wanted math help, he reminded himself. That's all this was. She'd only asked him because they happened to share a desk. Even so, he was, at that moment, walking through the halls with the most beautiful girl in the entire school.

Joan didn't seem to mind his silence. He could see her being an ice queen if you stripped that name of all its cruel intent. She carried herself that way: regal and cool. So many of the others here were loud and boisterous and expressive. If they felt something, they let you know it. Joan was different. She didn't talk all the time, and she didn't expect him to talk. She and Robert were people who could be quiet together.

The library was one of the few rooms in the building that wasn't cramped, probably because the administration didn't spend a lot of money on adding new books to the stacks. He checked his watch. Fifteen minutes until they had to be in their first class. This early, Robert and Joan had the place pretty much to themselves.

"Where do you want to start?" he said.

"Let's trade notes and see if we can figure out what he'll ask."

Joan pulled her chair next to his so that their elbows occasionally bumped. Or kissed. Could elbows kiss? Robert decided that they could and that he would continue to believe that until anything came to prove him wrong. He hoped desperately that nothing ever would.

He flipped through his notes, trying to find the start of the unit, but she was so close that he could feel her breathing next to him. She might be an ice queen, but her skin was warm. He imagined trailing his fingers down the long bones from her shoulder to her fingertips, and the thought made him dizzy.

"Wait a minute." She laid her hand on his to stop him flipping more pages. "There. Circles." Her touch was so light it scarcely seemed to touch at all. He was sweating. Not gross sweating, thank God, but enough to dampen his palms and forehead. He stole a glance at her as she ran her pink fingernail under his notes.

The first warning bell rang, startling him. "I guess we didn't get very far," he said.

Joan ignored the bell, scanning over his pencil marks and turning pages. The rate at which she read was dazzling. She paused at a formula and said, "Do you have this right?"

"What?"

"I have r squared, but you just have r."

Robert flipped to the page in their math book. "Sure enough," he said, "r squared. I thought I was supposed to be helping you study."

"We're helping each other," she said, smiling down at the notes with a warmth that shattered any thoughts of ice. He could melt from her radiance, leaving him nothing more than a puddle on a chair. A happy puddle. A puddle who wouldn't have to worry about math or Maurice or mothers or brothers or any other nonsense at all.

"We've got three minutes before we really have to go," Joan said. "Did I have anything different?"

Her pencil marks were barely darker than the paper. Her letters were small and square, precise as those from a typewriter. Looking now, he realized she was good at math. Really good.

Better than he was. She jotted questions and observations in the margins that predicted each new section, her mind moving faster than the book, independent of lessons.

"He'll definitely ask questions about triangles," Robert said. "It's all he ever talks about lately."

She nodded. The second warning bell rang. She said, "If Maurice does come at you, what's your plan?"

"Honestly, I don't know. I don't have a plan at all."

"If you fight, don't use weapons and don't break any bones. They'll let you get away with some things, but not those."

"I hadn't really planned on breaking bones."

"Good. It'd be better still not to fight at all." She took his hand quickly and squeezed it. "If you get expelled, I won't have any friends in this school."

She turned and ran to class and Robert stood there, watching her go, his mind buzzing and snapping. She thought he could break a bone. She squeezed his hand. Squeezed it! She hadn't needed his help at math. She just wanted to be with him. Alone. Sure, she'd used the *friend* word, but she squeezed his hand! He kept circling back to this. Squeezing it not like a friend because you didn't squeeze a friend's hand.

Everything inside him was bubble and fizz. He broke into a run towards biology. His hand would be warm forever.

ONE TEST

Joan was already at the desk when he got there, flipping through the neat stack of pages in front of her.

"Want to trade again?" he said.

"Sure."

Not a single thing was sinking in, but he didn't care. His eyes traced the figures she'd drawn on the paper. Math notes had never been so sexy. Every curve seemed to offer a promise. Every digit whispered in his ear.

"Put your books away and get out a pencil," Mr. Burns said as he shut the classroom door. If ever there were words to kill hope, those were the ones to do it. Robert suddenly remembered what he had known last night but forgotten this morning: this test was actually important.

He rifled through his bag looking for a sharp pencil. Mr. Burns was already silently handing stacks to the front row, but Robert could hear his words echoing in his mind. *I don't really think you want to go down a level.* No. No, he didn't. Not when Joan was here.

Mel's jacket made its weird noises as she turned to offer him the stack of tests. He took one, passed the rest, and tried to remember how to breathe. He looked at the first question.

For two long seconds, he panicked, certain that they'd studied the wrong chapter. Nothing looked familiar. Nothing made sense. But then he read the question one more time and the panic rolled away like fog over the sea. Easy. He worked the problem through the formula and wrote the solution. In his mind, he could see the clear, fine printing of Joan's notes. He answered the next question and the next. Everything he needed to know was all there inside him, neatly stowed in pockets of his brain waiting for the question to access it.

He finished the test with ten minutes to spare and looked back over his answers. He exhaled a long breath. He'd aced it. He'd never been so certain of anything in his life. In spite of Sean and the babies and smooth-skinned girls who smelled of raspberries, in spite of *Slayers* and banjos and English quizzes and bus rides across town, in spite of every failure in his life, he'd not failed this. He met Mr. Burns's eye as he handed in the test. Mr. Burns almost seemed to return Robert's grin, though his lips never moved and his eyes remained steady.

Robert hazarded a glance at Joan, but she had finished well before he had and was now too busy reading to notice him walking back to their desk. Which meant she was a nerd, too. He was finding his people.

He reached for his English book, figuring he might as well get a jump on things there. He had some recovery work to do. He'd answered every question on that morning's quiz with "I prefer not to," "I prefer not to," the only line he could remember from that stupid story and one sure to piss his teacher off, but maybe it wasn't too late to turn this year around. Out of all the guys in the school, it was just possible that Joan preferred him.

Robert was surprised that he could read with her so near, but actually, it was easy. Joan carried a stillness that made the air around her go quiet. He could imagine the whole rest of high school spent like this: the two of them snuggled up on the couch reading together or working out problems or going to watch TV with Jerome.

Only when Joan nudged him did he realize the bell had rung. "Good book?" she asked. He could tell she was laughing at him but only a little and in a way that maybe meant he was somehow endearing.

"Just English."

"You seemed pretty enthralled."

I am, he wanted to say, looking deep into her eyes to show that it was her he was enthralled with, not the book, but he just shrugged and lifted his bag.

"Why did you break that girl's rib?" he said, and immediately wanted to suck the question back out of the air and into himself, where he'd be content to leave it. It was as if he'd been so busy guarding against saying one thing that the question spilled from his mouth before he could stop it. Her expression was shocked and hurt, and he'd done that, and he couldn't take it back but would try. "You don't have to answer," he said. "It's just, you don't seem like that kind of person."

"Where did you hear that I'd broken someone's rib?"

"Isn't that why you were expelled?"

"Jesus."

Fucking Ricky and his rumors. Just because people said something didn't make it true—why did he have to keep learning that? He didn't begin to know how to apologize. "No wonder it didn't make sense. I'm such an idiot."

"Whatever. I get it. You didn't know me and you believed what you heard."

"I shouldn't have."

"Christ. Why did you even *talk* to me if that's what you thought?"

"I wanted to know you."

Her eyes were on his, searching for truth, but the rest of her seemed poised to leave him forever.

"You're kind of a bad ass, you know. I guess I figured, if you had fought some girl, then you had a good reason for it."

"A reason to break someone's rib? I thought you were nice, but you're just like every other dumb shit here. What could possibly justify that?"

"No, please." He grabbed her arm. He had one chance to not blow this. He weighed his words, looking for ones heavy enough to hold her. "It's not coming out right. What I mean is that I trusted you."

"You didn't know me."

"I know you now—at least a bit. I know you're the smartest girl in our math class and that you feel like you don't fit here, just like me. I know you're lonely because why else would you talk to me? And I know you're nice. That's why the story didn't make sense. That's why I asked. Please don't leave."

She looked down the hall. Half of her seemed already gone, but the other half hesitated. Under her breath she said, "I grabbed my mom's lunch bag."

"What?"

"That's how I got expelled. It had a steak knife."

"They can't expel you for that."

"Not every school is like Garvey or Oregon or whatever. Things were strict there—zero tolerance—and they'd already made one exception. You're not supposed to make the same mistake twice."

"You got expelled over a lunch bag?"

He hadn't meant to be funny, but he noticed a small smile tug at her lip in spite of herself. "I know. It's dumb."

"Why didn't your mom get different colored bags?"

"She did. My mom leaves early, though, and she's always a little loopy before her coffee. She mixes them up all the time. Usually, it's no big deal."

"Well, I'm glad it brought you here." It wasn't his smoothest speech, but she curled her fingers around his hand, her silver bangles skittering against his wrist.

The minute bell rang. A blush spread over his face as she hurried away. Things had gone so wrong for so long that it seemed impossible that this one thing might go right.

Jerome was well into his Fritos. "What took you so long? I was starting to worry that you had got jumped."

"Sorry," Robert said. He could still see the sway of her hips as she'd rushed down the hall.

"Well?"

"Well what?"

"Well, does she like you? What happened?"

"We studied."

Jerome stared at him before saying, "You are one exasperating S.O.B."

"What do you want me to say? We were in the library. We had fifteen minutes."

"A lot can happen in fifteen minutes in a library."

Robert laughed in spite of himself. "I think I aced my math test."

"What is that? Is that code? Are you trying to tell me something did go down with you and the ice queen?"

"No, man. I'm trying to tell you that I think I got an A on Burnsie's test."

"No one gets an A on a Burns test."

"I think I just did." His mind went soft at the edges, like the ripples in Joan's hair, knowing that he might just have succeeded in keeping his spot in the class with the desk they shared together.

FIGHT OR FLIGHT

Robert had made it the whole day, but now, as they walked home, Maurice was walking behind them, flanked by friends and wannabe friends and trailed by kids who just wanted to witness blood. Robert didn't turn to look. He didn't need to. Even before Maurice said a word, Robert could feel him there among the rush of voices, a solid force, a moving wall.

"Look at the faggoty-ass way he walks," Maurice said to anyone listening. Robert's Converse scuffed the broken concrete. The words were stupid, but they created new truths. Now, one of them had a faggoty-ass walk.

One block from school, and everything was hard edges and concrete. There wasn't a tree or a hedge or even a pot on a sill. The only things growing here were the beaten-down weeds sprouting in the cracks of the sidewalks, but looking at them, Robert remembered his theory about perseverance and stretched himself tall towards the broad blue sky. Jerome started to speed up, but Robert did not. He would not walk even one little bit faster for Maurice. If you were a Flannigan, he decided, running had one place, and that place was the track and field. Run there, and you were a champion. Run from problems, and problems chased you down.

Robert stopped and turned. Inside, he heard Joan's voice when he asked about the broken rib. *You're just like every other dumb shit here. What could possibly justify that?* But if there was another way besides violence, he couldn't see it.

In the television version of this moment, standing up would have been enough. Maurice, surprised, impressed by Robert's bravado, would clap a hand on his shoulder and say he was all right. They wouldn't need to throw a single punch. Instead, they walked shoulder to shoulder into an alley where they could fight this thing to the end. The shuffling feet followed them, every kid certain that Maurice would win. He'd have to stop soon, to turn and see them waiting for him to fail. Which he would.

The afternoon sunlight abandoned them. In the building shadows, the air reeked of stale urine and fetid dumpsters. Why did every hidden corner of Philly smell like piss? Robert had never actually witnessed anyone peeing on a building, but to smell the place, you'd think a whole fleet of guys whipped their dicks out every night. He imagined them, some sort of reverse garbage men, there to ensure the place stayed filthy. They'd wear blue jumpsuits with elastic-belted waists and a patch shaped like a penis on an embroidered yellow splash on their chest, just to the left side of the zipper. At any other time, this thought would have made him smile.

Robert turned, settling his weight into his feet, trying to find some kind of stability in the sidewalk beneath him. With his split lip healed, Maurice didn't really look all that menacing. If anything, with his white teeth and smooth skin and freshly trimmed hair and clean polo shirt, he looked downright dashing, but Robert only saw that the guy was an asshole. This whole thing was about shoving a kid down stairs when he wasn't looking. This was about handcuffs and nakedness and laughter. This was about staring disaster in the face and refusing to flinch. This was about knowing you'd lose but fighting anyway. This was about what Sean hadn't done.

Hit first.

Before he'd even finished the thought, Robert found himself rushing at Maurice, swinging before the guy had time to put up his hands. Maurice ducked, but not soon enough. Robert felt the knuckles of his right hand drive into the boney shoulder, twisting Maurice to the left as Robert's other hand came up to meet Maurice's chin. All hell broke loose, a chaos of shouting and movement. Robert fought like a berserker, flinging his fists randomly, hoping his punches would land.

Maurice was knocked to the ground, but launched himself back up, tackling Robert with a shoulder to the chest. Robert heard the whack of his own skull against concrete, and then the world blurred and darkened. The alley sound dulled behind a wall of static, distant and obscure. Maurice's next punch startled Robert back to some kind of consciousness. Blood oozed through his hair. Maurice straddled him, swinging away in a flurry of slugs. Robert absorbed them all, feeling each one from his teeth to his knees.

The crowd noise dulled as Maurice's punches weakened. Robert gathered his strength and shoved Maurice away. He rose to a crouch and fought for breath. Blood filled his mouth. His teeth felt loose and his gums were foreign.

In a week, his family would lose everything. In a week, his father would be one year dead. In a week, none of this would matter: they'd be moving to another neighborhood, another school. Perhaps these thoughts should have stopped Robert from fighting, but they fueled him on. Robert swung, hitting the ribs, but Maurice ducked his follow-up. Robert was getting slow. No one ever told him that fighting was so exhausting. They'd been at it a minute, two at most, and already, he just wanted it to be over, to lie down, to sleep. Every muscle ached.

Robert blinked rapidly to clear his eyesight, and Maurice landed another punch to his gut. Robert crumpled, the air rushing from him, and Maurice kicked him hard on the shoulder before pausing to catch his breath.

He towered over Robert with a bloody smile. "Stay down," Robert heard people saying. He glanced around him, but the faces were only hallway faces, passingly familiar at best. After everything they'd been through, Jerome was gone.

Robert understood the triumph in Maurice's stance. The Chum beat at you every day, but you didn't have to stay beaten. Not if you could pass it on. Shit might roll downhill, but you didn't have to lie in the trough—not if you could push someone else below you.

"Stay down," they said, "stay down," but Robert rolled to his feet and stood against a gravity that had never felt so heavy. This time, Maurice swung first and Robert partially blocked it before offering his own upper cut, catching Maurice in the ribs. Robert's muscles had come together again the way they'd done when he killed the rat, and Maurice folded. Robert knew he could follow it up, but with the memory of that afternoon also came the rat guilt, and he hesitated.

"What the hell is going on here?" The voice boomed off the walls. At the mouth of the alleyway, a man—a giant—strode in on a glare of sunlight, a piece of discarded two-by-four swinging from his hand.

Robert locked eyes with Maurice, and for a second, he would have sworn he saw relief. Around them, people streamed from the alley. Maurice turned and ran, joining the tide flooding out.

And then Jerome was at his side, his arm on Robert's shoulder, saying "Easy, man, easy," and Sean was standing behind him, tall and powerful as ever. The giant. Of course he was.

"You'll be okay," Sean said, but Robert flinched when his

brother ruffled his hair, and when Sean held his hand to the light, it was red with blood.

"I'll get him home," he told Jerome.

"You need a hand?"

"I got it from here."

Jack fell down and broke his crown. There was no Jill to tumble after. Jack fell dead and broke his head. Jack was jacked. The thug slugged. He slugged Jack down and stole his crown. Except there was no crown and had never been a crown because this was democracy, all things being equal. Jack blabbed at school and broke his skull. And there was no Jill and no Jack either, only a Jerome and a Robert who was sometimes a Bobby. But Jerome was gone now, and Sean was leading the way home. They were heading home.

Heading home? *Head* was a strange word. Robert felt himself heading out of his head, though head should be home if any place was because it was the only room you always took with you. They would head down the street and up the stairs and through the hall to home. Halls: the long rooms between rooms. He liked the word *hall*. He liked its stretchiness. *Haaaaaaaalllllll.* A bubblegum kind of word. He liked how the word was like the place: it could go on as long as you needed it to. The opposite of *street*, which you could stretch in the middle maybe but which always came to a hard end.

There was their building, solid on the street in front of them.

Home. A word with a hug in it, like love, like mom.

Robert and Sean went upstairs to find a stranger standing in front of their door. Robert would have to think clearly, though he was enjoying the fog. The floatiness of it. It let the ache stay back.

The stranger startled the world back into focus.

"Sean Flannigan?"

Pit sweat damped the man's rumpled shirt, and his bright odor acted like smelling salts, bringing Robert to. The stranger stood in front of their door, barring the way, shifting papers from one hand to another. His eyes were fixed on his brother's.

"You *are* Sean Flannigan?"

How convenient of the world to send men to remind you of who you were.

"It seems you owe quite a lot of money."

Sean glanced at Robert, as if *he* might know what was going on, and then looked again at the man. "What are you, some kind of shake-down guy?"

"You haven't returned our calls. We have received no indication that you plan to pay."

The pain was starting again in Robert's head. It felt like the thing in *Alien* that clamped onto people's faces and planted a baby alien deep in their chest, only this one had clamped on the back of his head and was forcing its way through the bone of Robert's brainpan. The fog had rolled back, but in its place was a bonging, echoing ache.

"We want you to understand that we know where to find you. We know where to find your mother. No one hides anymore. One way or another, debt gets paid."

"Are you making threats?"

"I'm explaining to you how it is."

The man held out the sheaf of papers for Sean to take.

"This is a copy of the letter we sent you two months ago. It lists all that you owe to your various creditors, including the interest and fees accrued on those accounts."

"And if I can't pay?"

"Then we go to court, and you pay those costs as well."

The blood in Robert's shirt collar was growing gooey.

He wanted to be clean again. He would unwrap a fresh bar of Ivory soap—already, he could smell it—and pull a clean washcloth, softened from years of use, from the cabinet and soak it in steaming water from the tap. The ache wouldn't go, but it would be a start. The first step towards fixing himself up. He liked that phrase, *fixing himself up*. But this man was standing in the way of it.

"We want to be reasonable." The stranger held forth the papers again. "We're giving you options. Of course, the best option is to pay in full and be done with us, but we understand that most people can't do that."

The way he said *understand* had snakes in it. It slithered.

"As you can see, you can pay just ten percent now and we can take installments from your mother's paycheck. Of course, there's a fee to cover the extra administrative costs, and your debt will continue to accrue a compounded interest, but that may be more convenient for you."

"And more money for you."

"Ten percent down. Surely you can find that much. Nice kid like you has friends, relatives, co-workers…"

Sean's head bowed as if he were yoked. He accepted the papers.

"That's our offer. We need to hear a decision from you soon. I would hate to see this go badly for you."

The man offered a weak smile and left them there.

Sean stood a moment breathing, then crumpled the papers into a ball and hurled them at the door, where they bounced away to sit with the other trash collecting in the dusty hallway corner.

Sean sat back on the sofa, gathering himself for a good old Big Brother moment. Any second now, he would start spouting something filled with experience and wisdom, perfectly scripted words that would allow Robert to learn his lesson from this day and go on to be a fine, upstanding young man. It made Robert want to puke. The fight was supposed to put an end to things, to let it be over, but now, "over" was only temporary. An unfinished fight was a debt, and debts had to be paid.

"Mom is going to shit when she sees you," Sean said. "You have a plan about what to tell her?"

"I was thinking I would go with the truth."

Sean sighed and shook his head, like that was just the answer he suspected a dumbass little brother to give. "Prepare to get lectured. You're going to hear a list of all the ways she's disappointed in you."

"Like you'd know." Every muscle throbbed its own story of hurt. His head beat with his pulse. He staggered into his bedroom where he could get some peace—or, at least, where he would have been able to get some peace if Sean hadn't followed him.

Robert pulled out his banjo. He didn't want to play it. He just wanted to hold its neck in his hand and feel its weight, something solid.

Sean said, "You seem to forget, I just saved your ass."

"I would've been fine without you."

"Like hell."

"Leave me alone."

"Why should I? You didn't leave me alone. You dragged me home and now I'm supposed to be, what? Some innocent bystander? Some shadow on the wall?"

"You? A shadow?" Robert snorted. "No, I never expected that. You're the big shining star. I'm the one who's the shadow."

"That's what this is about then? You're jealous?"

"I wish I *had* left you at St. Anthony's."

"You wanted mom's attention, so you thought you'd start

fighting for it, is that it?"

"You sound like a TV psychologist."

"I'm trying to help."

"You can't even take care of your own problems."

"We're not talking about me."

Robert bit his lip to keep from speaking. They'd moved here for him, taken his babies. They would lose their home for him, sell what little they had for whatever they could get, move to some shitty quagmire of a neighborhood that sucked you down and down until you couldn't get out, not for college, not for anything at all. They would sacrifice everything, over and over, but Sean would still think he was the one who saved them, who was saving them still.

From their mother's room, Deacon started to cry. The noise hit Robert like a slap. "You left them? Again?"

"What else was I supposed to do?"

Sean's anger flashed to the surface, but it was a different thought altogether that pulled Robert to his feet. The apartment was quiet when they came in. It shouldn't have been quiet.

"Where's Bridget?"

"Watching *Sesame Street*," Sean said, but the color drained from his face, and for once, his shine was gone.

Robert flung open the door to Bridget's room, his mother's, the bathroom, the kitchen. The apartment was empty of everyone but his brother and the crying babies. Robert ran to his own room again, putting the banjo away. There was nothing solid, nothing stable. Was there? He hesitated before grabbing the gun and shoving it into the waist of his jeans, pulling his shirt down to cover it. His head's throb left no room for thought except one: Bridget.

In the living room, Sean's hand was on the doorknob. He said, "I'll be right back. She can't have gotten far."

"No. You need to take care of Sammy and Deacon."

Robert wondered why he still needed to tell Sean that. He brushed past his brother and through the open door, charging down the stairs. There was no sign of her on the street. Only Jerome, sitting on his stoop, soaking up the late afternoon sun. His eyes fell on Robert. "Shouldn't you be sitting under those old frozen beans or something?"

"You seen Bridget?" Robert called.

"No." Jerome was already on his feet, waiting for the cars to clear so that he could cross. Robert started running the moment Jerome was at his side.

"We'll try Veronica's. Then the park."

They didn't say another word as they ran down the block, each footfall echoing in Robert's skull. Robert banged on the door harder than he meant to, and Veronica's mother opened warily, peeking at him under the chain, as she always did. Mrs. Ortiz was a big woman—almost as tall as Sean and twice as wide—but she seemed to live in constant fear of a mugger at her door.

She smiled when she saw it was only Robert and eased the door closed and open again as she unfastened the chain. She didn't speak but raised her eyebrows, staring at his bruises and the blood crusted at the rims of his nostrils. She reached a gentle hand to his cheek and tsked softly.

"I'm sorry to bother you," he said, speaking as slowly as he dared to give her time to translate, "but my sister didn't come here, did she? Bridget?"

"No." Worry deepened in the creases of Mrs. Ortiz's forehead. Her English might not be the best, but the gravity translated. "She no come here today."

"Thank you anyway."

Mrs. Ortiz stopped him from turning away with a hand on his shoulder. "You need help to find her." It wasn't a question, and she wasn't waiting for an answer. She pulled her handbag and a thin sweater from a teetering coat rack and called something back into the house in Spanish.

"We were going to try the park," Robert said.

"Yes, go," Mrs. Ortiz replied, shooing him with her hands. "I talk to the women."

"Thank you."

Robert fought his body to produce anything resembling a sprint, pausing only at intersections. There was always too much traffic. He didn't want to imagine Bridget trying to cross this on her own, so sure she could do everything by herself. But if she'd been hit, there would still be evidence, right? Or did little girls killed by cars clean up fast?

For months, he'd been thinking about everybody else. Sean, his mother, Maurice, the babies, Angela, Joan. He'd accused his mother of forgetting him, but that was just what he'd done to Bridget. Sure, he'd picked her up from school on the days he was supposed to. Sure, he'd talked with her when she'd gotten in his face. But when had Bridget really been at the front of his mind? When had he wondered how her day went, or whether she, too, was scared when Sean disappeared, or how she was adjusting to their mom working, or how many times a day she thought about their dad? When had he put what she wanted to do ahead of what he wanted to do? And now, because he hadn't been watching, she was gone. He hadn't even realized he was being selfish.

The small lot teemed with children, fresh out of school that beautiful October day and hopped up on after-school snacks. Robert couldn't remember when the park had ever been so crowded. Children covered the metal slide and the jungle gym. The playground equipment must have been installed when his mother was a child. It was the tall, steep, metal stuff that was being ripped out and replaced with heavy plastic and gentle corners in every other place. Every place with money. But as Robert looked at the park now, he wasn't paying attention to the vials that cracked underfoot. Instead, he noticed fresh paint and greased hinges—the work of the neighborhood association. The maple was freshly trimmed. The oiled swings arced high as children pumped their legs in delight, jumping from insane heights and landing on their feet in a spray of wood chips.

Robert started on the right and Jerome on the left, working their way through the delighted faces. They looked into the eyes of every sailing child, every boy hanging too high from one hand, every girl teetering from a totter or flying from the long silver tongue of the slide. The children were happy and laughing in the face of self-imposed dangers, and none of them were Bridget.

BRIDGE

By the time Robert and Jerome passed back through the neighborhood, half of the people living on the block were outside, sharing descriptions of Bridget and making plans to fan out. Robert found Sean with the twins in the stroller.

"We're going to check her school."

"I'll come," Sean said. "We can cover more territory."

But the crappy double umbrella stroller just slowed them down. Whenever Sean pushed faster, the whole thing shimmied so violently that it threatened to shake Sammy and Deacon out onto the sidewalk.

The sooner they found her, the sooner Robert could really rest. Lay down his head and heal. Ice and ibuprofen. With each mincing step, his frustration grew. Sean was holding them back. Again. Sean was the anchor they couldn't cut, the one who loosed his own child anchors on them when they became inconvenient. Whatever thing it was in him that filtered his thoughts, that determined when to be silent and when to speak, seemed to be broken. He said, "I can't believe you left her."

"I couldn't exactly stay, could I? Not with you thinking you're the next Mike Tyson."

Sean's foot caught on the wheel and jerked the stroller. He was blaming Robert then, seeing everything as his little brother's fault. The thought melded into the ache, inseparable from each other, inseparable from this moment. Even though Robert had been blaming himself not a moment before, that didn't matter now. *Poison*, his mother had called it when he'd spoken the truth about Sean. Maybe it was. Every frustration he felt was festering, turning vile and venomous. He wanted to yank the gun from under his shirt, hold it high, pour bullets and bullets into the air.

"You figure out how you're going to pay the collector?"

"This is hardly the time, Robert."

"We're running *out* of time. A week."

"Jesus. Lay off."

"You've had days. Have you called Mr. Murphy? Or how about your coach? You talk to him yet?"

"What?"

"At Hassler. Have you asked whether they might let you play again?"

"What are you even talking about? You're supposed to be focused on Bridget right now. That's what matters."

"Don't act like this isn't related. Like everything isn't related. Have you talked to him or not?"

Sean's jaw was a brick set hard against his brother. "No," Sean spit through clenched teeth, his own words ringing against his skull.

Jerome was purposely looking away, but Robert couldn't stop talking. "You had a full ride." He didn't want to be arguing anymore, didn't want to sound like a petulant child, but the words kept pouring out. "You had a chance—you were the only one of us who did. You ruined everything."

"Robert."

"You could have stayed in school this whole time, ridden it out, even with Angela and the babies. They were depending on you. We all were, and you bailed."

"What the hell do you know about it?"

"I lived it."

"You want to know the truth? Really? The truth is, I was never any good."

"You were a star."

"I was a big fish in a small pond. At Hassler, I rode the bench."

"It was freshman year! What did you expect? You could have worked for a place on the field. You could have tried."

"Fine! Maybe I could have. Maybe I made a mistake. What do you want me to do? How many times can I say I'm sorry?"

"Screw *I'm sorry*. Why don't you do something about it?"

"Some mistakes you don't get back."

Watching Sean walk those tortured, ridiculous steps, shaking and reddening with bottled rage, Robert realized for the first time just how big a coward his brother was.

"Fuck that. It's a phone call."

"I can't think about Hassler right now, Robert."

"Damn it, Sean. It didn't matter if you could play. You could have gotten a degree and a decent job. Instead, you fucked us all."

He had said it all now. Sean stared at Robert like he was a stranger wearing his brother's clothing. Robert was a stranger to himself. He'd spoken, and now all he wanted to do was sleep until everything was better. The blocks were endless at this pace. Robert couldn't imagine why Bridget would have gone back to school, but where else would she go?

The question shifted into a spotlight in the stage of his mind. Where *would* she go? That was the question they should have been asking in the first place. She knew the way to Veronica's and the park and her school. She wouldn't get lost going to any of those places. What if she'd gone somewhere outside the world she knew?

Robert pictured her watching *Sesame Street* when Jerome burst in. She would have heard him say her brother was in danger. Would she really have just sat there and waited for them? *His* sister? No. She would have followed them. Only Sean and Jerome would have been running, thinking and looking ahead of them rather than behind. They wouldn't have noticed her struggling to keep up, losing sight of them, not knowing where to turn, guessing wrong. And she *had* turned wrong somewhere, because if she hadn't, they would have passed her on the way back from the fight. Robert could see the whole thing in his mind, except for the location of her wrong turn. She was lost because of him.

They stood at the curb, waiting for the light. "We'll split up," Robert said. "Jerome and I can check by the high school."

"You're wasting time. She'd never go there."

"Like you said, we'll cover more ground."

After everything, Sean still saw him as some petulant little kid too full of his own anger to remember that his sister was in danger. Robert knew he had put on a pretty good impression of exactly that, but he wouldn't waste time now explaining. Already, his mind traced the maze of streets and avenues, boulevards and alleys, near Garvey. Each was dangerous in its own way, too wide, too busy, too dark, or too hidden. He thought of the buses barreling down Frankfort and how easy it would be to abduct a child from a side street.

"I never thought to look behind," Jerome said. "I didn't have one thought other than you and Maurice."

"None of us did."

"One little glance. It never even occurred to me."

"It's not your fault. If it's anyone's, it's mine. You told me not to go looking for trouble. You told me to mind my own business. My business was Bridget."

"It's noble to want to stand up for people." Jerome didn't add that he was capable of standing up for himself, but he didn't have to say it for Robert to hear it and to know it was true.

They stretched their legs and hit their full stride. Robert saw a map of the city in his head, like TV police maps, a small moving red dot marking their progress, moving towards a small white dot, a dot he didn't know where to place, that was Bridget. He shot glances down alleys. He was closing the gap, he was certain, now that they had ditched Sean, but by the time they reached Frankfort, there was still no sign.

Overhead, a plane drew a contrail across the sky above the high school. The world split along this seam. In one world, he knew where Bridget was and she was safe, and he didn't even realize how grateful he should be for that simple truth. He was in the other world.

They split up at the school, Jerome circling around the back while Robert took the front.

As he came around the stairs, Robert heard two people arguing. Something about blood, something about basketball shoes. It was difficult to make out. The angry voices were low-pitched, echoing off the wall. Blood pounded in his brain. He couldn't think, couldn't stop. He kept walking, rounding the wide beech tree.

The air pinched tight. Maurice stood with his back against the bricks. He hadn't seen Robert yet, either because of the tree trunk or because of the larger man in front of him. "I'll wash them," Maurice said. "No big thing."

"Blood don't wash."

"Then get me some new ones, if you so concerned."

The man answered with a fist. His punch flew so fast from his shoulder that Maurice had no time to duck. Robert's eyes were on the man's back muscles, the way, as his arm extended, his lat grew like a wing. Like freedom. Like maybe fighting was a kind of flying that could lift you right out of the Chum. Hit right, and you could soar away from the concrete and grime, loosed from whatever jesses held you there.

The man struck again and again with that same right fist, and with every new strike, Robert saw how useless it was: a kind of mad flapping. Maurice, already bruised and bloodied, cowered against the wall. His arms were up, shielding his face, but he took the blows to his arms and stomach.

The gun at his back pressed Robert on.

"Hey," Robert said. Car after car hurtled down Frankford but no one was slowing to help. An hour ago, Robert had been pouring every piece of energy he had into damaging Maurice. Now, seeing it from the outside, his stomach turned. The violence was inhuman, and it was deeply human—the ugliest part. The part that lived in him as well. The part that bristled just below his skin. He had the gun, he remembered. He could stop this. He said, "Have you guys seen a girl? Small, with brown hair that hangs in her eyes?"

The man turned. His left arm stopped just below the elbow. *Even meaner with one arm than he was with two*, Jerome had said. Maurice's brother. Andre. He looked calm for someone who had just publicly laid a guy out. Broad chested as he was, he could have advertised gym equipment or protein bars or PowerAde or steroids. He could have starred in action films. Even his stare was strong under his flat-brimmed ball cap, pushing Robert away.

Andre's eyebrows were low and straight like his brother's, but where Maurice's eyes held arrogance, his held sadness. Whatever sights Andre had seen growing up in the Chum implanted there and became the lenses through which he saw.

"She was wearing pink today, and blue jeans. Her shirt had a unicorn on it."

Was it Maurice's blood or his own that speckled those Grant Hill shoes? Maurice shifted at Andre's feet, but did not rise or glance up.

Robert tried not to stare at the nub where the arm stopped. The dimpled flesh was smoother than he would have imagined. Shinier. Stretched. He wondered if the ghost of Andre's lost arm felt things. He wondered if it hurt.

They were only shoes. They protected your feet as you went places. They kept out thorns and glass and rocks and anything painful. That was their only purpose. Shoes weren't for keeping clean like some kind of museum piece. They wore out and were replaced.

"Better move on."

"She's only little."

Andre squared on him. "You don't seem to understand what I'm telling you." He didn't elaborate. He let the breadth of his chest and the width of his biceps speak. Andre stepped closer. In the hollow of Robert's back, he felt the gun butt.

How much did one man have to witness for his eyes to fill with that particular kind of permanent sadness? To earn a gaze so wise and weary and bleak?

The gun whispered *power*. It whispered *control*. It said, *you need never be afraid again*. It made promises and promises and promises. In a corner of his mind, Joan whispered, *no weapons, no broken bones*. But she wasn't here.

The fight with Maurice felt inevitable, but facing down Andre was a choice. Robert felt every bruise on his face shining. He tried one last time: "Maurice could help us find her."

"Yeah? And why would he do that?"

"Robert!" Bridget's voice cut like a blade dropping between him and Andre. He could turn away now. Leave them. His only excuse for being here was gone.

Maurice turned from Robert, his eyes heavy and hopeless.

Bridget tackled her brother, hitting his leg from the side, but he stood firm. Her tears dampened his jeans as sobs racked her body. He rubbed her arm. They would leave now. They could go back to the apartment like nothing had happened. They would all be okay. Just so long as "everyone" didn't include Maurice.

Maurice was still his enemy. Robert needed to leave—it was so simple. Why couldn't he make himself do it?

"You best be going now," Andre said. He voice was bass deep with a rasp, with the resonant, rippling power of thunder.

"Let him up."

"You got your sister. Now, mind your business."

Business? Robert heard a voice from another of his father's old movies. *Mankind was my business.* Robert hated that he remembered his father by the words he had watched rather than the words he had spoken. Robert could hear an actor's voice in a moment, scraps upon scraps of mismatched quotations, but his father's voice was absent. Maybe people were all just the shavings of the things they loved, repacked and served as personality like a piece of pressboard, but Robert wanted his father to be more than that. He wanted to reconstruct the man. Robert wanted his father to live inside his own skin, not only as memory but as action, so that his dad wouldn't be so dead.

Andre turned and stepped to Robert. His breath, cheeseburgers and Coca-Cola, filled Robert's nose.

Robert again felt the itch under his skin, the Robert-animal responding, but the sight of Andre beating Maurice still churned in his stomach. Its repulsive brutality. He was genuinely scared now. More scared than he had ever been facing Maurice. His hand touched the gun. The grip's rough texture grazed his fingers.

Robert saw the possible scenarios:

1) He pulls the gun and fires. Andre dies. Success. ...Only, Robert goes to jail for murder and lives a meaningless life with no prospects of happiness while his mother cries herself to sleep over her failure to raise even one worthwhile son.

Andre stepped closer still, the buttons on his shirt pressing between them. His chest filled, emptied, filled, leaving no oxygen for Robert.

2) He pulls the gun and fires. Andre is injured but flies into a Hulk-rage, throttling Robert on the street before turning on Jerome, who is frozen by fear. Andre beats them both to a bloody pulp.

He curled his fingers around the handle and let them rest there. All he had to do was pull.

3) He pulls the gun and fires, but having no idea what he's doing, he misses Andre altogether. Andre laughs and slugs Robert in the stomach. The gun flies from Robert's hand as he crumples. Andre takes the gun for his own. He turns it on Robert, who is now even more powerless than he was before.

Bridget was crying again.

4) He pulls the gun and it backfires because, who knows, maybe it's a crap gun and that's why it was dumped in the first place, and what kind of idiot fires a gun he knows nothing about?

Fear had a smell, an acrid tinge tainting the sweat. Robert had never known the scent of his own terror, but he did now.

5) He pulls the gun and it doesn't fire because it was never loaded. Andre takes the gun and keeps it for himself.

He buys hollow points on the street and later shoots Maurice in some fit of rage over something as stupid and meaningless as tennis shoes, a fact that will haunt Robert for the rest of his life because as much as he hates Maurice, he doesn't want him dead. He just wants him to stop being an asshole.

"You seem to think you a man," Andre said. "You really want to find out?"

    6) He pulls the gun, just to scare the guy. Andre quakes briefly. No, scratch that. Robert knows too much of Andre already to believe that scenario. Try again: Robert pulls the gun, just to scare the guy, but Andre has already faced a gun and survived. Laughing, Andre pulls the gun from Robert's hand and things continue as in scenario #5.

The gun was the only thing that could save him—but it couldn't save him. Nothing could save him. Nothing would change. The street was the street, like Jerome had always said. His hand dropped empty at his side as he said, "I'm not leaving just so you can beat your brother to shit."

They were fighting words, which were maybe not the best ones to use when you had no intention of fighting. The gun could nudge and nudge with every shift of his weight, but Robert wasn't going to pull it. Its promises rang false. Pulling a gun was the act of an idiot or a coward.

"Find Jerome," Robert told his sister. "He should be somewhere around the back. Tell him I said to take you home."

Her eyes stared back, filled with what was maybe fear and maybe awe.

"I'll catch up."

"Robert?"

"Go."

* * *

The fist hit like a one-ton pickup, like a logging truck, like the log itself. The fist hit like an avalanche. It hit like a tornado. It hit like a knuckled brick. His fist hit like a moving truck. His fist hit like a building, collapsing. No, it was Robert collapsing.

Robert's head smacked the concrete. His thoughts flew like birds from a wire. He flew to English class, to the blackboard that was more of a gray board worn down by years. His teacher wrote quotations in the corner on Mondays to leave for the week. "*Cognito ergo sum*," or "It is not our differences that divide us. It is our inability to recognize, accept, and celebrate those differences," or "No man is an island, entire of itself." His teacher never addressed these quotations. They were never part of the lesson. She just left them there with a box drawn around them so that the janitors wouldn't wash them away. Around the border, she wrote SAVE ME.

Robert didn't see where Jerome came from, only that he was suddenly there, suddenly swinging at a man twice his size. Andre shoved him to his ass.

"Come on, man," Jerome said, scrambling to his feet again and latching himself onto Andre's back. "He's down. You won."

Robert couldn't see Bridget, no matter which way he rolled his head to look. Andre's foot slammed into Robert's ribs, lifting his body and forcing it back over the sidewalk. Robert decided the foot was a thunderclap because of the lightning strike he felt in his ribs. It struck twice, three times. A fist like a hammer against his cheek. *Save me.*

Jerome dropped from Andre and drove two square punches into his gut, only to have Andre's fist in his face. Jerome was on the ground. "You won," Jerome said again, through bleeding lips. "You won."

Andre paused, towering over them both. "You ain't shit," he said. "Neither of you. You not even the littlest speck of shit."

Robert squinted from the sidewalk, watching the feet

as they walked away, Timberlands in a pool of denim. Step, step, step.

The sidewalk turned its endless circles. Every muscle, so many micro-muscles he did not even know he possessed, pulled at a single screaming point in his chest. From the back of his head, blood oozed again, becoming a warm and sluggish trickle down his neck. Breathing stabbed him, but if he sat very still, it was better. Bridget ran to him. Her head on his chest threatened to snap him, but he took it because he was *alive*, and what else was there but to hurt and love?

Maurice sat against the wall, his voice dark. "Why did you do that?"

Robert didn't have the energy to answer. He felt the tears leaking from his eyes and he was embarrassed.

"You think you did me a favor?"

"You didn't deserve that," Jerome said, speaking for them both.

"I wrecked the shoes he bought. You'd be mad too."

"I don't know."

"I disrespected him. It's my fault."

"Okay."

"It's not like he's a bad person."

"Never said he was."

"He watches out for me. Not just the shoes either. No one fucks with Andre. Who you got watching out for you?"

Robert closed his eyes and drifted.

"Don't move, man."

Jerome and Bridget hovered over him, one on each side. The gun pressed in Robert's back, and he tried to turn, but the pain in his chest wouldn't let him.

"Did you not hear me?"

"I'm laying on it."

Jerome looked at him like he'd spoken something untranslatable.

"It's digging," Robert tried again.

Jerome slid his hand under Robert and felt the handle, his eyes growing large behind his glasses. He eased the gun out, and hurried it under his shirt.

Bridget craned to see. "What is it?"

"Nothing. Bridget, you stay with him. I'm going to call an ambulance. Don't move a muscle. And Robert, you stay with us. Don't you pass out again. Talk to him, Bridge. I need you to do that. Keep him here."

THE GREEN MAN

A week after the fight, everything still hurt. The rats were back in the walls. For this night, though, Robert was calling a truce. The flickering flashlight made shadows of him and Jerome. They'd kept him three nights in the hospital: a concussion and a broken rib. They'd taped him up, but only time could heal. For months to come, every breath, every turn of the shoulders, every lifting of his chin would send a jolting pain to his chest.

Jerome said, "You really need to rethink this whole savior thing. You're about as bad at fighting as you are at listening to sense."

"You're the one who did the saving."

"Me?"

"Uh-huh. So much for staying out of it."

"What was I supposed to do, watch you get killed?"

"You took on Andre."

"If you saw that, then you also saw Andre smack me down."

"That's not the part that matters."

"Tell that to my butt. Or to your own broken self."

"You stood up. You stopped him."

"He stopped cause he felt like stopping. That's the only thing that stops a guy like that."

The pineapple leaves flopped just as they always had. The gun's hidey-hole was unmoved in the wall. Rats moved in the walls, minding their own business. In their private corner of the Chum, nothing had changed.

Jerome said, "Maybe we saved each other."

"Maybe. And maybe, I should have listened to you from the start."

He remembered his dad driving to a logging festival, years ago. Robert must have been only seven. His father's thermos leaked just a little, so the Buick always smelled faintly of tea. The two of them had driven for hours to watch men carve bears with chainsaws and run on rolling logs and shimmy up greased polls in spiked boots. His father didn't stop smiling once that day. With his logging festivals and banjo picking, his dad had been a little hokey. Robert saw the strength in how easy his father was with being uncool. He hadn't let anyone define the terms of his happiness. His father wasn't scared to be a dork or a weirdo or a bit of a freak. His dad would be just exactly who he was.

Jerome pulled the gun from his pocket, the glow of the flashlight soft on its smooth, square barrel, and returned it to the hole in the wall.

"I can't believe you had that the whole time."

"Yeah."

"But you didn't pull it."

"It's like you've been telling me this whole time: if I pulled it, I'd be dead."

"At least you learn."

He didn't ever want to see the gun again or hear its false whispers. He wanted it a million miles from Bridget and the boys. He wanted it away from himself. The rats would safeguard it.

"Robert?"

"Yeah?"

"I'm glad you're not dead."

"Me, too."

They sat.

"Robert?"

"Yeah?"

"Would you think I'm for-real gay if I said I love you?"

"Only if you put it like that."

"Damn. That's cold."

"I love you, too. It's like you always say, we're brothers, brother."

"Thicker than blood."

"Always."

That evening, as he sat on the couch waiting for the ibuprofen to kick in, he looked up to find his sister staring around the doorframe. Bridget's eyes hadn't moved from his face all night. He patted the couch cushion next to him, but she didn't budge.

"You still don't look like you," Bridget said. Her voice was so small that it seemed to be crawling back into her as she spoke.

"I'll look myself again soon."

"Your face is green where the green man hit you."

"Just some kid," Robert corrected her. "Just some bruises."

"A fight with the green man and then into the hospital, just like Dad."

"A little like Dad."

She'd been edging closer as they spoke, but this was the wrong answer. Her chin went wobbly again. "He'll come back. They'll put you in a box."

"What box?"

"The box with the peas. The box in the ground, where the green man lives."

"Bridget, what are you talking about?"

"Like with Dad! The green man will eat you! They put

you in a box and he eats you."

"No, Bridge. That's just a nightmare."

"Then why did they say it? Why was it everywhere?"

"Say what?"

"The peas!" She was choking on her own words now, but she spit them out. "They said Dad would be in peas, then they put dad in the box where the green man would eat him."

And finally, Robert understood the full darkness of her nightmare. He wanted to hug her, but his ribs wouldn't let him. She tucked her head under his chin and he stroked her hair. "Peace, Bridget. They said Dad would be in peace. They meant he could rest forever and no one would ever hurt him again."

On the shelf in the living room was a large mason jar. For months, his mother had been stuffing it with one five-dollar bill per week.

The masking tape on the glass read BOSTON, but Robert knew his mother needed to save for more than one marathon. She'd run five days a week all through winter, training for Philly so she could qualify for her dream. The jar was for everything: entrance fees for both races, the Boston hotel, train fare, and the shoes that she always wore for too many miles because she had good feet and didn't mind a little pain. The jar needed to cover every expense she saw coming and every unpredictable incidental.

And the jar was for more than that. Sitting on the living room shelf, there in plain sight, the jar was a reminder that dreams have a price.

Sean had taken to adding whatever spare change he carried in from work. Not only had he called Goss Vending, Sean had broken down and called Hassler the morning after the fight. His old quarterback coach had coached him on debt as well. That was the deal: Sean could try out for a walk-on spot next fall, provided his finances were under control. They would give him a chance— and only a chance, nothing guaranteed—but they weren't about to risk an NCAA violation or the school's reputation unless Sean could get his shit together. The coach gave him the name of a consolidation company. The collector's activities weren't strictly legal, but apparently, that wasn't unusual. The consolidators negotiated new rates and worked out payments. The envelopes from Angela got added to this, and though they weren't much, they helped take a little extra chip off the total. And so, his mother had a jar and Sean had garnished wages and both had their own dream to work for.

What Robert had was less floor space. They'd sold his desk to buy the old mattress that now lay on the floor in its place, his brother's bed. Robert didn't mind so much about the desk. He'd always done his homework at the kitchen table anyhow. Sean was at work for most of the day, but Robert missed knowing that his room was his own, knowing that there was a space in the world dedicated just to him where he could play his banjo as late into the night as he wanted. He needed that sometimes. Maurice hadn't really let up. He might not shove them around so much, but he made up for it with rumors and innuendos. Jerome was right: nothing had really changed. And Jerome was wrong: Robert had changed. He didn't feel as scared or powerless, even though he was more aware than ever of all he couldn't fix. That was weird, but it was true nonetheless.

The apartment was as quiet as it ever had been. Sean and his mother had taken the kids to see a puppet show at Independence Hall. Bridget had spent all of Friday night cleaning her room to earn a water ice.

Now, Robert needed a sock. His own were too short. He wanted a tube sock, long and thick and preferably missing its match. He'd been digging around the room for twenty minutes. That morning, he'd promised to play for Joan, and only after hanging up did he realize that he didn't have a strap.

Jerome walked in to find Robert knee-deep in a pile of clothes in the back of the closet.

"You bring it?" Robert said.

"What you think?"

"Cool." A spring breeze drifted through the window, carrying with it the music and laughter that drifted through their block whenever the weather invited people out of doors.

"What you looking for?"

"This." Robert pulled a clean tube sock from the corner like a golden ticket. "We're taking this show on the road."

He cut off the toe and wove strands of twine, threading them through a doubled-over layer of sock. The Chum had never struck him as a banjo kind of place. The neighborhood thrived on fronting. If you weren't cool you, faked cool. If you weren't violent, you pretended violence. The banjo required him to strip himself bare. When he lifted it from its box, coolness slipped away. The banjo was a pacifist's weapon. Guns worked on fear, but the banjo required fearlessness.

These were not Philly kinds of thoughts. Faith in art was very hippie Oregon, he knew, but his thoughts had a place here if Robert had a place here, and today he was going to test exactly that. Better to be gunless and brave as his father than to put any more ugliness into the world. Better to find its beauty.

They had one stop to make before Garvey. The Philly PD was holding its first gun amnesty. They would buy the pistol for seventy-five dollars, no questions asked, which was good because Robert would have had no answers. He would hand the money to his mother to put toward the debt. Compared to what the banjo would have brought, it was nothing, but, Robert figured, it was the price of his future.

That afternoon, he sat on the wall in front of their school with Joan on one side and Jerome on the other, and his whole life rolling out in front of him like a picnic blanket. He picked at the strings, tuning one note from the other. Joan rested her hand on his thigh, and he started to play.

He wanted a song that contained all of Philly: its people, its heat, its aggression, its resolve. He'd call it "Scrapple," putting in all the bits and pieces, letting them flavor each other. He played in girls expelled for wrong lunch bags and boys knocked senseless by the brothers who should have loved them. He played a neighborhood pouring from their homes to look for a missing girl and he played children flying from timeworn swings. He played cheesesteaks and pretzels and pork roll. He played the dream of liberty that had conceded to slavery, the ideals and the failings. He played in gold shoes and magic ice cream mongers going broke and debt and debts paid. He pressed the scraps together, wanting to form something new, something better.

In every note, he heard himself failing to capture it all, but he played harder, experimenting with chords and rhythms, singing his own steel voice in harmony with Philadelphia's, the city that called him Bobby but gave him space to become Robert, the place that somewhere along the line became home.

THE END

ACKNOWLEDGEMENTS

First and foremost, thank you thank you thank you to the people who've loved me through writing: Nathanael, Gwendolyn, and Oliver Myers; Marie, Peter, and Megan Griffiths; and the entire Burns family. Even in my most obnoxious moments of self-involvement (and there have always been many), you were there for me. That you love me in spite of everything has made it possible for me to reach beyond.

Thank you to Kirsten Kaschock, Jennifer Mitchell, Jeff Newberry, and Kathleen Nishimoto for reading so many unfinished versions of this book while I flailed towards a workable one. Thank you, as well, to my peers and mentors at the Sewanee Writers' Conference, in particular John Casey and Claire Vaye Watkins, and the *Tin House* Writers' Workshop and my novel-writing mentor, Peter Mountford.

Thank you to my *Barrelhouse* family. I'm proud to be one of the cult. Patrick Swayze is dead; long live Patrick Swayze.

Special thanks to Kyle Poppitz and Matt Drollette, the writers and former soldiers who taught me how to shoot a Glock safely, along with several other pistols and one massive assault rifle. It was loud. It was terrifying. I never would have gotten through it without your patience, expertise, and enthusiasm.

Thank you to the Duplass family, for giving me two rent-free weeks in their beautiful cabin, where the final edits and revisions of this novel took place, and to Kaffe Mercantile, where so many of these pages were written...and re-written... and re-written. I challenge anyone to find a more beautiful, more welcoming coffee shop.

Thank you to the incredible team at Braddock Avenue Books, most especially Jeffrey Condran and Jan Nielsen without whom this book would not be a book. Their notes made the book so much better. Any missteps that remain are mine and mine alone.

Thank you to the city of Philadelphia for being exactly and unfailingly Philadelphia. No other city has welcomed me more into its home. You know what brotherly love means. It's not an easy or uncomplicated thing, but it is true and it is forever.

Thank you to you, the person who picked up this book and decided to buy it. I hope I made these pages worth your time.

Siân Griffiths lives in Ogden, Utah, where she teaches creative writing at Weber State University. Her work has appeared in *The Georgia Review, Prairie Schooner, Cincinnati Review,* and *American Short Fiction* (online), among other publications. Her debut novel *Borrowed Horses* was a semi-finalist for the 2014 VCU Cabell First Novelist Award. Her short fiction chapbook *The Heart Keeps Faulty Time* is forthcoming in 2020. Currently, she reads fiction as part of the editorial teams at *Barrelhouse* and *American Short Fiction.* For more information, please visit sbgriffiths.com.